New York Times and *USA TODAY* bestselling author **Bonnie Vanak** is passionate about romance novels and telling stories. A former newspaper reporter, she worked as a journalist for a large international charity for several years, traveling to countries such as Haiti to report on the sufferings of the poor. Bonnie lives in Florida with her husband, Frank, and is a member of Romance Writers of America. She loves to hear from readers. She can be reached through her website, bonnievanak.com.

Also by Bonnie Vanak

Navy SEAL Seduction
Shielded by the Cowboy SEAL
Navy SEAL Protector
The Shadow Wolf
The Covert Wolf
Phantom Wolf
Demon Wolf
The Empath
Enemy Lover
Immortal Wolf

Discover more at millsandboon.co.uk

HIS FORGOTTEN COLTON FIANCÉE

BONNIE VANAK

MIX
Paper from
responsible sources
FSC
FSC C007454

This book is produced from independently certified FSC™
paper to ensure responsible forest management

For more information visit: www.harpercollins.co.uk/green

Printed and bound in Spain
by CPI, Barcelona

MILLS & BOON

First Published in Great Britain 2018
by Mills & Boon, an imprint of HarperCollins*Publishers*
1 London Bridge Street, London, SE1 9GF

His Forgotten Colton Fiancée © 2018 Harlequin Books S.A.

Special thanks and acknowledgement are given to Bonnie Vanak for her contribution to *The Coltons of Red Ridge* series.

ISBN: 978-0-263-26589-7

0818

In memory of Sissy. Love you.
Miss you and your smile and your laughter.

Sissy's Creole Chicken
Recipe by Glenna "Sissy" Fischer

3 ½ pounds of chicken
1 clove garlic
6 slices bacon
½ pound of ham, diced
2 small onions, chopped
2 cups drained canned tomatoes
1 tablespoon chopped parsley
1/8 teaspoon Tabasco sauce
½ teaspoon thyme
2 teaspoons salt
2 cups boiling water
2 cups cooked sliced okra

Directions

Wash, clean chicken and cut into serving pieces. Rub skin side of each chicken piece with cut side of garlic clove. Place bacon in cold Dutch oven or a heavy frying pan and cook until crisp. Remove and crumble. Add the chicken to the Dutch oven or the pan, brown on all sides and then remove.

Add ham, onions, brown lightly. Then add the bacon, chicken, tomatoes, parsley, Tabasco sauce, thyme, salt and water.

Cover, reduce heat to low. Cook 30–60 minutes or until chicken is tender. Add the cooked okra the last ten minutes. Serves eight.

Chapter 1

Wedding cake and bombs.

Two thoughts sped through FBI agent West Brand's mind as he jogged along the main street leading out of Red Ridge. Chocolate rum cake with vanilla frosting and swirls of delicate pink flowers. And bombs made out of materials as easy to find as cake.

The cake, he didn't care about, but he wanted to make Quinn Colton happy. She was a real foodie and, as a caterer, weddings were her specialty. He'd be happy to eat a cake made from sprouts when they got married.

When they *could* risk a wedding. Red Ridge had a serial killer lurking, a psycho killing grooms right before their weddings. The MO was always the same: bullet through the heart, black cummerbund stuffed in the victim's mouth. Several men had been murdered. And with the Groom Killer still out there, he and Quinn had decided to keep their newly engaged status quiet, along with their relationship.

For now, he had to focus on bombs. His cop instinct tingled, warning things were too damn quiet and the tension in the city was about to explode.

High-powered explosives were West's specialty. He preferred to work alone and being on loan to the Red Ridge Police Department's K-9 unit hadn't changed his mind. West's partner of choice ran on four legs.

Cool air washed over him as he ran, the darkness pierced by the green glow of his sport-utility watch. Rex, his black Labrador retriever, kept pace alongside him. West always took him on his daily jogs.

Breath fogging the air, he let his thoughts drift to the missing fifty-five-gallon drum of highly concentrated hydrogen peroxide from a chemical warehouse in Sioux Falls, South Dakota. The owner had reported it missing two days ago.

Even though there had been no other bombings reported in the area, all West's instincts had gone full red flag.

Peroxide-based explosives presented a deadlier threat than ordinary C-4, which was much harder to obtain. Unstable chemical compounds brought the risk of blowing yourself up as you mixed and packed the ingredients, and quite possibly blowing up your unsuspecting neighbors, as well. Terrorists preferred the risk because they could easily purchase the ingredients without raising eyebrows or alerting the feds. Gone were the days when materials had to be smuggled past the eyes of authorities. These days, a kid could waltz into a grocery store and make a bomb with soda pop and nail polish remover.

The bad guys made it harder to do his job and keep people safe. So he kept learning and listening and reading, because long ago, he determined no one would ever die on his watch.

Not again, like when he was seventeen…

Don't go there. Focus. Did a daydreaming clerk misplace the drum or did someone steal it to make a bomb?

Red Ridge wasn't the type of town that saw the same kind of terrorist bombings as big cities. He'd bet that Dean Landon, the canine explosives specialist who was out on medical leave, had seldom seen many bombings in town. He was replacing Landon until the officer recovered from an injury and then it would be back to the city for him.

Maybe. Something else he had to discuss with his future wife.

He and Rex turned a corner down a dirt road toward the boarded-up building that once served as a hardware store. The store marked his three-mile turning point. As West started past the building and prepared to turn, Rex stopped.

The dog stared at the building.

"Whoa." He jogged in place, frowning as he squinted at the building in the inky darkness. Dim light from the nearly full moon showed ghostly shadows, thick weeds and brush, and a rotting wood storefront with a few two-by-fours hammered over the windows.

The abandoned building sat on the edge of town, a scrubby cousin to the sleeker Main Street buildings with their shiny windows, trim doors and flower boxes. It fitted in with Rusty Colton's nearby dive bar that reeked of stale beer, tobacco and dark thoughts.

He glanced down at Rex, the Labrador's nose pointing at the storefront, his body tense and alert. Then the dog sat down.

West clenched his gut. Rex had found something. Specially trained to sniff out bombs, the dog sat when he smelled suspicious odors.

Though he'd worked with Rex for three months and spent each day training with him, he still remained wary.

Maybe Rex saw something interesting. Or he smelled something fascinating, like a dead rodent.

"What is it?" he asked Rex.

The dog kept staring at the building.

Could be anything. Hell, even a ghost. Sure was eerie enough on this end of town, the sad, lonely building desolate and abandoned. Maybe a homeless person decided to camp there for the night and Rex sensed that.

The watch he wore on his right wrist insisted he had to get his butt back now into town in order to leave Quinn's place before the nosy townspeople started opening their shops. Last thing he needed was a gossip prattling on about how the FBI canine agent on loan to the RRPD was seen sneaking out of Good Eats, Quinn Colton's catering shop.

If he investigated, he'd be late. West swept his gaze over the building's exterior as he squinted in the dark. Heart racing from the run, he looked again at Rex.

Still sitting. Still alert.

That was it. West reached for his gun tucked into a leather holster at his side and prepared to go closer.

A flash of movement in the darkness. He tensed as something rattled inside the building.

A scrawny black-and-white tabby cat squeezed underneath one of the boards on the window, looked at them. It hissed at Rex, and then sped off in the direction of town.

Still, it was best to check it out. West did a quick patrol around the building, saw and heard nothing. He glanced down at Rex, who whined, his tail beating the dirt.

"A cat." West shook his head. "All that drama for a stray feline? C'mon, buddy. You disappoint me."

Tongue lolling out, Rex grinned at him.

Sighing, West patted his head. "Let's go."

They jogged back to the main road as a cool wind blew, rattling the shutters of the abandoned building.

When he reached Quinn's apartment above her store, he let himself in with his key. West poured Rex a bowl of fresh water and grabbed a bottle from the fridge, drinking deeply. The clock on the range read 5 a.m. If he hurried and showered here, he could make it to his truck, parked discreetly down the street, and drive out of town before Quinn's assistant showed up to open shop.

Leaving Rex in the kitchen on the pillow Quinn placed there for him, West headed into the bathroom.

Steam misted the air as he emerged minutes later, a white towel wrapped around his waist. He padded to the bedside and stared down at a slumbering Quinn.

He was one lucky bastard. After thirty years, thinking he'd remain a bachelor for the rest of his life, he'd found the woman of his dreams. Last night he'd asked her to marry him, and she'd readily accepted.

West removed a single red rose from the crystal vase by the bedside. Last night he'd given her two dozen red roses to proclaim his feelings.

It was all so new and marvelous. And uncertain and out of character. He wasn't impulsive. All he knew was that he adored Quinn, wanted to make her happy for the rest of her life and needed her like he'd never admit to needing anyone.

Not since his entire family had been killed had he allowed himself to be this open, this intimate with another person. He'd proposed because he was getting older and so was Quinn. He couldn't bear for her to get snatched up by another man. He'd already lost too much in life, and wanted to spend each precious moment with her.

He only wished she didn't want children so badly. Getting married to the woman of his dreams was one thing. Having kids was another. Being responsible to protect one life—Quinn's—yeah, he could handle that. But making sure nothing bad would ever happen to children? After what had happened to his sisters, he had quietly vowed to avoid having children and risking that kind of heartache ever again.

He sat on the bed's edge, gazing at his new fiancée, his heart racing with anticipation. Damn, she was so pretty when she slept. Even prettier when she awakened and gave him that sexy smile filled with promise, her brown eyes smudged with sleep and hard loving. West bent over and inhaled the smell of her: apple shampoo, delicate jasmine and the musk of sex.

Life was filled with the ugliness and violence of his job. Quinn made the brutality bearable, and eased the stress he bore. Coming home to her each day was definitely something he anticipated. Quinn made him laugh, lit up his life with her cheerful smile and saucy attitude. She was an eternal optimist who didn't let anything get her down.

Not even me.

West stroked the rose petals over her freckled cheek and she stirred. He set the rose upon the pillow next to her.

"Good morning, sleeping beauty," he whispered as she slowly opened her eyes and smiled up at him. She ran a hand through her rumpled curls.

Quinn took the rose and inhaled the delicate fragrance. "A flower on my pillow. What a lovely way to wake up. But not as nice as waking up to see my handsome man."

"You deserve a dozen fresh roses every day." He took the flower and tapped her forehead with it. *And more. Everything I could give you. I only wish I could give you the one thing we can't have now—no more secrets.*

As he replaced the rose in the vase, she sat up.

"You up to kissing speed yet?" he teased.

Quinn smiled. "Anytime with you, I am."

She cupped his face, her fingers stroking his cheek. "You shaved off your beard."

West rubbed his cheek against her playful caresses. "Makes it easier to get close to you, in all the right places."

A delicate flush ignited her round cheeks at the intimate hint in his voice. "I like it. Did you have a good run?"

"Not as good as staying here. But I had to get away from you and think. When I'm here—" he traced the edges of her lush lower lip "—I tend to get distracted from my work."

"What were you thinking about?" She yawned and stretched.

He admired how the motion lifted her breasts beneath the flannel T-shirt. "You." West reached out and tugged one of her corkscrew curls. It bounced back. "And triacetone triperoxide."

Quinn's forehead wrinkled. "What? It sounds like something my father would take for a hangover."

He laughed. "It's a bomb, sweetheart. TATP. Favored by terrorists. They call it Mother of Satan because it's so volatile to make and you risk blowing yourself up."

"I can give you something much nicer to think about." Her smile widened as she crooked a finger at him.

Forget the Mother of Satan. Here was pure heaven. Guilt flickered through him. Quinn didn't know his real purpose in coming to Red Ridge—to find Demi Colton, the main suspect in the Groom Killer case, who'd fled town months ago right after being initially questioned. Or that he'd been assigned to investigate Quinn and her half brothers to see if they knew where their half sister, Demi, was hiding.

I'll tell her. Soon.

And then her mouth met his and he forgot about all else.

Food costs and sex.

Quinn Colton tried hard, and failed, to keep the smile off her face as she bounced down the stairs leading to Good Eats, her catering shop. Sex with West was always fantastic, but this morning added a special, delicious urgency to their lovemaking. Certainly the sex was better than the inventory waiting for her downstairs, along with the stacks of bills for the latest restaurant order.

Thirty years old and in love. Never thought this would happen. Certainly not a whirlwind romance and a lifelong pledge in only three weeks. But her heart knew that West was the one meant for her. They were made for each other.

Quiet and strong, and handsome and rugged as a movie star. Her heart thumped a little bit harder each time he was around.

It hadn't been love at first sight. More like love at first fight, she thought as she reached the bottom of the stairs. Quinn unlocked the door—her private entrance into the shop—and then locked it behind her. The door opened to her storage area. She skirted two heavy sacks of whole-grain flour and frowned at the mess on the floor. Last week she'd reluctantly laid off Jeb Plimpton, the teenager who swept up and kept her store tidy. More things on her to-do list, when right now all she could think about was adding West to the list, permanently.

West was a muscular, intimidating guy who scowled. Except around her. From the moment the tall, black-haired man with the chocolate-brown eyes had first walked into her shop, sparks had jumped between them. In his low, gravelly voice West had told her he wanted to order a meal to go. *Something resembling red meat that isn't that green sprouts froufrou food I heard you're known for. Fresh roadkill will suffice. Don't take it personally, sweetheart.*

She'd set a kale smoothie in front of him and told him he needed "foo foo" in his tank because he looked like fresh roadkill. Run over twice. With a backhoe. And he should not "take it personally."

Instead of sneering, West had laughed.

Her smile grew broader as she recalled that deep, grudging laugh. It had sent a tingle down her spine and a curious desire to coax more from him. She headed into the shop.

Austin Jones was already in the kitchen, lighting the gas range. Tall and wiry, he had been her best friend for ten years, ever since they met while taking cooking classes at the local college. They'd partnered in business together when she'd opened Good Eats, but Quinn remained the principal owner.

"Morning, sunshine," he greeted her as he straightened and headed over to the counter, where a batch of fresh arugula waited. Austin began chopping and dicing, and snapped his chewing gum.

Quinn wrinkled her nose. "How can you chew that obnoxious stuff? If you're craving apple pie, bake one."

Austin patted his flat stomach. "Have to watch the waistline. This may not be dessert, but tastes as good. Apple gum. Besides, I need the wrappers."

Right. Quinn picked up the foil swan her friend had made. "Future Christmas gift?"

"Don't knock it. If business keeps going downhill like this, you'll be lucky to get one."

As she scanned the kitchen, her smile wilted like the greens she'd had to toss yesterday. "What happened to the Bernstein order? Shouldn't you get that ready?"

"Canceled. They called this morning and said they were headed home early."

Oh dear. The Bernsteins, summer visitors to Red Ridge, always hosted a huge end-of-summer bash for one hundred and fifty guests. For the past five summers, Good Eats had been their caterer.

"There will be other summer parties." Quinn hoped she sounded more buoyant than she felt.

Yesterday they'd had to throw out nearly a case of fruit

that had spoiled. Their main business came from healthy fruit and veggie smoothies, but she couldn't keep paying bills for long on over-the-counter items. The catering end of her business had slid into the red with the Groom Killer on the loose. The news that someone was still murdering grooms before their weddings hadn't been good for her wedding catering business, either.

Bracing her hands on the counter, she stared at the slim list of catered orders for the week. Quinn had counted on the Bernstein order to make payroll and pay for next week's wholesale shipment of vegetables.

"How are we going to survive like this?" Austin gave a deep sigh, putting his hand to his chest.

Quinn gave him a playful poke. "If you want dramatics, try out for summer stock. We'll get by."

"Such an optimist. Did you pay the rent yet?"

Although the apartment rent was due later than the store rent, Quinn got a discount paying both all at once. "I will."

If necessary, she'd dip into her savings account.

Austin set down the knife. "Quinn, do you want me to take care of it? I'd hate to see Larson start eviction procedures."

Noel Larson wouldn't evict. Not right away. He'd gloat over the fact she owed him, and then squeeze harder, putting pressure on her and humiliating her. Noel and his twin brother were real estate tycoons in Red Ridge. Their reach and their power made them nearly invincible. You didn't want to mess with them.

"No. Stay away from him. I have the money, Austin, and I don't want Larson thinking I'm dead broke." She softened her tone. "I appreciate your offer of help, but you know me. I refuse to hand Larson that kind of power."

"Pride goeth before homelessness," he quipped.

She smiled. "Don't worry. I'd never let that happen."

Quinn felt warm inside as her thoughts drifted to West. By winter, perhaps she'd be married. Maybe even on her way to starting a family. Humming, she bustled around the kitchen.

Austin's blue eyes twinkled behind the thick glasses. "You look so…glowing this morning. New boyfriend?"

She wished she could scream about her romance with West from the rooftops, but she couldn't. For his safety. "I had a love affair with a nuclear reactor," she teased back. "And a good night's sleep."

"I'm glad someone's happy," he muttered morosely as he set down the knife and scooped the greens into a bowl. "I can't seem to get a date with everything going on in this town. At this rate, I'll be more celibate than a monk on Mars."

She laughed, and the laugh cut short as she suddenly remembered. West hadn't used a condom this morning…

They'd been so eager, so tired from their jobs and so careful to make sure no one saw them together, they'd forgotten to be careful that way.

Anxiety arrowed through her. She checked the calendar on her Android phone. Too close to call. Pregnancy wasn't on her to-do list. No Bullet Journal for that, she thought as she tucked her phone back into the pocket of her apron. Never mind the fact that West stated he didn't want children, and she did. She longed to have two children, a real family with a mother and father who stuck around, unlike her shiftless dad, Rusty.

Maybe she could change West's mind about having a family.

I need breakfast if I'm going to deal with this. Quinn opened the stainless steel refrigerator and gathered the ingredients for a blueberry-peach smoothie. When it was finished, she took it outside in the cool morning air.

Up and down Main Street, shopkeepers were opening their stores and starting business for the day. Summer business bustled in August with tourists who wanted some late-season fishing or hiking, taking kids to see Mount Rushmore and the Black Hills before shuttling them off to school. But not this year. Maybe the visitors heard about the Groom Killer and decided to stay elsewhere.

The brick facade of her little shop was aged, and gave Good Eats a small-town charm, along with the flower boxes lining the big windows overlooking Main Street. Her store, at the very edge of town, backed onto a wide-open field where there had been talk of developing a shopping center.

Those plans had been abandoned by the developer after business started going south in town.

Quinn had dug into her slim savings and purchased wrought iron bistro tables and chairs where customers could sit outside and enjoy a hot cappuccino or a cold smoothie in the warm weather. Once, the drinks were icing on her store's financial cake; now they were the entire cake and frosting.

If she didn't get a big order soon, she and Austin would be in financial trouble.

Never. Austin was her bestie. She needed him in her life as much as she needed West. And her brothers and sister.

Where was Demi?

She had constantly wrestled with worry over her kid sister. A bounty hunter, Demi was tough as nails, fierce, and Quinn couldn't help wondering if her half sister really had snapped and killed her ex-fiancé and the other grooms. Her ex had been the first victim. There had since been many more. According to the RRPD—many of whom were related to Demi and Quinn in some way—Demi was guilty. Others said she was being framed. All Quinn knew was that Demi was alone out there, supposedly trying to prove her innocence. At least, she'd texted as much to their brother Shane a couple months back.

Since then: radio silence.

What Quinn couldn't stop thinking about was that when Demi had fled town, she'd been pregnant. She must have had the baby already. Or was about to.

Quinn sipped the shake and set it down on the table. Her phone buzzed and she reached into her apron to pull it out when a tremendous *KA-POW* split the air, startling her into dropping the cell phone and spilling her drink.

Shaken, she stood up, staring in the direction of the explosion. Her father's bar was down that way…

In the direction West had taken when he'd kissed her goodbye and then headed for work.

Chapter 2

The abandoned hardware store had been totally flattened. West thought it looked as if a giant stomped on it, squashing the roof, toppling the walls and shattering what was left of the broken windows.

West was so focused on solving the Groom Killer case, on finding Demi Colton, that he figured her into every crime that affected Red Ridge. Blowing up a building to take the focus off the murders would allow her to sneak around the city more easily, hunt down the grooms who'd refused to hide their love and relationships.

But Demi hadn't done this, unless she graduated to high-tech explosives.

Then again, Demi Colton was a smart woman, a clever bounty hunter, and anything was possible.

Lights flashed from RRPD patrol cars and fire trucks lining the dirt road in front of the abandoned hardware store. Nearby, several tent canopies sat over tables for collection of evidence—the command post—along with an industrial generator. Yellow crime scene tape had already been strung up along the perimeter, where a crowd of curious bystanders started to gather. He recognized some of the hard-core patrons from Rusty Colton's bar and gritted his teeth. Drunk civilians were a pain to deal with, and worse at a crime scene.

His pulse raced as he parked his black Ford truck. West grabbed his kit, climbed out and then skirted around the side to let out Rex. The Lab jumped out and stood close to his side as West surveyed the detectives and cops already milling around the scene—the abandoned building he and Rex had jogged by earlier this morning. He raked a hand through his hair and sighed.

At his side, the dog gave him a reproachful look as if to say, *I told you so.*

"Hey, I checked it out," he told Rex.

He took a deep, calming breath. Steady now.

Every time he investigated an explosion, he remembered that day when he was seventeen, and his entire family had been killed by a bomb. He had been the sole survivor.

Surviving only because he'd been out with his girlfriend, parked at the local lovers' lane. The sex had been good, and quick and forgettable.

What he saw when he arrived home had not been forgettable.

Focus. Priorities. Safety first. West took another deep breath and glanced at Rex.

"Let's do this."

Every inch of the scene had to be processed, numbered and documented. His dog would alert him where the most evidence of the bomb was, while other investigators would sort out the scene for shrapnel embedded in the building and dirt.

But not until he and Rex checked out the scene for unexploded devices.

Ducking under the tape, he headed for the staging tent and grabbed a white hazmat suit and put it on, along with booties. Then he took the specially made booties he'd ordered for Rex and attached them to the dog's paws, fastening them with Velcro. The booties would not only protect Rex's paws from broken glass and debris, but helped preserve the integrity of the crime scene, as well.

Chief Finn Colton saw him and headed to the tent. He glanced at Rex.

"We've divided the building into four quadrants. Need you and Rex to search for secondary devices. When you give the all clear, I want you to search for evidence in the fourth quadrant—the southwest corner."

"No prob." West motioned to Rex and they entered the blown-out building.

The bomb had been a big one. Glass windows had been shattered from more than two hundred feet away and the boards that blocked the windows were now shards.

Any hopes this was a prank pulled by kids were immediately dashed. Kids who liked to blow things up wouldn't cause this kind of destruction.

No, they'd take a pipe bomb into the woods and then explode it, watching the destruction from afar.

He recognized Cal Flinders from the district Alcohol, Tobacco & Firearms office. Cal was one of the few he trusted.

West nodded at Cal and gripped Rex's leash. Safety first. If there were any unexploded devices on scene, his dog would detect them.

"Find," he ordered Rex, still gripping the leash.

Rex combed through all the sectors, searching for secondary devices. When he finished, he remained standing. West stared at the wreckage. No bodies today.

Not like at his family's house, where he'd screamed and tried to break past the barricades, get to his father, mother, two little sisters...

Focus. Rex looked up at him expectantly. *All clear, we okay?* the dog seemed to ask.

"Quadrants one, two, three and four all clear," West called out.

Next, he began scouring the area of the building assigned to him. Rex sniffed through the debris. The bomb had detonated in the building's center, where the worst damage was, but shrapnel traveled far. Patterns of the damage indicated how powerful the explosion was. Fortunately, no one had been injured.

Rex nosed beneath a piece of wood and sat. West hunkered down and examined the evidence.

Caked with dust and soot, it was heart shaped and partly bent. A woman's gold compact, with a butterfly design. West photographed the item and then studied it. It was covered with a film of white powder.

Bomb residue.

A woman had been here. Possibly slept here, or at the very least, stayed here for longer than a few minutes. He started to put a marker by the place where it had been, and hesitated.

Maybe Demi Colton hadn't planted this bomb, but this suggested she might have worked with the unknown suspect, the unsub. Or another woman had.

His cop instincts tingled. The RRPD assumed he was simply an FBI canine officer temporarily assigned to Red Ridge while one of their officers recovered from an injury.

No one on the force knew he was secretly investigating to see if the RRPD and Chief Finn and the other Coltons were deliberately dragging their heels on the Groom Killer investigation. If this compact belonged to Demi Colton, it might vanish before it could even be processed as evidence. *Were* the Coltons protecting their own? He didn't know. Hell, he wasn't even sure if his own secret fiancée was keeping her half sister's whereabouts to herself. Better to be safe and bring the compact back to the district office to test it.

Looking around to make sure no one saw, West bagged the evidence and carried it separately instead of dumping it into the official evidence collection bag he carried.

Why blow up an abandoned building? What was the deal with the overkill? Was someone testing out how to cause as much destruction as possible?

Was it Demi Colton trying to diffuse attention so she could target her next victim without the cops on red alert for her?

He couldn't remain there staring at the debris. He had to do his job. An RRPD cop in a hazmat suit came over as West removed an item from his kit.

"Nice." The officer whistled. "You feds have the funding for the latest equipment."

West looked at him. "You're contaminating my crime scene."

"Chief sent me over to see if you need help."

"I don't."

Grunting, the cop left. West switched on the ion mobility detector and swept his assigned quadrant. The machine could pick up trace amounts of chemicals, helping him determine what kind of bomb had exploded.

The unit sucked in air to test for traces of chemicals. It didn't take long.

Swearing under his breath, he switched off the machine.

Just as he'd suspected, but the job required details, more details and more details.

Returning to the command post, he told Finn Colton what he'd found. Then West glanced at the man standing just outside the crime scene tape, staring with avid interest at the bombed building.

He jerked a thumb at the man. "Curious bystander?"

Finn shook his head. "Witness. He's already been interviewed. Drove right past before the bomb exploded."

After the chief summarized what the man had said, West decided to talk to the witness himself. Experience taught him it was best to get firsthand information himself, before memories grew dim. People's detailed memories got muzzy real quick. Besides, if someone saw something linking Demi Colton to this explosion, and that interview got buried…

West peeled off his gloves and chucked them into a biohazard container, heading for the middle-aged man.

Slightly chunky, with quick, eager green eyes, the man looked around as if this were entertainment arranged just for him. West knew the type—self-important, glad to help, wanted to get his name in the paper. Still, he took a moment to study the witness. Though West had been in town less than a month, he didn't recognize him.

West introduced himself and scribbled the man's name— Santo Nestor. A cigarette dangled out of the corner of his mouth. He puffed constantly.

Nicotine addict.

"What were you doing at this end of town?"

Keeping his voice mild, he studied the witness's eye movement. The man stared earnestly back at him.

"I was headed into the city to grab a bite," Nestor said in a thick Hispanic accent. "I'm a salesman. Thought maybe

I could scope the place out at the local eatery, make a few contacts. I sell aluminum siding for houses."

Better than bridal supplies in this town. West made a few notes. "What did you see?"

Nestor prattled on the same thing he'd told detectives.

"Black smoke after the explosion?" West asked.

The man shook his head. "White smoke. I was so afraid, I almost wet my pants. Oh, *Dios mío*, I was damn lucky, I was right in front when it blew. I've been all over the country, never seen anything like this. What kind of place is Red Ridge, anyway, with terrorists bombing buildings?"

West took a long, thorough look at the man. Puffy cheeks, thick, dark brows, and a bulbous nose.

Drinker, as well as smoker.

White shirt, rolled up at the sleeves. Black hair slicked back with too much gel. Slight paunch oozing over his cheap leather belt. No tie. Black trousers, cotton, a bit casual for a salesman, but it was August in South Dakota and warm. His gaze scanned the trousers. Rumpled, maybe from driving a long distance.

"Longtime smoker?" West pointed to the cigarette.

Nestor shrugged, tossed the butt and ground it out with his leather shoe heel. "*Si*. Road trips get long. My ex tried to get me to quit. No luck. Did get me to give up the Cubans. I love a good Cuban. You smoke?"

West shook his head. "Where is your next client?" he asked.

The salesman flicked a hand toward the west. "I don't have an appointment until next week in Cheyenne. I was checking out the town for prospects. Going to stay a couple of days. You know any places in town that are good?"

You mean ones that don't blow up? West shook his head.

After taking the man's cell phone and home address, plus the name of his company, West closed his notebook.

Santo Nestor returned to his car, tossed the cigarette butt out the window and drove off.

Litterbug. He loathed civilians contaminating the area anywhere near his crime scene.

Glancing with disgust at the cigarette, he bagged it and put it in his pocket as evidence just in case.

Then West returned to the rubble, again, picking his way through it carefully. White smoke suggested black powder, as in TATP, not TNT or C-4.

Don't jump to conclusions. But his instincts tingled. TATP was a low-heat bomb and it took more than five hundred grams to do this kind of destruction.

The distinctive bleach-like odor told him his gut was right. TATP didn't contain nitrogen and made the explosives easier to avoid detection by scanners.

When they found it, the packaging containing the bomb might reveal hard evidence. Tape or wires could also contain scraps of skin cells, sweat or even hairs. If they were lucky, the unsub left some kind of DNA on the fragments.

Was the unsub Demi Colton?

Who did this? Does it have anything to do with the Groom Killer? Upcoming wedding site? Maybe the killer wants to blow up wedding party members in the future?

As he continued to gather evidence, his thoughts flashed back to his family, the ruins of their home, the ruins of his former life. West deliberately thought of Quinn, her sweet smile, saucy attitude. It soothed him as he worked.

Relationships were all about power. He knew this even with Quinn. In bed, he dominated, but out of it, she ran the show. She held his heart and, man, he enjoyed every single moment of it.

Even though they were private about their relationship for now, he preferred to keep it that way. The less interference from her family, the better.

But he couldn't help but wonder if her half sister was behind this explosion, as preparation for something more deadly to come.

Working a crime scene was an arduous, grueling task. Shortly before one o'clock, the chief ordered takeout for everyone.

Takeout from Good Eats.

His heart raced as he glanced up and saw Quinn's white delivery van pull up in front of the tent. She jumped out and opened the back door. Someone hastened to set up another long folding table for the food. As she picked out the aluminum containers, her brother Brayden ran to help.

ATF agent Cal tracked her moves and whistled, making the outline of an hourglass with his hands. "Nice dish."

West wanted to smack him. *Hands off. She's mine.* He only grunted, and at the low sound, Rex growled.

Cal glanced down at the canine. "Easy, boy. I'm not going to take your chow."

But I'll take your head if you even try to touch her. West gripped Rex's leash harder. Hell, it was tough enough concealing the fact he was secretly investigating the RRPD's efforts to find the Groom Killer. Hiding his relationship with Quinn was agonizing. His instincts were to draw her away from the admiring glances, put an arm around her waist to signal that she was taken. Exclusively. By him.

And he didn't even dare do more than nod at her when he helped carry a warm container of something that smelled like roasted lamb. Their fingers touched as she handed it to him, and familiar sparks jumped between them. West sucked in a low breath.

Damn, he could smell her amid the chemicals and the dust and the delicious odor of grilled meat. Real meat, too, not that tofu she also served.

His fiancée smelled like apples and spice, everything delicious.

Quinn finished setting up the containers and unpacked the paper plates and plastic silverware.

"All set, Chief," she told her cousin. "There's grilled lamb and rice, salad and butternut squash linguine with fried sage." Quinn tossed West a saucy, knowing look. "For those who prefer froufrou food."

Damn if it took every inch of his control not to laugh. Not to toss aside his plate of grilled lamb and stride over to her, pull her into his arms and kiss her senseless. Letting everyone know she was his and they belonged to each other. He didn't need healthy food for fortification. He needed only Quinn, and her vivacious spirit and wholesome smile.

Cal drifted over and thanked her. The ATF agent jerked a thumb at West.

"Don't mind Grumpy, Miss Colton. West doesn't like healthy food," Cal jested. "He's a red meat man."

"Takes all types," Quinn's brother Brayden remarked.

Ignoring them, West took his plate and a bottle of water to his car and sat on the hood of his truck to eat. He watched Quinn talk with Brayden at the table where most of the others ate. West noted that Finn Colton and Brayden worked closely with the Gages on the squad, despite the famous feud between the Colton and Gage families.

Did Quinn know where her sister was? What if she was hiding Demi? When he'd asked her about how close they'd been, Quinn had only shrugged and said she loved her sister, but they weren't close and barely knew each other. Demi concentrated on her job as a bounty hunter and Quinn was invested in establishing Good Eats and trying to make a good rep for herself in town.

His radar went on full alert as a sleek, expensive car

pulled up to the perimeter. Out from the driver's seat climbed Devlin Harrington. West looked down at the excellent meal Quinn had prepared. It turned to cardboard in his stomach.

Harrington was a wealthy, entitled lawyer who worked in his father's energy firm. The man oozed money. Probably used one-hundred-dollar bills as kindling in his fireplace each winter.

His father, billionaire Hamlin Harrington, was equally money hungry. He offered to save Colton Energy from bankruptcy, but only if Layla Colton, a bigwig at Colton Energy and the owner's daughter, married him. Layla's father, Fenwick, desperately needed the cash.

And the Red Ridge Police Department needed Fenwick to continue funding the large K-9 unit and training center. But Hamlin had called off the wedding to Layla until the Groom Killer was caught. Fenwick, who doubled as mayor of Red Ridge, was beside himself and breathed down the chief's neck on a daily basis to solve the case. It didn't matter that Fenwick was related to Chief Finn Colton. Fenwick needed money.

West understood Hamlin being nervous, canceling the wedding and calling off the engagement to Layla Colton. With a killer out to slay grooms, who would dare host a public wedding in town?

What he didn't get was marrying for money, not love. He didn't understand it. His own mother and father had been happily married for more than twenty-four years before a killer snuffed out their lives. He and Quinn wanted to marry because they loved each other, crazy as it seemed after barely meeting a month ago. But he knew Quinn was the right woman for him. She was intelligent and witty and caring, and he'd do anything for her.

Layla, Quinn's cousin, seemed like a smart, kind woman,

concerned about her family and savvy about business when he'd interviewed her about Demi Colton. Was she that dedicated to her family and saving her father's company that she'd sacrifice her own personal happiness?

Life was short. He'd learned that at seventeen when his world blew apart. And marriage lasted a long time, or at least, it should.

West's scarred hand felt tight today, as it did each time he worked a crime scene, reminding him of the night his family died in the bomb blast. He flexed it as he watched Harrington approach Chief Colton, wondering what the man wanted.

Wealthy lawyers usually didn't visit crime scenes. Not unless they were ambulance chasers. He'd bet a case of hundred-year-old brandy that Devlin Harrington had never chased an ambulance in his life. Not with that cash cow of a rich daddy, who probably paid him a salary that made West's modest income look laughable.

Wearing an expensive gray silk business suit, with a red power tie and starched shirt, and expensive leather footwear, Harrington looked out of place with the cops in their bunny suits, tactical vests and grubby, scuffed shoes.

The lawyer stood by the table where Finn Colton ate. He scrutinized the scene, shook his head. "Chief, this is most upsetting. Now we have a bomber in Red Ridge? I'm sure this is related to the groom killings. If there is anything I can do, any help I can offer, please let me know. I want to help. If you need assistance, I'm here."

To his credit, Finn didn't take the bait. "It's too early in the investigation to tell anything. We're doing all we can. Every man on this force is dedicated to catching the killer."

"But you must admit this is terribly suspicious timing." Harrington swept a hand over the crime scene tape. "If the killer is graduating to bombings, she must be caught.

I wanted to let you know I'm offering a $100,000 reward for the capture of Demi Colton."

West nearly choked on his forkful of rice.

Finn didn't even blink. "Oh?"

"She must be found and brought in for questioning. If she's innocent, she's innocent. But if she's guilty…" Again with the hand gesture. "Then the killings, and this kind of violence will end."

Was the guy running for office? West snorted as a newspaper photographer snapped Harrington's photo. He could envision the headline now: Billionaire Lawyer Offers Six Figures of Own Money for Capture of Suspect Demi Colton.

He hated it when civilians messed with an official investigation. Offering that much money for Demi's capture would send everyone eager for the reward out searching, giving the department more headaches and more false leads to chase.

And make a desperate Demi harder to catch. Hell, half the town would be searching for her now, eager to claim even a share of the reward.

West knew he had to question Quinn further on her sister. If Quinn even had a remote inkling of where Demi was, he had to know immediately.

"I'd like to see the official ad you're running in the newspaper," Finn told him, giving him a level look. "For the record."

"I'm very busy this afternoon." Harrington took out his cell phone, texted something. "But I'll send an Uber to drop off the notice at the station."

Sending an Uber to deliver a damn paper? Typical Harrington. You can't take five minutes to stop by on your way? No, that's too much trouble.

West knew some attorneys back East, hardworking,

congenial men and women who dedicated themselves to the law and society. Harrington was not one. He did it for the money.

Harrington flashed those pearly whites at everyone and glad-handed the officers sitting at the table.

"Thank you for all you are doing to catch the Groom Killer. If you need anything, anything at all, my office is at your disposal. We all want Demi Colton caught so life can return to normal. My father will be most grateful when Demi is found and arrested and weddings can resume in Red Ridge. He's most eager to marry Layla."

He spotted West sitting by his lonesome, walked over and stuck out a palm. "Agent Brand, so glad to see the FBI is working with our fine force. We certainly can use your services."

Giving him a cool glance, West nodded and ignored the hand. He picked up his fork and continued eating. Harrington's smile only got wider.

"Have a good day," the lawyer told him.

He strode off toward his car. West caught Quinn's worried gaze. If she was concerned about her sister before, she must be worried sick now. West made a small gesture at Harrington's car speeding off, then did an eye roll. She flashed a brief smile.

West ate quickly, tossed away the plate and plastic silverware, and then returned to the crime scene. The sooner he finished, the faster they could find who did this, and clues to where the bomber would strike next.

Whether or not it was Demi Colton.

Two hours later, Quinn unloaded all the catering dishes and brought them inside to her store, placing them on the counter near the sink. With a rueful smile, she noticed her hands were trembling.

West did that to her. Even being within one hundred feet of him set off her female parts. They tingled with anticipation, and her nerves jumped as if the annual Fourth of July fireworks exploded inside her.

Her smile fled as she recalled the extensive damage to the building, and the sneers of her father as he swigged back a bottle of beer and watched the cops work the scene.

Rusty had a habit of making the worst things worse. He liked his beer and criticizing other people and bragged about both.

Like her brothers and Demi, Quinn worked hard to overcome the reputation of being offspring of the town's notorious bar owner and womanizer. It was why she elected to serve wholesome food at Good Eats, to differentiate from the greasy bar food her father dished out.

She picked up the mail the carrier had dropped through the slot in her front door. As she walked to the counter, Quinn sorted through the stack. Bills. More bills. And a white card-size envelope that resembled an invitation. The envelope had a cute red heart stamped on it.

A wedding invitation?

Maybe an engagement announcement? Who would be crazy enough for that?

Taking the mail into the kitchen, she found a knife and went to open it. Hesitated. It looked innocent. Pretty stationery. What if it wasn't?

There was no return address. Quinn felt the envelope. She had never been the suspicious type, but dating West turned on all her precaution sensors. No return address could mean something dangerous inside, intended to harm.

Quinn studied the postmark. Red Ridge. From here in town. What if the Groom Killer had decided to reach out to new targets?

What if it was Demi, and she was sending a secret message?

Thoughts tumbled through her head. The possibilities were endless. So was the worry. She set the envelope down. Maybe it was better to wait for West. He had experience, perhaps there was some fancy instrument in his bag of tools he could use to scan the contents.

West had been working too hard lately on this Groom Killer case. Late nights, early mornings. A couple of days off in the mountains sounded perfect.

She went into the tiny cubicle kept as an office and opened the desk drawer to find the key Tia had given her. As a favor for delivering her meals on time every day, Tia Linwicki gave her the code to unlock the front gate and a key to one of the cabins in Pine Paradise, a property she owned. As long as no one rented the cabin, it was Quinn's to use.

She'd told West about her privileges with the cabin and how Tia entrusted her with the key. It would make a terrific weekend retreat with West. Quinn hunted for the key, but couldn't find it. Maybe she'd left it upstairs in her apartment. With all the confusion lately, the scrambling to find clients, she felt slightly scatterbrained.

She left the office and went into the store's front just as her brother Shane entered.

Smiling, she gestured to the counter. "Need an afternoon pick-me-up?"

His nose wrinkled. "Kale shakes and fruit smoothies? No thanks."

"I can make you a late lunch." Quinn's smile widened. "Something that will put hair on your chest. Make you attractive to the ladies."

He laughed. As if he needed that. With his sandy-blond hair, blue eyes and tall, muscular body, Shane was drop-dead gorgeous. For a while Quinn had envied him. Surely he didn't get those good looks from their father.

No, Shane had inherited their father's tough streak, though.

And besides, Shane was hot and heavy with someone, a dog trainer at the K-9 center. It was easy to forget because Shane, like everyone in town, kept their relationships on the down-low.

"Came to see how you are. And maybe if you baked some of those blueberry muffins."

Food costs had soared, but for her brother, she'd bake another dozen. "Go outside and sit. I'll get everything ready."

Humming as she buzzed around the kitchen, Quinn realized how much she enjoyed her job. Working for someone else might pay the bills, but she loved being her own boss. Books rested on a shelf above the stainless steel table where she did food prep. One was only a notebook with her handwriting. Those recipes she'd invented on her own, adding this and mixing that.

She'd hate to have to follow orders from an employer. Red Ridge was a good place to live…well, until lately.

Good place to raise a family. Quinn ground to a halt before reaching for a bottle of water for Shane. She and West had briefly skirted the topic of children.

He didn't want kids.

She wanted two.

Impasse, for now. Quinn kept reasoning with herself that they could compromise. Maybe he'd change his mind.

She brought a tray with the treats outside and joined her brother. Shane munched on a blueberry muffin made from coconut flour, while she drank her strawberry smoothie. Sunshine still peeked through the puffy white clouds, but indigo dotted the horizon, indicating a summer storm approached. Quinn didn't mind the rain on hot days like this, except the rain drove away the customers who made impulse purchases of organic snacks and shakes.

"That explosion." Shane shook his head and took a swig of bottled water. "Damn scary."

"Do they have any clues?" Despite being on the crime scene and serving lunch, Quinn couldn't discern any information. But Shane worked as a private investigator and informant for the RRPD, and he was savvy at picking up information on the street.

"Not yet. Everyone's speculating."

"Maybe it was some local kids, fooling around."

"I doubt it." Shane's gaze looked troubled. "There's buzz it might be a test run of something bigger to come."

"Terrific. I hate this." She toyed with the straw, glanced up and down the street. "Some days it feels like we're living in a war zone, not knowing what will happen next, who's doing all this. My business is going from bad to worse. Summer's nearly over and what am I going to do when winter comes? This is my busy season."

Quinn leaned back, trying not to fret. The rent was overdue and she didn't know how to make her budget. "Maybe I should move to Sioux Falls."

Shane's eyes widened. "You? The girl who vowed to stay in Red Ridge, no matter what?"

West's home was near Sioux Falls. It might be a good place to settle after they married. Or get married there, far away from the dangers of the Groom Killer. Maybe West would change his mind about children if they lived away from Red Ridge.

"Everyone changes. I'm getting older, I could find a good job with another catering company."

"You can't. Where would I get my blueberry muffins?"

She rolled her eyes and shook her head as he grinned

at her. They'd never been close, barely knew each other growing up, but lately she'd drawn close to her brothers. She wanted to have relationships with them, and since Demi's disappearance, Quinn realized how precarious and unpredictable life could become.

Her thoughts went to the mysterious envelope in her kitchen. "Have you heard anything more from Demi?"

Shane coughed on his bite of muffin. He swigged more water, avoided her gaze. "Why would I?"

Leveling with him might be best. "I'm really worried about her. She's all by herself, with a baby...and since she's on the run, she could be staying in places that aren't safe."

"I'm sure she's fine." He ate the last of the muffin and wiped his mouth with the linen napkin she'd given him.

Quinn wished she'd been closer with her younger sister. Maybe then Demi would have contacted her, asked for help. And now that she and West were engaged, she wanted to tell someone. Anyone. A sister, who could keep a secret, a sister who would laugh and roll her eyes as Quinn went into poetic professions of how she adored West, what a wonderful, generous man he was, what a cute butt he had...

Speaking of the devil. West's familiar pickup pulled up on Main Street, parked. He got out, let out Rex and then locked the door.

Shane sniffed. Quinn didn't care for the sound. It indicated her brother didn't have a high opinion of the new guy in town.

The new guy who happened to be secretly engaged. *To me.*

"Nice dog," she murmured.

"I like dogs." Shane's voice remained level. "Better than cops and better than FBI agents."

West did a fine job of ignoring them both sitting across the street and staring at him.

"What do you think of him? I mean, he's an FBI agent, but he seems okay." She tried to keep the question casual, but couldn't help peeking at West as he stopped to enter the small boutique where she knew he liked to buy Rex treats.

Shane shrugged. "I try not to think. He's FBI, and feds aren't any better than cops."

"Our brother," she began.

"Wasn't talking about family." Shane's too-observant gaze sharpened. "You certainly seem interested in Agent Brand."

Uh-oh. Quinn gave a little laugh. "It's a small town. New people are always fascinating. And these days, I can't afford to alienate potential customers."

"He doesn't seem like the organic type."

Oh, I don't know. He sure did like that farm-raised honey he put on me two nights ago when we...

"You okay? You're blushing." Shane finished his water.

Quickly she fanned herself. "Fine. Just hot."

"It'll rain soon. Cool things off."

"I hope it doesn't destroy the crime scene and the evidence."

Her brother cocked his head. "Now you're sounding like a cop. What gives?"

Quinn busied herself with cleaning the table. West's lingo had filtered into her life. Soon she'd be talking in acronyms like he did. She needed to be more careful.

"Just a concerned citizen who wants things to return to normal, so I can stay in the town I love."

Shane sighed. "Don't go making any hasty decisions yet. You need money?"

Deeply touched, she shook her head. "The Larsons gave me an extension."

Now her brother looked mighty angry. "Those rip-off artists are cons, Quinn. Don't trust them. Extension today on the rent, double the price tomorrow."

"I'm fine." She waved him off. "Go investigate someone else."

To her surprise, he gave her a quick peck on the cheek. "Thanks. See you."

Inside the kitchen, she looked at the clean counter, the neatly stacked bowls. A kitchen shouldn't be this tidy. It meant no business. The lunch for the RRPD would help with the smaller bills. But the rent still remained the huge question mark.

I'll think about that later.

She picked up the envelope she'd received in the mail today and held it to the light. Nothing. Shook it. No telltale sound of something floating. She wished she'd remembered to show it to Shane. She'd have West check it out tonight.

The back door opened and Austin walked through.

"Where have you been?" she demanded. "I had to set up everything myself at the crime scene for the cops."

"I went fishing for business. Great news. I found us a gig for tonight. Yoga studio is hosting an open house and they need gluten-free hors d'oeuvres and fruit smoothies for two hundred potential clients. We need to be in Sullivan Falls by nine tonight."

Delight turned into dismay. "That's forty miles away!"

"And they promised cash on delivery. So let's hustle." He pushed his glasses up his thin nose. "Plus some free lessons. You could use a little flexibility to loosen up."

Quinn set down the envelope for later, along with the pile of bills. They had work to do, and money was tight.

* * *

It had been a hell of a day and he was exhausted.

Shortly after midnight, West parked his truck in the usual spot, the parking garage one street over from Main, and ducked down a back alley leading to Quinn's shop. He went through the service entrance, skirting the green Dumpster. Rex, who normally stopped to sniff around the garbage, loped eagerly alongside him and darted inside as he opened the door with his key.

"Yeah, you're as beat as I am," West murmured to his dog, bending down and scratching behind his ears after he locked the door. "How about some treats?"

Part of Rex's training involved food. Rex never ate from a bowl because each time he found explosives while training, West fed him. But he also gave him treats after a long day.

Upstairs, he found the dog biscuits Quinn had hidden in her pantry just for Rex. Leaving Rex to happily munch, he headed into the bedroom.

Sitting at her antique dressing table, Quinn brushed her curls. West felt a tug inside as he watched. He adored the way her mouth softened as she gazed into the mirror, and how it sparked when she caught sight of him.

As if he were the only one in her world who could light her up inside.

Leaning against the doorjamb, he watched her, all the day's tension sliding off him. "You didn't have to wait up for me, sweetheart."

"Are you hungry?"

"Grabbed a sandwich in town."

Her gaze twinkled. "I like waiting up for you. I like watching you, too. Saw you on Main when I was sitting outside with my brother."

"You were eyeballing my very fine ass," he teased.

The ensuing blush assured him she did the very thing. "It's quite nice to watch. Long day?"

"The worst. But it's better now that I'm here with you." His voice went husky. "You make all my troubles go away."

Except the biggest trouble, and that was finding Demi Colton. Finding the truth about her. Today's explosion deeply worried him, and not simply because he'd ignored the warning sign this morning.

Explosions like that from TATP bombs indicated professionals. Someone intended to do much, much worse. And there was no way to predict where, and when. If Demi Colton did have a hand in it, he needed to know ASAP if Quinn and her brothers were hiding intel on their runaway sister.

"Can you believe Devlin Harrington is offering a hundred thousand to capture my sister?" she asked.

Careful now. West considered. "He seems all about the money. What's he really like?"

"Rich. Powerful. Very nice when you meet him. He started dating my cousin Gemma a few months ago. That's what the gossips say." Quinn sighed. "I'm not close to Gemma. Unlike me, she's from the right side of the tracks."

"And you think you're from the wrong side? I don't think so."

Quinn gave him a wry smile. "Being the daughter of Rusty Colton carries a certain stigma in this town, West. Especially with the rich branches of the Colton family like Gemma's."

"Maybe, but not from what I've seen. People respect you for who you are, honey. And your excellent cooking, even if you make tofu," he teased back.

He strode behind her and gently took the brush from her hands. West began to brush her hair as she smiled at him in the mirror.

West scanned the items on the table's polished surface, fishing for an opening to bring up her sister.

"Did Demi ever brush your hair when you were kids?"

Ever so slightly, she stiffened. "We didn't live together. And my mom and hers didn't exactly get along."

He kept brushing, while racking his brain for a way to bring up her sister again. But for now, it felt wonderful to be with her, to ease the pressure of the job with the simple enjoyment of Quinn's company.

West wished the job and his personal life didn't have to collide.

Her eyes closed and she made a sound of pure pleasure. "That feels so good. You're a good man with your hands, West Brand."

A faint memory tugged at him. Once the grief had been a sharp blade, but now it had eased into a painful ache. "My sisters used to beg me to brush their hair at night. It was one of my chores. I'd sit down with them, listen to their day, brush their hair and then our parents would tuck them into bed."

Quinn's eyes met his in the mirror. "You don't talk much about your family, honey. All I know is that they were killed in an accident. I don't want to pressure you, but I'd like to know more about your childhood."

"I'll tell you. Some day." A vague promise. He would. It was still too raw, even after all these years, because the sting of guilt was a constant barb, waiting to rip open old wounds once more.

But he'd give her an opening, because maybe in talking about his sisters, she would open up about Demi. And the sooner they found Demi and the Groom Killer, the sooner he could really open up to Quinn.

"We used to go camping in the Black Hills. Dad didn't have much of a chance to take us, because he was always working, but when he did, it was wonderful. Sometimes we'd stay at cabins in the canyon instead of tent camping, when Mom decided camping was a little too rustic and she needed a real vacation from roughing it. She wanted us to experience nature and the great outdoors, but working plumbing was a terrific invention."

Quinn smiled softly. "Your mother sounds like she was a special lady."

The ache in his chest flowered, hit like a hammer. West took a deep breath. *Focus on the job and Quinn.* "Did you ever go camping with your family?"

"There was a cabin I rented in Spearfish Canyon last year when I needed to get away from work." Quinn frowned, as if trying to remember. "Lovely place. It was called Pine Paradise. It was the most peaceful, serene spot I'd ever visited."

She turned her head and he stopped brushing. "You know that feeling, where you're outside in nature, the birds chirping, the wind blowing through the trees and you feel like you're the only soul in the world?"

"Yes," he said quietly. "I know it."

Places like that kept him sane when the job grew too intense and the evil he'd witnessed threatened to erode his soul.

"It was a good place to get away from the pressures of the city. I invited Demi to stay with me. I was trying to get to know her better. She always loved the outdoors and I thought it was a good place to bond with her."

"Do you think she would ever return there? Did she enjoy it?"

"I have no clue," she muttered. "She didn't stay long."

"That's too bad."

Quinn sighed. "She was in a hurry to leave, as usual. Loaned me her leather motorcycle jacket. It's still in the closet. I keep meaning to return it, but hoped she would stop by. That was long before everything went down with the Groom Killer."

He stopped brushing her hair, took a curl between his fingers and pulled it down slightly. West watched it uncoil and spring back up. Then he went into her closet, sorted through the clothing and found the jacket. Leather motorcycle jacket, with a broken zipper. He whistled.

"Nice." West replaced it in the closet, returned to her. "I have a much better way of keeping you warm. You and me at Pine Paradise. A few days hiking, trout fishing."

Quinn smiled, her earlier displeasure gone. "Fishing? And I'd cook the fish."

"All organic," he teased.

She caught his right hand, kissed his palm, her mouth moving over the old scar tissue. Quinn rubbed her cheek against it. "You never did tell me about how you got this. Was it on a field assignment?"

"It was a long time ago. I'll tell you, someday."

West thought about her sister. Relationships that failed, bonds never formed. At least he'd shared that with his sisters, much as he missed them.

Memories helped ease the grief on days when it hurt.

"I always longed for a brother. Do guy stuff with, like camping, football, basketball, but my sisters were…special to me. I never regretted any of the time I spent with them. They could be pests, like little sisters are, but they were great kids."

He paused in brushing her hair, the acid creeping up his throat. His sisters deserved a chance to live, a chance to have boyfriends, share a first kiss, marriage, babies. They never had it.

"I love children." Her gaze met his in the mirror. "I want a family, West."

Damn. *Let's not go there tonight.* West's circle was tight and small. He thought of it as he thought of investigating crime scenes. *Work it from the perimeter out.* On the outer fringes were coworkers and casual acquaintances. On the inside were those close to him.

There weren't many of those relationships. He kept it that way.

Once, it had been expanded to include his family, a flock of friends and relatives. After the bomb, he shut down most of those relationships.

Kids meant having innocent, fragile babies who couldn't defend themselves. What if he failed to keep them safe, the way his own father had failed his daughters?

Including Quinn in his circle? Yeah. Kids? No.

"I don't want children." There. He stated it. Would this provoke a fight? But Quinn only looked away, her mouth tight.

"It's late. Let's discuss this later," he told her. As in ten years. Or twenty.

"I would have loved having a little sister when I grew up. I always wanted to have a close relationship with Demi." Quinn sighed.

Okay, let's try for subtle. He placed the brush on the table.

"When you last saw your sister, did she have a gold compact? Heart-shaped?"

Yeah, subtle, alight, Brand. Subtle as a locomotive.

Quinn picked up the brush he'd set down and began to toy with it. "Funny you should mention it. A few years ago, when I met her for lunch, I brought her a gift like that. I saw them in a store in Sioux Falls and bought two."

West's heart skipped a beat. He jammed his hands into the pockets of his Dockers.

"Does she still have it?"

She leaned her elbows on the table and looked at him in the mirror. "Why are you asking about the compact? And Demi? Does this have to do with her disappearance?"

West knew he had to tread lightly. Offer information, but no details. "Maybe. It could be a clue to where she went."

"I don't know. I wasn't in the habit of checking her purse." Quinn's voice was sharp.

He pressed on, because he suspected the gold compact now was definitely a sign that Demi had been in the abandoned building. Maybe she'd dropped it while mixing the chemicals to blow up the place, cover her tracks before she went to her next destination.

"What does your compact look like? Was it like hers?"

Her full mouth flattened. "West, why all these questions?"

He squatted down by the table and took her hand into his, brushing a kiss against her knuckles. "We need to find her, Quinn. But I promise you this, when we find her, I will let you know."

She blinked rapidly, moisture filling her lovely brown eyes. "I wish we had been closer. I really do. I'm so worried about her."

He held her tight, stroking her back in circles. West hated seeing her this upset. Hated that he was the one making her cry, because he had to ask all these questions. It was his job, and he had no choice.

Not that he could tell her that.

"What does your compact look like? If it's like hers, I might be able to track her down." He wiped away a stray tear. "Don't tell your brothers. This is something I'm working on my own."

"To find Demi?"

At his nod, she swiped a hand over her eyes. He didn't

like the frown denting her brows, and the suspicious look she gave him. "Not because she's my sister and you know how worried I am about her. Because she's a suspect."

He blew out a breath. "She is a suspect, Quinn. The sooner we can find, and question her…"

"The sooner you can arrest her."

West clenched his hands. "The sooner she'll be safe. Now, will you help me?"

Quinn bit her lower lip. "All right. I'll tell you whatever you need to know, as long as it will help Demi."

"Is your gold compact like hers?"

"Not exactly." She frowned, and toyed with the brush again. "Actually, now I remember. Hers wasn't gold. It was silver, with her initials on it. And round. I got a round one for her to engrave her initials on it."

Damn.

"Mine was heart shaped."

West went still. A chill raced down his spine. "What exactly does it look like?"

His heart dropped to his already-churning stomach at her next words.

"It's gold. With a butterfly emblem on the front."

Chapter 3

How the hell had his fiancée's compact ended up in a blown-up building? Quinn acted as surprised as everyone else to learn about the explosion. And worried, too. Could she possibly have been in the building—helping her sister set up explosives? Come on.

He couldn't risk sharing details with the RRPD just yet. The following morning, he drove east to meet with his supervisor. Special Agent in Charge Mikayla "Mike" Ryan ran the satellite office near Sioux Falls. She had worked with him in the field for the three years since West had moved to South Dakota.

Before meeting Quinn, he'd had the itch to move again.

The diner where he'd chosen to meet Mike was off the main grid, a small, but clean greasy spoon between Sioux Falls and Red Ridge. With her mousy brown hair, glasses, petite and trim figure clad in a blue pantsuit, Mike looked more like an accountant than a woman who knew how to take down bad guys. She was already there in a quiet back booth by the large picture window, sipping coffee and digging into a big plate of fried eggs and crispy bacon. His nostrils twitched with appreciation. Since dating Quinn, he hadn't eaten anything "unhealthy," but his taste buds sure did remember those days.

West slid into the booth across from her.

Mike glanced up from her forkful of eggs. "You look like hell, West."

"Nice to see you, too."

Beneath the table, he handed off the brown paper bag containing the bagged evidence of the gold compact, along with a plastic bag with a few strands of Quinn's hair taken from her brush last night. Mike tucked it into the tote bag sitting on the seat beside her.

He signaled for the waitress and ordered black coffee. Stomach too tense to even try food, he watched his boss eat as if it were her last meal. Mike amused the hell out of him. How she stayed so thin while eating artery-hardening grease was a mystery. She was sometimes too sarcastic and loud, but a hell of a good field agent and manager.

West sipped his coffee and waited. Mike wasn't the type to rush headfirst into conversation. She liked to give the agents a chance to collect their thoughts, assess the situation.

And then hammer them. He'd already filled her in on the explosion and the investigation.

"Anything on the RRPD?" she asked, wiping her mouth with a paper napkin.

Same question she asked yesterday. Mike was like a dog, worrying the same topic to death.

"Nothing so far." West stared out the window of the diner. "I can't get a bead on the Coltons. They're good at their jobs, and keep to themselves."

"Like you." Mike stirred more cream into her coffee. "Anything else I should know?"

Guilt flickered through him. *Yeah, I'm engaged and in love with the sister of the suspect. But you don't need to nose around my personal life.*

He clenched and unclenched his fists. "I need you to run the evidence for DNA and match against the hair sample I've provided."

Mike didn't even blink. "Victim of the blast?" She leaned forward, her green eyes sharp behind the glasses. "Or personal acquaintance, of the female variety?"

West cringed inside. "What makes you say that?"

"You look like you haven't slept all night, and what sleep you did get was in your clothing. You want me to process this separately from the routine investigation the RRPD is already conducting, so it's got to be connected to the Coltons or a Colton, and…"

He waited.

"You have a love bite on the right side of your neck."

Inwardly, West cursed, and slapped a hand over the telltale mark. Knew he should have worn a collared shirt, but he'd been in a rush.

"And you shaved off your beard. You never shave your beard. So it has to be a woman."

West rubbed a knuckle against his cheek. "My personal life is none of your damn business."

Mike's gaze narrowed. "It is if your personal life interferes with the job, West. You're a good operator. I asked for you on my team because that's how good you are. You're focused and private and that's fine. But don't let a woman get in the way of finding Demi Colton. I'd hate to see you trash your career over good sex."

"Great sex." He locked gazes with her, and flattened his palms on the table.

Her mouth curled into a smile, and then she gave a short, grudging laugh. "I'm glad someone's getting something. Fine. Do whatever you must do. But do your job, as well. And don't hold anything back from me."

Mike was not his father confessor. "You're on a need-to-know basis. That's how we set up this op. So when you need to know, I'll tell you. For now, know this. Whoever blew up that hardware store probably is the same person who stole the fifty-five-gallon drum of peroxide from the chemical warehouse in Sioux Falls. This could have been a test for something bigger, with massive human casualties."

Now he'd succeeded in diverting her attention away from his face and neck. Mike glanced at the bag in her tote. "Another TATP bomb? Demi Colton trying to create a distraction, or blow up a whole damn wedding, groom and bride this time?"

"I don't know. My gut says whoever did this, the hardware store was a test run, to see how volatile the explosives were and how much was needed for the real thing. If it was Demi Colton, she's gone beyond shooting grooms." He took his notepad out of his back pocket where he'd scribbled details about Quinn's sister and what he had learned about her.

Quinn hadn't been close to her half sister. She'd told him as much. But that had been growing up. Giving Demi the gift of the mirrored compact told him Quinn reached out, tried to forge a bond with her sibling.

"Have you gotten anything out of the Colton brothers?"

"Not yet. They're closemouthed and haven't said much to me."

"What about Quinn Colton? Has she said anything at all about her sister?"

He hadn't been a smooth operator all these years to give away answers with his facial expression. West thumbed through the notebook. "She's worried sick about her sister and the baby. She also thinks it's possible that Demi could be the Groom Killer. If Quinn was in touch with her sister, she would coax her into surrendering to authorities."

I hope.

Had Quinn helped Demi hide in the abandoned building, giving her food and water, and then they'd blown up the building to hide evidence? Too far-fetched, but why the hell was his fiancée's compact in the rubble? He had no answers, only questions.

West shoved his notebook back into his pocket and glanced at his watch. He had enough time to grab lunch, and a few necessities, before arriving for the afternoon shift. The chief had granted him a half day after he'd worked the crime scene a full fourteen hours yesterday.

"Got to go. Call me as soon as you get a hit on that evidence." West slid out of the booth.

Mike nodded. "And you check in every other day now instead of once a week. I don't like this development, West. Or being left in the dark. You know what I do when I'm in the dark."

"No worries. Will do."

As he headed out of the diner, he knew the intent behind his boss's words. Mike wouldn't be satisfied with the meager information he'd given her. If she felt he was holding out, she would yank him off the case and replace his sorry ass. Or worse, go undercover herself to team up with him. In working close with him, she'd be certain to find out about his relationship with Quinn.

He could only hope he had answers to give her soon, before that happened.

Vegan meals were easy for Quinn to make. The hard part was the delivery, and the finicky client—Tia Linwicki.

Tia, who owned her own real estate agency on the edge of downtown, was very fussy about her meals. She had sent Quinn a specific list of foods to prepare. If the food was too hot, she complained. If it was too cold, she complained.

But she paid cash each day and didn't mind the surcharge Quinn put on there for the special delivery fee.

Or, as Quinn privately put it, "The Bitch Fee."

This morning she'd made Tia a special vegan garlic pasta with roasted tomatoes. The smells had been so enticing, they even made Quinn's mouth water.

Then she slid the pasta into a special heated dish, covered it with the insulated food carrier and left her store.

Tia worked a good distance from her, but it was such a nice day, Quinn decided to walk. The insulated container would keep the pasta at the proper temperature and cool it slightly by the time she reached Tia's office. If she drove, her client would complain the food was too hot to eat right away.

Humming, she walked past the stores, her practiced eye noting the lack of customers out on such a pretty, sunny day. Normally downtown was bustling with tourists. Not now.

Her business wasn't the only one suffering.

The heels of her flat-soled shoes clicked on the pavement as she walked. At the corner drugstore, she saw West coming out, a paper bag in hand. Her heart beat faster.

Quinn nodded at him. "Afternoon, Agent Brand."

"Miss Colton, a pleasure to see you," he murmured, tapping his index finger to his lips. His eyes sparkled as he held up the bag.

Oh yeah, she knew why he had been in there. Condoms.

She continued walking, unable to keep the silly smile from her face. The finger-to-the-lips gesture was their secret code for he planned to spend the night with her. Oh yeah, great sex on the horizon always chased away gloomy thoughts.

Her smile fled. Condoms for tonight, but they'd been reckless recently. She might even be pregnant now. If so, West's choice about kids would be removed. Well, that was a worry for later.

The early-pregnancy test kit she'd bought still sat in the bathroom. Soon as she returned home, she'd screw up the nerve to take it.

Later, she'd also worry about all the questions West had peppered her with over Demi. She was happy he'd finally opened up about his family, and sensed it was a deeply sore subject, but she wanted him to share with her about his childhood. Surely there were good memories, as he'd indicated last night. Quinn couldn't imagine losing her entire family all at once. West had only told her it was an accident. Probably a car wreck.

Quinn wished she had shared a closer bond with Demi. Maybe her sister would have turned to her for help instead of running off. Pregnant, alone and probably scared.

Her thoughts drifted back to the cabin at Pine Paradise Tia had given her the key to. It would make a perfect place for her and West to honeymoon before Tia sold the property. Or share a day or two alone, away from the prying eyes of her neighbors. This business of him sneaking in and out of her apartment was taxing.

Shifting the covered dish in her hands, she saw Tia's office. Tia had a small storefront at the edge of downtown, next to Lulu's Boutique, a small shop offering imported Italian clothing and accessories. The closed sign hung on the boutique. Lulu usually closed shop at noon and drove home to feed and walk her two dogs.

No such lunch break for Tia. Tia never stopped hustling. Like the Larson twins, Tia liked money. Once or twice she'd seen the twins in Tia's office. Not surprising. Tia had a harsh personality, as pushy as the Larson brothers.

Perhaps they talked shop, or looking for bigger and better deals. Yesterday she'd overheard Tia on the phone talking about Pine Paradise. Tia was not a happy person during that convo.

She peered through the front window of Tia's office. The vertical blinds were drawn almost all the way across. Odd. Tia loved to leave them open, wave to pedestrians. Look important, doing deals, making money.

Making money for her clients.

Quinn shaded her eyes. The office was dark inside, but she could barely make out Tia's desk. The woman wasn't there. But a man dressed in a suit stood by the big mahogany desk Tia had bragged cost her a small fortune. The overhead fluorescent lights picked up the shining gleam of his black hair, worn long, down to his collar.

He turned, showing his profile, his expression slightly cruel, cold. A shiver raced down Quinn's spine. She looked at the unruly cowlick sticking up from his hair. A cigar stump dangled from his mouth.

He didn't look friendly, or welcoming. More like the type who threatened. Then he ran out the back door, fleeing as if the hounds of hell were chasing him.

Quinn hesitated. Wasn't she being judgmental? The lighting inside could have made him look mean. Maybe Tia wasn't working as hard as she claimed and she had a new love. Perhaps he didn't want anyone knowing they indulged in a session of afternoon delight.

Tia, you could have picked a better lover. This guy looks like he gets off on playing it rough. Gooseflesh sprang out on her arms.

I've seen him before. But where? She frowned. Maybe at Tia's office?

None of her business. Only delivering the meal was.
And getting paid.

Quinn set down the food carrier to fumble with the doorknob. She opened the door and grimaced as the stench of cigar smoke wafted outside. As she went to pick up the casserole, she saw a flash of white as an enormous *KA-POW* slammed the air. A giant hand punched her with a hammering fist, hurling her through the air back into the street. And then the world went dark and she felt no more.

Chapter 4

The shift in air pressure and the tremendous explosion rattled windows and made the ground shake. West instinctively dropped to the sidewalk, spilling the paper bag, and covered his head.

Screams filled the air. He waited for a few seconds, but it felt like minutes, before rising and looking at the edge of town.

In the direction Quinn had strolled. His heart dropped to his stomach and he raced to his truck, where Rex sat in the front seat, the air-conditioning running. West opened the truck, grabbed Rex's leash, but the dog needed no coaxing.

They both ran in the direction of the explosion. Locals stared at the building, now engulfed in flames. West was already running, phoning for backup. No need, for the whole damn county must have heard the blast.

Not Quinn. Please, not Quinn. Let her be far away, hell,

in the next town. Not Quinn. Not when he'd finally found her, allowed himself to feel again after all these years...

The real estate office was leveled, white smoke pouring from it. Safety first. It had been drilled into him, but that was for cases. Not for the love of his life.

Boards and rubble lay everywhere, shards of glass sharp enough to slice through skin. Flames licked at the back of the building. Ordering Rex to stay back, he picked his way through the rubble.

Quinn always delivered Tia's meals in person...putting them on her desk. He had been there once, knew the agent worked at an expansive desk in the back. Everything in the back was splintered, fragments of a profession...of a life. Smoke billowed through the air.

Where the hell was Quinn? He'd seen her head in this direction, knew she was delivering Tia's lunch. Maybe she hadn't entered. *Please*, he prayed. *Let her be okay.* He whistled for the dog.

"Rex, find Quinn," he yelled out.

Rex nosed through the rubble toward the front of the shop, clambering over boards and debris.

Rubble was everywhere. Rex barked, the signal for finding a human. Boards and a chair covered a petite figure sprawled on the ground. West lifted the board and tossed it aside to find a woman lying on her back. A shattered food container, and mangled bits of pasta, was nearby.

Quinn. She couldn't be dead. His breath hitched, and then he saw her chest rise and fall. Relief made him weak, but he got a grip.

Alive, but unconscious, bleeding heavily from a laceration to her head. Blood streamed down the side of her face. West shrugged out of his jacket, tore off his white T-shirt and held it to her head to stanch the bleeding.

Not daring to move her further, in case of a neck injury

and shattered vertebrae, he held his shirt against her head, his hand trembling.

"It's okay, baby. It's okay. I've got you," he whispered, everything inside him bunched up in knots. Rex licked her face.

People were running toward him. The whine of sirens grew louder. Help was arriving. *Hurry.* In his mind's eye, he flashed back to that terrible night when he was a teenager. House burning, broken glass littering the front yard, his screams echoing through the night as the sirens wailed a mocking song… *Too late, too late, too late…*

Not too late. Quinn was breathing. Alive.

EMTs rushed forward. One medical professional squatted by him, opened a kit. West was dully aware of the man trying to shoulder him aside.

"We've got this," the paramedic assured him. "Let us treat her."

Let her go. They're professionals. But everything inside him screamed to hold on and not let go of Quinn because if he did, he could lose her.

She might die, just like his mother, father and little sisters.

She will die if you don't move it, Brand.

Dragging in a deep breath, he stood and stepped aside.

With quiet, swift professionalism, the paramedics went to work, swapping out his soaked shirt for real bandages, putting a neck brace on her to prevent her head from moving, starting an IV, taking her pressure. He heard a buzz of words, saw them slide Quinn onto a backboard and then lift her onto a gurney.

She's going to be okay. Has to be okay. I can't lose her.

Everything inside him fought to run back to his truck, race after the screaming ambulance. Follow her to the hospital, make sure she got treated, hover until she opened her eyes and looked at him.

West clenched his hands and unclenched them. Using a breathing technique he'd learned from a therapist who'd treated him for PTSD, he centered himself and his thoughts.

The best way he could help Quinn was by doing his job. The sooner he helped catch the bastard doing this, the safer she and the town would be.

"Brand!"

He turned at the sound of Finn Colton's voice. The chief looked at the departing ambulance, his expression grim. "What happened?"

West told him about finding Quinn, as others arrived and began to work the scene.

He knew cops, knew the tight brotherhood. Quinn had been injured—one of their own, family—and they were going to work this case hard.

West didn't need to get insider information on the local cops to ascertain this. He knew human nature.

Finn gave him a hard look. "Brayden and Shane are on their way to the hospital, and they'll question Quinn if she wakes up. I need you to stay here, work the scene."

West nodded, though he fought the instinctive need to rush to the hospital with the chief. He turned back to his truck to fetch his equipment.

No one knew what Quinn meant to him. They had kept their relationship secret on purpose. But right now, as he jogged back to his truck, Rex at his side, he was the one who could openly claim her and join her brothers at the hospital.

Firefighters had quickly doused the flames and now the cops were working the scene. Someone had marked Tia's body.

What was left of it.

He saw a high-heeled red shoe attached to a section of bloodied leg sticking out from beneath half a large-screen television. High heels. Quinn had not worn high heels. Not during the day. At night she liked wearing them when they met in secret outside town. Dinner, a show, good times.

He liked her in high heels, and when she wore them to bed last week…

Was she okay?

Focus, Brand. Focus.

West dragged in a breath and studied the body with cool, professional detachment. Tia lay on her side. One of her arms had been torn off in the blast, and her torso was horribly mangled.

Burns covered her body and part of her head…

He looked at Tia's head, noting the head injury and exposed brain matter with analytical coolness. If she had died before the explosion, the autopsy would confirm it.

"Find," he ordered Rex, his death grip on the leash making his palm sweat through the latex gloves.

Rex combed through the building's rubble to search for secondary devices. Nothing found. But near what had been Tia's desk, West found pieces of the bomb, including the detonator.

Cell phone. Same kind of burner phone used in the first bombing.

Until the pieces were tested, he couldn't be certain, but he suspected it was the same type of bomb that had gone off earlier in the abandoned building. The first bomb was a trial run, probably to see how much damage the unsub could inflict.

But something had gone wrong. The killer hadn't known that Quinn delivered lunch here every day around noon. Nor had he anticipated the device wouldn't totally destroy evidence.

Or had he? Quinn had told him that everyone knew her schedule—that every day she hand delivered lunch to Tia, one of her best clients. Tia always ate at twelve thirty sharp. The woman ran a tight schedule.

He returned to his truck, fetched his equipment. With methodical care, he combed through the scene. Gray file cabinets were dented, some of their contents blown out. The computer was in shards, but if Tia backed her files up to a cloud, they could access them.

Maybe one of her clients had a grudge. Damn, it was better than thinking someone had it in for Quinn, or wanted to cause more than one injury.

In the rubble, he found the thin stump of a cigar. West bagged and tagged the evidence. Tia smoked. A fact Quinn relayed to him previously, her pert nose wrinkling in disgust. Tia even liked to light up Cubans after hours. But everything had to be looked over.

Something glinted among the rubble in a shaft of late-afternoon sunshine.

West crouched down and studied the fragment. The edge of a key chain, rounded, with the etching of a pine cone. He could just make out part of an address.

#5 Pine P.

Pine Paradise? Acid crept into his throat. Too much of a coincidence.

He knew this.

Pine Paradise specialized in cabins in the thickly wooded canyon south of Red Ridge.

After Quinn had told him she had a key to a cabin there, he planned to take her for a weekend. Maybe taking Quinn with him for hikes in the woods, long bouts of lovemaking into the night. He liked that area of South Dakota; it was quiet, peaceful, and enabled him to think and find peace. Get away from all the people in town and the nosy neighbors. He could use his gray matter to fit together pieces of a complex puzzle called the Coltons, figure out if they were covering up evidence of Demi Colton's whereabouts.

Question her further.

Pine Paradise offered quiet, small cabins near a creek reputed to have excellent trout fishing. Each cabin was set back from the road, nestled in the thick woods. Isolated and accessed only by a dirt road, they were far apart from each neighboring cabin to offer seclusion and privacy.

When he'd first arrived in town, he'd asked Tia, Red Ridge's reigning queen of real estate, about renting a Pine Paradise cabin. She'd haughtily informed him that the cabins were occupied. *The property is unavailable, Mr. Brand. Got it?*

The woman was just…nasty. He could understand why she mistrusted him for being an outsider and FBI, to boot. Some locals had looked at him with suspicion. Small town, strangers. But Quinn had told him the real estate agent was one of her best clients and a cold, demanding person. It wasn't him. It was Tia's personality.

Did that personality get her into trouble? Had the real estate agent gotten into a squabble with someone who decided on permanent payback by killing her?

Until the autopsy was performed, they could not confirm his suspicion that Tia had been killed prior to the explosion, and the killer had used the bomb to cover his or her tracks.

There was another troubling idea in his mind. Maybe Quinn had been the real target.

In his gloved hands, West fingered the evidence, his mind clicking over the facts like a computer.

What if there was a connection between the killer and

this property? He needed to find out exactly what other properties Tia owned.

But Pine Paradise was a good, isolated place to hide while experimenting with making bombs, far away from the inquisitive locals. Someone who wouldn't hesitate to blow up buildings and kill innocents like Quinn to cover a larger crime.

But what if this bombing was connected to the Groom Killer? There was no evidence yet to link the two crimes, but as an investigator trained to be thorough, he couldn't rule it out. He had to look at all angles.

Maybe the bomber wanted to kill Quinn because she was related to Demi Colton.

Even without the autopsy report on Tia, West's instinct warned whoever had planted the bomb didn't do it to kill the real estate agent. Bombs were tricky. Sometimes they didn't detonate, so as a means of killing someone, they were unpredictable.

The killer hadn't used enough explosives to totally destroy Tia's body. He'd planted the bomb in the wrong place. Maybe he—or she—had been in a hurry. Or perhaps the bomber's intention had been to destroy evidence.

Or unfamiliar with exactly where to plant a bomb in order to do the most damage, and destroy the evidence one wanted to cover up.

And then Quinn had interrupted the crime. That meant she was a witness, and whoever did this would want to erase any evidence.

Eradicate any witnesses, especially one Quinn Colton.

Later, he and Rex would take a road trip to Pine Paradise. But not for trout fishing.

Fishing of a different sort—searching for Tia's killer.

Chapter 5

West couldn't wait to get to the hospital to check on his fiancée. As soon as his shift ended, he would see her.

Quinn had to be okay. She was a fighter.

He drove to his apartment in town and dropped off Rex. The dog looked up at him and whined, sensing West's emotions. He hunkered down and patted Rex's head.

"She's going to be fine, boy. She's going to be fine."

Maybe if he said it enough times, it would be true.

Anxiety tightened his stomach. Driving to the hospital, West wanted to break every speed limit in town. Not possible. No one knew of their relationship. Had to play it cool.

Doors to the Red Ridge Community Hospital ER swished open. He flashed his badge at the front desk, asked for Quinn Colton.

The nurse barely looked up. "She's still in the ER. Room three. But you can't see her yet. The chief called, gave strict orders only family can be with her."

The hell with that. "Who's with her now?"

The nurse kept scribbling on a pad. "Her brothers."

Maybe he was a stranger in town, and Finn Colton held the power with the hospital staff. But nothing would prevent him from seeing his love.

West ignored the nurse, went straight to the closed doors leading from the waiting area to the nurses' station. A burly security guard narrowed his eyes.

"You have a pass?" the guard asked.

"The only pass I need." He flashed his badge. "FBI. I work with Shayne and Brayden."

"The chief said—" the guard began.

"Family only. We're brothers in arms. I found Quinn in the rubble. Need to check on her."

He stared down the guard and the man nodded. "All right."

The security guard pressed the button and the doors swished open to admit him.

Smells assaulted him as he entered the treatment area. Antiseptic, bleach, sickness.

Death.

I'm sorry, West. There was nothing we could do.

Gritting his teeth against the memory, he arrived at room three, where the nurse said he'd find Quinn. Shane, her brother, hovered outside the curtained area.

"Why are you here? Finn gave orders only family is to stay with Quinn." Shane gave him a suspicious look. "Shouldn't you be on the scene?"

"I came to check on her."

Shane turned more wary. "Brand, we'll take care of interviewing our sister. She doesn't need extra stress right now."

Deep breaths. "How is she?"

Shane glanced at the closed blue curtain. Murmurs came from within.

"Brayden's in there. She finally woke up."

Well, thank the good Lord for that. "What other injuries?"

"Lacerations, left wrist may be broken, but X-rays aren't back yet. Biggest problem is the head injury. We don't have answers yet." Shane folded his arms across his chest.

West paced, hooking his thumbs in the belt loop of his jeans. "Where's the doctor? When will we know anything for certain?"

"A major car accident and the bombing have the hospital staff split. We'll need to sit tight."

West didn't care if the entire town suddenly needed medical care. All that mattered was Quinn. "Damn it, what's taking so long?"

"Cool it," Shane snapped in a low voice, his stress and worry about his sister obvious. "If you want to be useful, go back to work and find this bastard who hurt my sister. You're not needed here."

"Yes, I am. She had a bad head injury." He stopped, tried to peer past a slim crack in the curtains. "She has to make it. And if I get my hands on the bastard who did this, I'll break his neck."

Shane frowned. "What's it to you?"

Telling the truth hadn't been in the game plan. They'd wanted to keep their engagement a secret. But with two protective brothers, and a hospital staff who wanted to allow only family in to see her, he knew something had to give.

Still, he hesitated. "I'm the one who found her. Maybe even saved her. I'm concerned."

Shane relaxed. But he narrowed his eyes. "You may be on the level. But still, you're a fed."

West didn't care what he thought. He needed to see her. Now. "I'm going in," he announced, as if the room were an active crime scene filled with danger.

Danger of a different sort now—because he was scared as hell of losing the woman lying on that stretcher. Shane started to protest. He ignored him.

Lifting the curtain with one hand, he stepped inside the room.

Brayden sat by Quinn's bed. Her eyes were closed and a huge white bandage covered her head. Red stained the bandage. West saw red himself, red rage at the bad guy who'd hurt his woman.

Her left wrist was splinted, and she had a bruise and some cuts on her face. But she was alive, breathing. He watched her eyes flutter.

"She's awake?" he asked.

Brayden looked as wary as his brother. "Why are you here?"

"Came to check on her. I found her." West crouched down, staring at her too-pale face. "Where's the doctor?"

"They had a trauma case come in. I'm supposed to make sure she stays awake."

Relief filled him. Awake was good. From experience, he knew she shouldn't fall asleep again until the medical staff felt confident she could hold a conversation, and her pupils weren't dilated. The injury could get worse.

"What did you see when you arrived on scene?" Colton demanded.

West briefed him. "She must have been entering the building. Judging from the position of the detonator, the bomb went off on or near Tia's desk."

"If Quinn had been at Tia's desk, she'd be gone."

Nails and bolts churned in his guts. "How is she? Does she remember what happened?" West asked.

"Give her a minute, she only woke up a little while ago." Brayden gripped her hand. "We're still waiting on tests. But she's alive. I wanted to question her soon as she fully wakes up."

Finally Quinn's lovely eyes opened. She moaned, and Brayden hastened to soothe her.

Colton didn't know he and Quinn had dated. But what mattered most right now was the woman on the stretcher. West smiled at her.

"Hey there, sleeping beauty." Maybe using his secret nickname for her would trigger a smile. "How are you feeling?"

Her hand went to the large bandage on her head. "It hurts."

"I know. Must ache something awful. But it will get better." He squatted down to eye level with her. "You're going to be fine. Up to kissing speed in no time."

Brayden frowned. Well, that would puzzle the guy, and he'd set things straight with the man later. All his attention zeroed in on Quinn.

And then his heart dropped to his stomach as she stared at him with no glimmer of recognition. "Who are you?"

His stomach knotted. The woman he adored and loved had no idea who he was. No memory of first meeting him. No memory of the laughs they'd shared, the stolen moments of togetherness, the lovemaking...

The fact she'd agreed to be his wife.

He was a total stranger to Quinn Colton.

Chapter 6

Her head ached, and so did her throat. Her left wrist throbbed. It felt as if someone had shoved sand into her eyes, as well.

She wanted to wake up, sit up, but her body wasn't working properly. Everything felt sluggish, as if she were swimming upstream in thick oil.

Beeping machines. Sterile, awful smells. Voices murmuring near her. A thick pressure on her arm, and then it eased off. Blood pressure cuff… She recognized the sensation.

What happened? From the morass of confusion in her mind, she pulled out a name. Quinn. Her name was Quinn and something horrible made her end up here. The pain was incredible.

Quinn blinked hard, wishing someone would pull out the rail spike driving into her head.

"Easy there," a deep male voice said. "Quinn, do you know where you are?"

"No." She blinked hard, trying to focus.

"Do you know who I am?"

She stared at the concerned, handsome face of the man at her bedside. "No." Panic rose up, threatened to squeeze her chest. "What happened?"

"You're in the Red Ridge Community Hospital ER. You suffered a head injury." The hand covering hers squeezed gently. "I'm Brayden Colton. Your brother. You don't remember me at all?"

Brother? She blinked again, hating this void in her mind, the fact that everything felt so foggy.

Her gaze flickered to the other man in the room. Tall, handsome, his dark gaze burning with intensity. The man who'd called her "sleeping beauty."

He shoved a hand through his already-rumpled hair. "I'm West. West Brand. You don't remember me?"

Quinn started to shake her head, but it hurt too much. "Give me a mirror."

West hesitated.

"Now. I have to see."

They hunted one down, and West handed it to her. She stared at her reflection.

Two large purpling bruises, one eye swollen. "Why can't I remember?" Quinn began to cry.

"Easy," said the man who was her brother. "Try not to move around too much. I'm going to get Shane."

With a hard glance at the man named West, he pointed to her. "Stay with her. Don't question her yet. Just watch her."

Nausea curled in her stomach. She put a hand over her mouth. "I don't feel good."

The tall, handsome man searched around, found a small pan and held it under her mouth. She waved it aside. It hurt too much to throw up.

West's palm covered hers. Warm. Strong. Caring. Why did he care? He wasn't family.

Quinn closed her eyes.

"No, honey, don't go to sleep. I know it must hurt, but you've got to stay awake."

She opened her eyes, studied him. Dark hair, round chin, sculpted mouth. Handsome, strong face. Expressive brown eyes filled with worry. Worry about her? What was she to him?

The curtains jerked aside and another stranger entered. Quinn blinked hard as he introduced himself as Shane, her other brother.

"Do we live together at home? Where are my parents? Why aren't they here?" she asked.

Brayden and Shane exchanged glances. "We're actually half siblings. Our mutual dad is Rusty Colton. He's… different," Brayden told her.

West snorted.

"Your mother is Marcia and she moved to Denver a few years ago when you opened your catering business. She works in sales for a tour company. I called her, but she's out of the country for the next ten days," Shane said.

"Don't worry, Quinn. We're here for you," Brayden added.

Brothers. At least she had some family. But this tall, muscular guy with the worried dark eyes seemed even more concerned than her brothers.

The curtains parted and a man in blue scrubs and a white coat walked inside. A bright splash of red dotted his scrubs.

He checked the bandage on her head, looked at a chart.

"Miss Colton, I'm Dr. Cairns, the attending ER physician. You were seriously injured." Dr. Cairns was young, had horn-rimmed glasses and a brisk, professional air. "We're running some tests to see the extent of the damage."

The doctor started rattling off technical terms that made her head ache even more. Quinn held up a hand. "How was I injured?"

Gaze flicking away, he glanced at the man sitting by her. "The police, and your family, can fill you in. I've scheduled a CT scan for you. The technician will be up shortly to take you upstairs."

Dr. Cairns pulled out a slim flashlight, shone it in her eyes. It made her wince.

"Pupils dilating and reacting normally. That's good," he said. "Do you know your name?"

"Quinn…Colton." Surely her last name was Colton if these were her brothers.

Next, the doctor asked her what month and year it was, which she got right, but she had no idea what day it was.

"Where do you live?"

She put a hand to her head. "Here… Red Ridge? I think."

"Do you know where you work? Anything else?" the doctor asked in his grilling, calm voice.

"No." Tears burned the back of her throat. "What's wrong with me?"

"Standard for a serious head injury." He patted her hand, looked at her brothers. "I have to check on that trauma."

Then the doctor left. Her brothers followed, like puppies trailing their mother. She didn't like being left in the dark, no information, no one willing to tell her what had happened.

The tall man named West did not leave. He kept staring at her. He must know her. But he meant nothing to her.

"Why are you here?"

His dark brows knit together. "I…found you, honey.

You don't remember me at all?" He took her hand again, and the sensation was comforting, if odd.

Strangers holding her hand.

West lowered his voice. "I'm West Brand. FBI, working temporarily for the Red Ridge Police Department. And your fiancé."

Now her head hurt even more. She was engaged? "I'm sorry, I don't know you. Can my brothers confirm we're going to marry?"

This man might say he had a relationship with her, but at least family she could trust. West? Unknown.

West looked uncomfortable. His gaze flicked to the closed curtains. "They don't know. No one in town knew we were dating."

An even bigger mystery, and right now the pain was too intense to contemplate it.

"What happened to me?" she whispered. It hurt too much to form many words.

Silence draped the air, with only the sound of beeping machines and the aching pain in a mind that remembered nothing of her past.

"You're Quinn Colton," he finally said. "You own Good Eats, a catering company with a kitchen on Main Street. You live above the store."

A warm smile touched his full mouth. "You cook frou-frou food."

Nice smile. Such a good-looking man. She tried to think. Vague memories of cooking, a little apartment over a kitchen, flickered into her mind. Quinn Colton.

Trying to remember hurt her head. She wished the pounding ache would cease. Maybe then she could think straight.

Maybe then she'd remember this tall, handsome man

who claimed to be her future husband. And what happened to land her here?

"You're not telling me why I'm in the hospital?" she asked.

"Try to rest," he told her gently. "I'll tell you soon."

He was no help. For all she knew, he could be someone other than the love of her life. Wouldn't she remember such a love?

With considerable effort, Quinn turned her head away from West Brand.

"Please leave," she said dully. "I want to be alone."

He'd known it was going to be bad, but not like this. And damn, it hurt deep inside, getting rejected.

Quinn was obviously distressed. Remembered nothing of him. Gone was the trust, the love, the affection.

Well, she was alive, and he'd find solace in that fact. She'd get better.

Outside the room, West paced, checking his phone for voice mails, for texts. For any information the others on the unit had found and shared.

This is personal now.

Her brothers left the nurses' station and joined him.

"What did the doctor say?" he demanded.

Brayden glanced at him. "Nothing yet. We're still waiting for him to finish with that trauma case. We didn't give her details on the explosion. No reason to upset her even more."

Not exactly procedure. Were Quinn an ordinary witness, West knew the others would grill her relentlessly until family objected. This time they were the family, and the Coltons were keeping to themselves.

"Good," West told them. "I didn't, either. She'll find

out soon enough. You sure there's tight enough security in this hospital?"

Brayden's expression tightened. "There will be. I called for a friend to guard her."

Dr. Cairns came out of another room, saw them.

West didn't like the grim look on the doctor's face. "Is she going to make it?" he blurted out before her brothers could speak.

Dr. Cairns raised his brows, but nodded. "However, there are complications."

"What kind?" West asked.

Dr. Cairns glanced at Brayden, who nodded.

"Miss Colton has a concussion. The blow to her head has caused retrograde amnesia."

West's heart dropped to his stomach. "What can she remember?"

"Nothing significant. You heard. She knows the year, and her name, where she lives. Little else. Nothing prior to the injury."

"So much for being a witness," Brayden murmured. "How long will it take to clear up?"

The doctor shrugged. "We'll run more tests, keep her here for a while. I've scheduled a CT scan. Until I receive the results, there's no telling when she'll regain her memory. The human brain is a delicate, tricky matter. It could be hours. Or days. Or even months."

Curling his hands into fists to hide their shaking, he turned away. He'd give her time, but she had to remember him. Remember their sessions of hot loving, and the sweet kisses they'd shared. Remember how he'd professed all his feelings.

Remember their engagement.

How could she forget all that? West blew out a breath.

Worse, he didn't know if the bomber intended to kill her as well as Tia.

Quinn still remained in danger. Maybe her own damn sister wanted to blow her up. In that case, everything became even more complicated.

As the doctor left, he gestured to Quinn's room. "I'm going to question her. With the right questions, she may regain some memory."

Shane's mouth dropped open. Brayden started to protest. He knew what they thought—that this was business.

Sorry, sweetheart. The cat's about to be released from its bag.

West met their angry gazes head-on. "Quinn isn't a witness to me. She's much more. We've been…dating. Seeing each other."

Yeah, he had to tell them something, but the full truth? Not now.

Both brothers blinked in surprise. "Wow," Shane murmured.

"I had no idea," Brayden told him.

Encouraged, he jerked his head toward the nurses' station, where nurses and doctors talked and worked on computers. "Appreciate you both keeping this on the QT. Quinn and I decided to be private about our relationship because of the Groom Killer. Just in case the killer decides to start targeting other couples in town. Or women who date cops."

He gave them a level look. "She might have been a target if that were the case and someone found out we're together."

Both brothers visibly relaxed. "Good idea to keep it quiet," Brayden said.

"No offense," Shane told him.

West gave a sharp nod. Maybe they were family, but, damn it, he loved Quinn.

He'd taken charge here, and the brothers had let him. They understood. Quinn was his woman.

He went into the room again. Quinn picked absently at the sheet covering her. Tight lines of strain showed on her freckled face. West couldn't imagine the pain she suffered.

Showing no interest in him, she muttered, "Can't I get something for my head to stop pounding?"

West pulled up a chair next to her stretcher. "Not until the CT scan, honey. They'll be here soon and then you can get the good stuff."

He pulled out a small notepad from his back pocket. "I'm a K-9 bomb specialist. It's my job to analyze evidence, comb through crime scenes. I have some questions for you, Quinn. Do you remember anything about arriving at Tia Linwicki's real estate office?"

She blinked. "Is that where I was? Where the accident happened?"

Locking gazes with her, he watched for any sign of recognition.

"It wasn't an accident, Quinn. Someone set off a bomb in Tia's office. You got caught in the blast. Tia's dead."

Tears filled her eyes, making his chest ache. He hated upsetting her, but she had to know. "Oh my God. Someone was killed?"

"But you weren't. You're alive."

"Did I know her?"

He nodded. "She was a good client of yours. You brought her lunch every day. Vegan meals. You were on your way to deliver it in person when the blast happened. You're probably the last person to see Tia before the explosion, which is why I need to ask you some questions."

He softened his voice. "I know you're in pain and this isn't easy. Maybe you can remember something that will help us in the investigation. Do you know anything about

Pine Paradise? Did Tia say anything to you about the cabins?"

"Cabins?"

"Rentals. You had rented a cabin and invited Demi to join you there. Do you recall anything about Demi?"

"No. I don't know anything about a Demi. But a cabin. That sounds familiar."

West leaned close, searching her expression. "We talked about renting a cabin together."

"I remember…something." She stared at his lips. "Not a cabin. Kissing… Someone was kissing me. He had the most amazing mouth. It was…wow."

West glanced at the closed curtains, and felt a flush heat his body. "That was me, Quinn. I'd suggested getting away to a cabin for a weekend, just the two of us."

"Some kiss." She studied him, and put a hand to her head. "I remember that."

Her mouth pursed in a cute little pout, the type he adored. Couldn't help himself. Hell, maybe it would trigger something.

West leaned down, gently pressed his lips against hers. Only for a moment.

A sigh fled her as he eased away. And then she looked intrigued, and then scared.

"I don't remember anything else."

Okay. That was a sweet memory. Not useful for the investigation, but encouraging. Because if she remembered that kiss, perhaps she'd recall other little details related to Tia. And eventually, Demi.

But then an orderly arrived to take Quinn upstairs for her CT scan. Questioning her further would have to wait.

West checked his watch. He'd return to the crime scene, get briefed by the others and return later.

Chapter 7

Austin Jones. She kept repeating the name to herself as the man with glasses talked with her.

It was scribbled on the notebook she kept on the bed tray. Otherwise, she wouldn't remember who visited.

Having a visitor who professed to be her best friend was wonderful. Quinn still felt terrible, but she was determined to recover, and determined to find out what happened to her and why. Last night she'd managed to sleep in an opiate-induced haze. Nightmares assaulted her—whiteness, a huge bang, flying through the air and never landing, her head splitting apart…

Darkness.

Shaking, she'd awakened with sweat dampening the hospital gown, her palms cold and clammy. Quinn forced herself to go back to sleep.

Only to experience another dream. She was naked, rolling in bed with a dark-haired man who kissed her as if his last breath depended on it. Pleasure shot through her like a rocket, such incredible passion. She had never felt anything like it.

Quinn had awoken from that dream sweating for a different reason. For a long time, she'd remained staring at the ceiling, trying to find an anchor.

The morose, but friendly man now in her hospital room claimed to be her business partner.

She wrote that down, as well. And the name of her business—Good Eats.

Austin was the guy who secured all the accounts for the catering business. The catering business that was losing money, he informed her with a sad face.

He'd come today to visit, two days after her "accident" and the first day she stayed in a regular hospital room.

No one but her brothers and West was allowed in ICU, where she'd been transferred after the ER. Quinn had spent one night there. Fortunately, the doctor had decided she was recovering nicely, and had her moved to the third floor. Private room. No nurses constantly hovering, checking her every five minutes. Her nurse helped her out of bed earlier today to sit in the chair. Quinn felt proud of herself as she'd walked up and down the hall, her nurse at her side in case she suffered a dizzy spell.

The earlier exercise left her exhausted.

Quinn listened as Austin talked. Left wrist taped up tight—no broken bones, only a sprain—cuts and bruises on her body, she ached, but the pain was manageable. She felt fortunate to be alive after what happened, for Austin told her things West did not.

The bomb blast leveled much of the building. Knowing how close she'd come to punching out made Quinn's hands shake as she reached for the glass of water, took a sip through the straw.

Much as she hated the constant interruptions with nurses coming in all the time to check on her, the hospital felt safe. The room offered a window view of the town she no longer remembered. Earlier, her brother Brayden had informed her they'd paid for privacy and an off duty cop to stay outside her room at night.

During the day, with all the nurses and orderlies running about, no one would threaten her, Brayden assured.

The CT scan showed she had no serious brain damage. The neurologist felt confident she would recover with rest and time.

Pen in hand, Quinn scribbled notes as Austin talked. When he finally came up for air, she asked him the burning question.

"Austin, who exactly is Demi Colton and why would the police search for her? Did she set off the bomb that hurt me and killed Tia?"

Austin squirmed in his chair. "Um, no one knows who set off the bomb, Quinn. The police are investigating. As for Demi Colton, that's something your brothers should answer."

Terrific. Brayden and Shane sidestepped the name of *Demi*, but West Brand kept bringing it up, asking her if she remembered the woman.

And when she denied knowing a Demi, he refused to share anything more about this mysterious woman. Instead, he asked different questions.

All these questions, when she had some of her own that weren't answered. And her brain still felt foggy, her life filled with uncertainty.

"Who is Demi?" In frustration, she raised her voice.

Reeling back, he held out his hands. "Okay, okay! Demi is your sister. Your half sister. She's the one everyone in town thinks is the Groom Killer, going around and killing men before they marry. There was evidence linking her to the first murder, but she fled town. She's been missing awhile now. No one knows where she went. She was pregnant when she left."

In dumbstruck disbelief, she listened, scribbling down notes as he talked. Her sister. Brayden and Shane never mentioned her.

West only wanted to know what she knew of Demi.

"The first groom murder was Bo Gage, her former fiancé." Austin leaned close, his voice lowered. "Bo was marrying Hayley Patton and his bachelor party was at your father's bar. When Bo's brother, Carson Gage, arrived, he found Bo dead, a black cummerbund in his mouth."

"And everyone thinks my sister, Demi, killed him?" Quinn tapped her pen on the page.

Austin shrugged. "Even you told me a while ago you weren't certain if Demi was the Groom Killer. Although she's pregnant, probably with Bo Gage's kid."

Quinn frowned. "My sister is pregnant?"

"Was. By now she's had the baby. She was seeing Bo and then he dumped her and was set to marry Hayley three months later. You were pretty worried about Demi being on the run and alone with a newborn. Even though you weren't close, you had tried to have a relationship with Demi."

Her friend squinted at her through the thick lenses. "You sure you don't remember any of this?"

"No," she snapped.

Head aching, she set down the pen and notebook. Austin pointed to it. "Does that help?"

"Yes," she muttered, her earlier good mood evaporating. "Remembering would help more."

The therapist they'd sent in to work with her had told her writing things down was best with memory loss. Another one kept asking her questions, only these questions proved more frustrating because they were simple. *Who are you? Do you know where you are?*

Quinn felt like a child locked in a cell, unable to free herself.

The door opened and cute, tall and muscled West Brand strode inside. Here was one fine man she wished she could remember instead of hearing she had a business sliding deeper into debt. Today he wore jeans, a black T-shirt, heavy work boots and a lightweight jacket. He saw Austin, hesitated. Nodded.

"Hi, Miss Colton," he said in his deep voice. "I stopped by to see how you were doing, and ask you a few more questions."

West removed the jacket, folded it neatly and placed it on the corner chair. Quinn's heart skipped a beat with pleasure. The action triggered a faint familiarity. Not a memory, but something close.

A pistol hung from his belt. Black, lethal looking. It gave her comfort, knowing he carried it, because this quiet, strong man seemed determined to protect her.

Quinn didn't know why, but her instincts told her West Brand would put himself into danger to keep her safe. Going on instinct was all that guided her presently. Until she could get back into her home, and try to piece together the fragments of her life, she had little to aid her in regaining her memory.

West held a bottle of water and took a sip. His sharp gaze roved over her bedside tray, as if he checked to make sure everything was a-okay.

"Do you need anything?" he asked.

"I'm fine," she told him. "Austin and I were chatting."

He'd been the same way last night, and held her hand as she fell asleep last night in the ICU.

Sympathy softened Austin's expression. "We were talking about Demi Colton."

If she hadn't been studying West's face, she'd have missed the slight tensing of that chiseled jawline. West looked at her. "What about Demi Colton?"

"Apparently she's a sister I don't remember," Quinn muttered.

"Half sister. You stayed in cabin number seven last year." Austin heaved a dramatic sigh. "I remember because you left me alone with temps to fill the orders. I threatened to hunt you down and drag you back to work."

The smallest glimmer of…something…surfaced. And then it fled again. "I stayed at Pine Paradise with my sister?"

"Don't you remember?" Austin looked sheepish. "Sorry, Quinn. Yeah, you rented a cabin in the early fall. You told me it was a great place for peace and quiet and to try to get to know Demi better. Isolated, and far away from people. You even kept her jacket, hoping she'd return to the store and pick it up. She never did."

West shuffled his feet. Austin stood. Her friend pushed his glasses up his nose. "Well, I'll leave you two alone now."

"Leaving me alone with the big, bad FBI agent?" Quinn teased.

"I'm sure you want to spend time with him. He is your boyfriend, after all. Probably your husband in the future."

West choked on his sip of water. Quinn frowned. "How do you know?"

"Yeah, how?" West demanded.

Mischief twinkled in Austin's gaze. "I saw you late one night, sneaking up to Quinn's apartment when I returned to the store. Forgot my cell phone."

"So much for discretion," West muttered. "We were keeping it secret."

Her business partner stared frankly at West. "Secret engagement? Can't blame you, in this town."

West compressed his mouth, but Austin grinned. "Aha. Knew it. Well, congrats, you two. My lips are sealed."

Although Austin's confirmation of West proved soothing, it remained frustrating. Quinn sniffed. "It's all a secret to me now, because I have no memory of it."

"You will," West assured.

Austin made a large X over his heart. "Don't fret, either of you. I won't tell. Cross my heart. Never mentioned it to Quinn because I figured if she wanted to tell me, she would. It's your personal life."

Then her friend looked gloomy. "There's enough trouble in this town trying to have a relationship with people dying and things blowing up. Me? I'll stay single. Safer that way."

Austin blew her a kiss and waggled his fingers. "Later, sweets. Gotta secure that order and keep the dough rolling."

When he walked out, she gestured to West to sit. He didn't, but paced.

"Do you need anything? How do you feel?"

"So many questions. I'm fine and I feel better."

Much better than when her head felt like someone was stomping on it with nails and her mind was foggy. Thanks to the morphine drip she'd received, the pain had diminished.

"Did you find anything out? Anyone who might have done this?" Quinn pointed to her still-bandaged head.

"No. Nothing yet." West pulled up the chair, reached through the bars on her hospital bed for her hand. Held it, the way he'd held it last night.

It felt good.

"Anything coming back to you? What about Demi?" West studied her in his intense manner. "You tried to get close to her, once."

Demi again. But at least she knew who Demi was. "My sister, Demi?"

West blinked. "You remember Demi and who she is? That's great!"

"No, Austin told me, since you and my brothers were reluctant." She bit her lip. West had been nothing but kind and sweet to her, despite the questions. "I have a few flashes of memory here and there. Maybe I am getting better."

"Of course you are," he told her.

She was loath to tell him about her morphine-induced dreams. Dreams of making love with this man, passionate kisses, amazing sex.

It could be wistful thinking. Maybe West Brand was only a decent lover and her imagination filled in the rest. But, wow, what an imagination!

Feeling overheated, Quinn reached for her water. He was there, handing it to her.

"You need anything?" he asked.

Quinn set down the cup, decided to level with him. "Information. What have you found out so far? Was someone trying to kill me?"

West's jaw went tight. Quinn pressed. "Well?"

She had to know. Information was her best defense right now. Being in the dark, coddled by her brothers and this man who called himself her fiancé, was not.

"We don't know. The investigation is in its early stages."

Same answers as before. "Then hurry up."

Anger flashed in his dark gaze. "That's not how it works, sweetheart. You have to be methodical and pick through every single part, otherwise you miss critical evidence. A tiny fragment can be a crucial clue. What will help us is if you remember something. Anything, about what you saw prior to the blast."

"Nothing yet." She yawned. "I'm tired."

"Sleep, honey," he soothed. "Rest will help you recover. I'll stay here with you for a while."

Quinn dozed off. Real sleep was impossible, with the nurses checking on her, the sounds from the hallway. She awoke a few minutes later, feeling hungry. Lunchtime soon. But she kept her eyes closed because it was easier than opening them and facing the reality of this horrid fogginess.

And then she heard West's deep voice, close to her bed.

"Yeah, Mike, I'm at the hospital. There's a witness. Quinn Colton. She survived."

Quinn strained to listen as his boots scraped the floor, indicating he walked farther away from the bed.

She caught snatches of conversation. *Suspect. Unsub.* And a word that made gooseflesh spring out on her bare arms.

Autopsy.

Tia had died in the same incident that caused her amnesia.

Who was Mike? Another FBI agent? Quinn's suspicions rose. But she kept her eyes firmly shut.

Boot heels shuffled closer to the bed. No conversation. Maybe he was listening. Then he spoke in his deep, confident voice, quiet, but she could overhear every word.

"My loyalty is to the Bureau, damn it, Mike."

Silence, and then he raised his voice. Angry. Biting.

"I don't know if the Coltons are hiding Demi. Shane admitted to hearing from her a while back. If Quinn has information on her sister, she hasn't shared it with me. She sure as hell won't share it now because she's lost her memory from the explosion. You have to give me more time."

Her stomach pitched and roiled. Oh God. What was this man doing? Investigating her family? Was West searching for Demi and thought she knew something?

And remembered nothing now?

She remembered that kiss. Smoldering, passionate, making her toes tingle and her blood race. Clearly, there existed a hot attraction between her and West. The man was smoking.

And he had a wonderful, tight butt beneath the blue jeans he wore.

But was he her lover because he loved her? Or was he trying to coax out information about Demi?

Confusion filled her. It seemed much easier to deal with individuals like Austin, gloomy as he was. Austin was simple and straightforward.

No attraction there. No subterfuge, either.

"Goodbye, Mike. I'll be in touch."

Sounds of West walking away. Quinn kept her eyes shut.

She felt the soothing brush of warm, firm lips against her forehead. "You sleep, honey. I'm going for a cup of java juice. Be right back."

The door opened and closed. She was alone.

Quinn fiddled with the remote for the television and turned it on, flipping through channels. There, someone at a desk talking about the news. Something about Congress. An interview with a politician with a big, wide smile talking about improving things.

Right. She changed the channel.

Local news. They mentioned the bomb blast at the real estate office. Quinn squinted at the television, not sure if her dizzy spell was from the head injury or the fear curdling in her veins.

Because the film they showed of the wreckage looked horrible. Shattered glass, yellow crime scene tape everywhere, bits and pieces of wreckage.

Of someone's life that had been snuffed out by a killer.

And she'd survived that.

I don't know anything about my life, who I really am and who I can trust. How can I trust this West, who's supposed to be my future husband, when he's talking about me as if I'm under investigation?

She turned off the television and reached for the cell phone Austin had brought her. Scrolling through the contacts, none of the names looked familiar.

Maybe they were clients. Or friends. She had no clue. Quinn swiped through the photos, hoping it would trigger something.

Many photos of herself with West. One at a fancy dinner, with candlelight, both of them smiling at the camera. One of them at an outdoor bazaar. A few more of West, his shy grin, as he rode a horse.

So, they'd been horseback riding. She must have enjoyed that. And shopping and eating dinner with him. The photos proved they shared a life or at least spent significant time together.

If so, why was he checking on her as if she'd done something wrong?

Quinn took her notebook and wrote down questions. Demi seemed to be the common factor in everything that happened, even the loss of business for the catering company.

The pen paused in midscribble. *What if Demi is the person who blew up the real estate office? What if she wants to hurt me?*

Having a sister who was on the run, suspected of killing grooms, did not endear her to Quinn. Having no memory of her felt worse, because she had no basis to make her own judgment of Demi, only what others told her.

She studied the other notes she'd made about family. Seemed as if she had a slew of Colton cousins, from the police chief, Finn Colton, to his kid sister, Valeria. Yesterday in ICU Finn had told her Valeria wanted to visit, and might be by today or tomorrow.

Valeria must be a cousin she liked, Quinn decided.

In the contacts section, she found Valeria's number and went to dial. Hesitated. Best to leave that conversation in person, so she could judge facial expressions.

With the information Austin had relayed, she realized it wasn't a simple matter of losing her memory.

She'd lost her memory in a town where a serial killer roamed, and was now setting off bombs.

The door to her room remained open after Austin left. There was a slight knock, and then a good-looking blond man in a charcoal-gray business suit walked inside. Clutching a vase of roses, he looked sleek and professional.

Tucking the phone beneath the sheet, she studied the visitor. "Hi."

"Hi, Quinn. I'm Noel Larson." At her look, Larson added, "Your landlord."

Well, this was news. Quinn sat up, wishing her hair wasn't mussed and her brain all scrambled.

"Came to collect on the rent?" Quinn gestured to the lines feeding out of the IV port in her hand. "I'm a little unable to sign a check now."

"No problem." He set the flowers on her nightstand. The fragrance was lovely, but overwhelming. "I know you're good for it. Eventually."

Noel Larson. The name was unfamiliar. Still, a tingle rushed down her spine.

Don't trust this one.

"Why are you here?" she asked.

The smile on his handsome face seemed false. "Visiting to see how you are. It was a bad explosion and I was concerned."

Right. I may not remember much, but I know enough to trust sincerity. You're as sincere as that politician on television. Except you're more dangerous.

If she reached for the phone, he'd get suspicious. Instead, she kept the nurse call button within reach. The nurses on this floor responded quickly.

"They say you don't remember anything about what happened."

Quinn found herself fascinated by his hands. Elegant fingers, polished nails and smooth hands, as if he held a desk job. Not like her brothers or West, who worked in the field.

"I don't. What do you know?" she challenged.

A shrug in that well-fitted gray suit. "Only what the gossips say. The office was destroyed. Poor Tia. She's dead. You were quite fortunate."

"Maybe I'm more than fortunate. Maybe I saw something happening, and ducked out of the way, only I wasn't quite quick enough."

Inside, she groaned. Why did she bait him like that? But she watched his expression widen.

She'd surprised him. Startled him, in fact.

"Perhaps you did. Too bad you can't seem to remember."

"Maybe my memory is coming back. Or not."

There. *Want to play games?* A flash of memory—laughing and clapping as she sat at a table with an older woman, playing a game called Monopoly. Her mother?

Feeling more confident, Quinn fiddled with the button.

Noel came closer to the bed, the overpowering scent of his cologne making her want to gag. After the hospital antiseptic smells and the smells of medicine and machines, she didn't need something else clogging her senses.

He picked up the IV line leading to the pole by her bed and studied it. "So many lines and needles. So much pain. Poor Quinn," he murmured.

She was helpless, lying in bed, unable to defend herself. He could pick up a pillow and smother her and she'd be dead before anyone came.

Silly. Why would a businessman want to kill her? Or cause her any harm? He was her landlord. A dead tenant couldn't pay rent.

Unless there was something else he needed from her more than money.

Silence.

Screams wouldn't attract anyone. In frantic alarm, she pressed the nurse call button as Noel started to touch the morphine bag…

Barely seconds later, not a nurse, but West Brand strode into the room. Coffee in hand, he dropped the cup and rushed over to the man.

"What the hell are you doing here?" West got into Larson's face. "And touching her drip?"

Noel Larson lifted his hands as if to say, *I'm innocent.* "Just checking to see the medication, if it needed changing. Wanted to be helpful. I've had relatives in the hospital and I know how it is, how it's hard to get nurses to do anything."

"Not this hospital," Quinn cut in, needing West by her side and needing him to believe her. *Don't leave me alone here with that man. Forget the fact I owe him money. He scares me.*

Noel's sly gaze flicked over to her and then back to West. He shrugged. "Good to hear. I'm just a visitor. I heard what happened and brought her flowers. What's wrong with that?"

"Two things." West's fingers played with the butt of the lethal-looking gun sticking out of a holster on his leather belt. "You're. Here."

Noel's smile didn't meet his eyes. "West Brand, the new FBI man in town. Man of few words."

West scowled. "Here's one more word. *Leave.*"

Noel nodded at her. "And so I leave. Goodbye, Quinn. Feel better."

The man left as West glared at the door closing behind him. West went outside, returned a minute later.

"From now on, there's someone outside your door 24/7. No visitors except myself and your brothers. And anyone authorized by us."

Her tummy did a funny flip-flop, partly from nerves about the odd encounter with Noel Larson, and partly from West's nearness.

He sat in the chair by her bedside, his anxious gaze holding hers. "Did he do anything to you?"

Scared me. "I'm fine. He seems slimy." And yet Noel Larson hadn't been the one to talk about investigating her. West had.

Her gaze went to the gun hanging on his belt. Was it a weapon to protect her? Or force people into talking and revealing information they were loath to share?

"He's worse than something you scrape off your shoe," West told her.

"Why? What's wrong with Noel Larson?" Was this another person she had to worry about?

She already worried about a relationship with West, the man who proclaimed to love her.

Proclaimed it to her face, and then whispered in her room he was trying to find out information from her.

Could she trust anyone in this town?

"Everything. The man is a con, and a liar. All he cares about is money." He jammed a hand through his short hair. "He's also your landlord. Was he pressuring you for the rent?"

"N-no. He asked if I remember him. I told him no."

West gave her a level look. "I also believe he had something to do with the bomb blast that killed Tia. Just a gut feeling. And you're the only witness, so he's not allowed back. I'll pay your rent."

Quinn shook her head and winced. "No. I pay my own bills. At least, I think I did. I don't want any help."

"Fine. Then when you get home, give me the rent check and I'll keep him from breathing down your neck and give him no reason to have any contact with you. None."

West continued, checking her IV and nodding. "And the fact he had his dirty hands on your morphine drip gives me mighty cause for worry, sweetheart. He might have tried something."

Fear tightened her stomach. The pretty red roses on the nightstand suddenly looked ominous. Not pretty and an offering of friendship to a sick person.

She gestured to the flowers. "He gave me these. Can you get rid of them?"

West studied the flowers, sniffed one. "They're probably nothing, an excuse for him to visit. I'll send them to the lab, just in case."

Quinn wished she could recall something. Anything. She felt like a person navigating through a minefield. Anything could blow up in her face.

Anything already had. Who could she trust? Not this Larson fellow. But West was trustworthy. Certainly he seemed up-front and honest. Except he'd talked about her to that mysterious Mike person, as if his interest zeroed in on her ability to find Demi.

Yet there was the memory of that kiss. Had West Brand seduced her to find Demi, her sister?

Chapter 8

After leaving Quinn's hospital room, West was due at the police station for a briefing.

The chief, her cousin Finn, had given him a lot of latitude with work because he knew West had experience with questioning bombing victims. Only Shane and Brayden knew that he and Quinn had dated.

Dropping off the roses she'd been given by Noel Larson at the lab, with strict instructions to be careful of poison, he headed for the briefing.

Inside the squad room, the other members of the Red Ridge PD milled about, quietly talking as they waited for Chief Colton to appear. Surprised to see Demi's half brother Shane Colton, he realized the PI probably was there to share street intel. Sometimes there was more than a grain of truth in what town gossips said.

West nodded gruffly at the others, grabbed a cup of coffee. Still shaken over seeing Larson in Quinn's room, he preferred to remain alone. K-9 unit detective Carson Gage gave him a scrutinizing look. West didn't care. In this force, everyone always looked at him as if they couldn't quite make him out, trying to figure out what he was doing here. He was an outsider, regarded with respect, but not admitted to anyone's inner circle.

Fine with him. He had a job to do.

Brayden spotted him, wandered over. He didn't quite trust Brayden, but the man was okay in his book.

"We spent last night combing through the surveillance video from the convenience store across the street from Tia's office." Brayden's jaw tightened. "Nothing. Camera was too far away."

"Whoever did this knew the area, knew Tia's routine." His troubled gaze met the other man's. "It could have been someone intending to hurt Quinn, as well."

He stared at the whiteboard with the photos of the Groom Killer's vics and bombing vic Tia. Someone was setting up a PowerPoint presentation on the laptop to show on the screen in front. And then Chief Colton walked in.

Everyone took a seat. West chose one away from the others. He didn't care to socialize or share information other than what was related to the crime.

Uncomfortably aware that he was there to secretly investigate the Coltons and their knowledge of Demi's whereabouts, he couldn't risk being buddies with any of them.

Finn sat on the front desk, legs dangling over the side, cup of coffee in hand. "The autopsy on Tia concluded she died from blunt force trauma. Not the explosion. Someone bashed in her head first."

He'd figured as much. West gripped his coffee. The news made him a little more relaxed because it meant Quinn wasn't the intended vic.

Still, he couldn't discount Quinn in all this. She'd been there, and the unsub might have intended to kill her with the bomb, as well. The timing was too slick, too perfect.

The PowerPoint presentation started, showing the evidence markers at the scene. Dozens of them.

The body of Tia.

A photo of Quinn, the only known witness.

Heart slamming against his chest, West winced. She looked so fragile, so vulnerable lying in the hospital bed. Curls mussed, face pale and drained.

"Quinn Colton has yet to regain her memory. Brayden will discuss the detonator now." Finn handed the laser pointer to Brayden.

Brayden stood, gestured to the slide showing the detonator. "The cell phone was a burner, type you could purchase in any retail outlet. We also found fragments of metal ball bearings embedded in the filing cabinets. Whoever made this bomb wanted us to think it was a terrorist incident."

Shrapnel bombs, especially ones with ball bearings, were common with terrorists, who wanted to injure and maim as many people as possible.

Shane snorted. "The hell it is. Talk on the street is the Larsons had a hand in it. Noel had dated Tia, things went south. Maybe he wanted to make it a permanent breakup."

Heart dropping to his stomach, he tried to keep his cool.

Finn looked at West. "Report?"

He went to the front of the room, took the pointer and gestured to the slide on the screen. "Rex found residue of TATP on the carpet near Tia's desk, and the front door. We determined the seat of the bomb originated from Tia's desk. The bomb was housed in a cardboard container. Postblast damage includes the window shades in front, which were drawn at the time, front windows, office equipment and several files on the victim's desk, as well as the victim herself."

West clicked to the next slide. "The blast was powerful enough to embed this pencil into the wall."

He droned on, going over what his dog had discovered, what evidence was present. No fingerprints yet pointing to the unsub.

As the chief thanked him, his gaze flicked over to Brayden. "There's something else."

Everyone waited.

West scrubbed a hand over the bristles on his jaw. "Noel Larson was in Quinn's hospital room this morning."

Every head in the room stared. Brayden glared at him as if West had personally escorted the man inside. Guilt and anger knotted his guts. "I sure as hell didn't invite him. I was downstairs, grabbing coffee, and caught him fiddling with Quinn's morphine drip. I kicked him out."

"Larson might have intended to finish the job. My sister could have been his next victim," Shane grated out.

"Either way, Quinn is in danger. She's the only witness and once she regains her memory, whoever did this will want her silenced," Finn said, frowning.

More murmurs, but West ignored them. His gray matter was spinning off facts and what he knew about the Larsons.

"If Larson killed Tia, it wasn't over a failed romance. He'd give it his own spin. He's slick enough. This was over something much more important to him." West scanned the room. "Money."

He used the laser pointer to gesture to the next slide. "I found this key chain in the rubble. Pine Paradise Cabins."

Telling them what he'd encountered with Tia, and leaving out the part about wanting to rent a cabin with Quinn, he concluded, "Property like that is worth millions."

Shane stretched out his legs. "Rumor has it Tia owned

the property and planned to sell to Larson. But the deal fell through."

"Why?" West asked.

Shane frowned. "No one knows for certain. Tia backed out at the last minute. She was selling for a cool two million dollars. She hated the headache of managing all those cabin rentals."

His mind clicked over the facts. If Tia had backed out, either she didn't trust the twins, or she had good reason to cancel the sale. Maybe the cabins offered another source of income.

His gaze raked over the Colton officers in the room. Maybe income from blackmailing a certain Colton, on the run with a baby, rumored to be the Groom Killer. Or Tia wanted to protect Demi from being found.

Could Demi Colton be hiding out at Pine Paradise?

On impulse, he decided to throw out a nugget. See how the others reacted, especially the Coltons. Maybe some of them did know where Demi Colton hid.

"Maybe the Larsons aren't connected at all," he told them.

Continuing to stand in front of the room, he snapped the pointer shut. Looked at all the expectant faces, waiting for him to speak.

"What if Demi Colton decided to hide out and Tia was helping her? Maybe Tia wanted to kill Larson for dumping her."

His theory was off the charts. Hell, he didn't believe it.

His crazy theory didn't matter.

Their reactions did.

Silence draped the room. Blank shock on the faces of most of the Colton K-9 detectives. Brayden looked secretive and guarded. Shane's expression smooth and blank.

Finally Carson Gage spoke up. "That's ridiculous. Demi

and Tia had no real connection. Tia socialized in different circles than Demi."

West shrugged. "I wouldn't know. I'm a stranger to town. Just thought I'd toss out an idea, seeing there's already one serial killer in town."

Murmurs started about Demi Colton. Nothing overt, nothing new. Chief Colton waved a hand. "Enough already."

Finn made a note on his pad. "Check out for certain who now owns Pine Paradise."

The chief's gaze hardened. "Tia's cell phone is missing. We searched her house and nothing turned up."

West figured the unsub took it. He hoped they could find it. Phone records would show who called Tia last. It was all standard operating procedure.

"I want a guard 24/7 on Quinn Colton." Finn stared at the others. "Not because she's my cousin, but she's the only witness we have, and once she gets her memory back, we could have a suspect."

As the chief dismissed them, West's concern centered on Quinn.

Because if the Larsons were behind this bombing and the killer screwed up in leaving a witness behind, she would be next to die.

Chapter 9

"I'm headed home today. Alone."

There, she'd said it.

Quinn paused in gathering from her hospital room the plethora of cards, cheerful greetings and handmade drawings by local schoolchildren.

"No, you're not." West shook his head. "You heard Shane and Brayden. I'm coming with you. And Brayden and Shane hired a security guard to watch the store and guard the apartment. No one is getting in or out without him knowing it."

Doubts filled her. That phone call she'd overheard had changed everything about West. Although the faint recollections of terrific sex and smoldering passion had been more frequent, she couldn't be entirely sure of him. "Why should I let you come home with me? I don't even know you. At least my brothers, the men who say they are my brothers, share my last name."

She wouldn't meet his gaze. Couldn't. Quinn had nothing to guide her.

Truth was, she was plain scared. If someone had planned to kill her, they would surely try again. Anyone could be suspect.

Even this man, who professed he knew her. Loved her, even.

But could she trust him? It sounded as if he were investigating her family over this mysterious Demi. What if West professed to love her only to get closer, get information?

And then get out of town, abandoning her?

"I can handle things alone," she retorted, wishing she felt as confident as she sounded.

"No, you can't. You had a major head injury. The doctor agreed to release you only on the condition you have someone at home to help you out." West tapped his muscular chest. "At your service."

Home had to be better than staying at the hospital. Even if it meant she headed to a place she didn't know was a palace or a pigsty.

He helped her pack all the cards, letters and artwork into a small suitcase. "Quinn, honey, I know this must be scary for you. You don't know if I'm one of the good guys. All I have to prove it is this," he said, and flashed his badge. "But I promise you, I'll do everything in my power to keep you safe."

Finally she looked at him. Determination shone in that dark gaze. He had the most incredible eyes. Behind it lurked some lingering sadness, shadows she couldn't identify.

She moistened her lips. West stared at her mouth, as if he wanted to kiss her.

Quinn frowned. "Stop staring at me."

He blinked. "Sorry. I was…remembering the times we had together."

Glad someone can remember. If only I could. Quinn felt adrift, without an anchor or a compass. She didn't know who to trust. Could she trust this man with the burning gaze and the quiet, steady air?

Her brothers told her West was a guy who liked working alone. But he was rock-solid.

"Give me one good reason why you are a better protector than one of my brothers."

Tension knit his brow, showed in the tautness of his strong jawline. "Because they have their own lives, and other concerns. You're my top priority, Quinn."

She moved and winced. Her head still ached at times. West immediately strode over, rubbed her temples with soothing strokes.

Such a small action. But his touch was gentle, and he riveted his attention on her, unlike Brayden and Shane. They talked with her, worried about her, but hadn't shown this attentive concern.

Maybe she was a fool, but she had to start somewhere. Her brothers thought West was okay. She pulled away. "All right. You can come home with me. You can sleep on the sofa."

West nodded slowly. "And Rex will be with me. He's a good watchdog. He's crazy about you."

Terrific. Yet another thing she didn't remember. Quinn pressed her fingers to her temples, wishing she could force her mind to work.

"Give it time," West said quietly. "The doctor said it's not permanent. The amnesia will fade with time and rest."

As she started to reach for the water cup, West was there, filling it, bringing the straw to her lips. Quinn drank, pushed it away. West held the cup in his big hands as if cradling something precious.

"Deal?"

Such hope in his deep voice. This had to be difficult for him, if they'd shared the relationship he claimed.

"Deal. As long as I'm free to kick you out if I feel the need. And you keep to yourself."

He held up two fingers, pressed together. "Scout's honor. And if I'm anything less than a gentleman, feel free to sic Rex on me. Better yet, serve me some of that gluten-free pizza you were always pushing on me."

A faint smile touched her face. "I have a feeling you'd rather face an angry dog than a meal you can't stand."

His grin was wide. Endearing. "You got it."

So cute. Handsome and charming. Could this FBI agent really be hers?

Or was he pulling a trick to try to get close, get to know her, maybe get something out of her?

The nurse came in, bearing a sheaf of papers. "Doctor's ready to discharge you, Miss Colton."

Quinn eyed West. "All right. Let's do this. Let's go home."

Wherever home was.

Two hours later, West pulled up to a small storefront on Main Street. Dismay filled her. She was hoping for some rambling, big house where she could have plenty of space to herself. And avoid close contact with this man, who seemed determined to stick to her.

"This is it?"

"You live above the store. Got a break in the price from the Larsons for renting both the storefront and the upstairs apartment." West switched off the engine. "I left Rex upstairs, waiting for you, guarding the place. If anyone tried to break in to plant another bomb, Rex would have him for breakfast."

Good thinking.

"It looks old," she murmured, studying the front.

"The historical flair to the building is one reason you liked it. The apartment is quaint, but the kitchen has been fully modernized for your business."

West Brand knew more about her business, and her home, than she did. Before she could even open the door, he was outside, sprinting around the truck to open it for her. Instead of assisting her out, West scooped her into his arms.

Blinking in stunned amazement, she watched him kick the door shut with a foot. "I'm not an invalid," she told him, scowling.

"No, but those stairs are steep, so let me be your elevator."

What did you say to a charming man who insisted on carrying you like a bride? Quinn felt too weary to argue.

Brayden and Shane pulled up behind West, and her brothers opened the door to the shop.

They all walked inside. The big, burly man with the gun at his hip standing near the entrance introduced himself as Tom, an old friend of Brayden's. He would stand guard over her shop and the apartment during the day, while another man replaced him at night.

Quinn took an appreciative whiff of the air. The faint smell of spices and food teased her appetite, but nothing looked familiar.

Brayden and Shane studied her. "Anything?" Shane asked.

"No." She frowned. "Please stop staring at me as if I'm a monkey in a circus."

She pointed to the floor. "Please put me down. I need

to see my store. You two—" she pointed to her brothers "—can go upstairs."

"Bossy," Shane said, grinning.

"As ever. Guess this means she's feeling better." Brayden winked.

"We'll stay here." Shane sniffed the air. "Maybe you still have those amazing blueberry muffins around some-place, Quinn."

After West set her on her feet, Quinn looked around the shop, and then shuffled into the kitchen. Nothing triggered any memories. Her head ached slightly, but thanks to the medicine she took, it wasn't terrible.

The lack of remembering felt worse.

A white envelope sat on the stainless steel counter near the stove. West picked it up, frowned. "What's this?"

"I don't know." Quinn pressed two fingers to her temple. It was important, she knew, but why? Why hadn't she opened it?

"There's no return address." Lines formed in his brow as he studied the envelope. "Brayden, get in here."

Her brothers rushed into the kitchen. When West pointed to the envelope, Brayden's genial manner dropped. Her brother looked equally concerned.

"I don't understand. What threat is an envelope?" she asked.

"No return address is dangerous, honey. Especially after what happened to you, I'm not taking chances," West told her.

New worries. "Is it dangerous?"

"Could be. Might even be another explosive." He set down the envelope carefully, dialed a number on his cell phone.

Minutes later, the Red Ridge bomb squad showed up. "Check her apartment, comb through everything in case Rex missed something," West instructed.

Waiting on a kitchen stool, Quinn felt exhausted. Suddenly her safe apartment did not feel quite so comfortable anymore.

When the bomb squad left with the envelope, she felt off-kilter. "They really put bombs in envelopes?"

"Anything is possible." West studied her. "Even a few grams of the right explosive can detonate under the right conditions. And you work in a kitchen with gas burners."

Upstairs, Brayden opened the door and West carried her inside. He set her down, as if she were made of glass, on a narrow green sofa.

A large black dog came out of the kitchen, tail wagging furiously. He loped toward the sofa.

"Rex, sit," West ordered.

When he did, she patted Rex's head. He panted with pleasure, pink tongue lolling out. Tired of being an invalid, Quinn stood and began to explore her home.

There wasn't much to see. Sizable living room with a sofa and two armchairs, a bookcase and a wide-screen television hanging on one wall. Hallway leading to the one bedroom.

King-size bed, covered with a white comforter embroidered with blue forget-me-nots. A window overlooking the street, with lacy white curtains, and a bureau holding a small wood jewelry box, an alarm clock and some perfume. A desk squeezed into one corner, holding a laptop computer.

Quinn studied the bed, felt West peering over her shoulder. Her nerves tingled. If they were lovers, they surely shared that bed.

Not now.

West headed for the desk. He opened a drawer, withdrew a notebook and set it on the desk.

"In case you wish to take more notes to jog your memory," he explained.

Instead, she hunted through the drawers, found a checkbook, flipped through the register to see the last rent check. Quinn studied the balance. She knew she must have been an organized businesswoman. There was enough money to cover the rent. Whatever other bills needed to be paid would have to wait.

She wrote another check. She tore it off and handed it to West.

"Can you deliver the rent check to Noel Larson? It's already late." Quinn felt her chest tighten. "I don't want Larson to think I'm not good for it and I'm any more helpless than he saw me in the hospital room."

"I'll take care of it," he promised, folding the paper and slipping it into his wallet.

A bathroom held a shower and a mirrored medicine cabinet filled with lotions, creams and ordinary pain reliever. It looked clean, neat and totally impersonal.

Two toothbrushes were in a holder decorated with a smiling mermaid.

The cabinet below the sink held other items, including a man's razor, shaving cream and deodorant. Quinn removed the cap, sniffed it. A faint memory clicked.

It smelled a little like West. Masculine, spicy and appealing but not overpowering.

If she wanted proof West had shared her life, surely this was it. Her sense of smell hadn't been distorted by the bomb blast.

Maybe it could aid recovering her life.

Quinn opened a drawer. Organized, neat, containing extra toothpaste and…

She took a step backward, blinked. Then she reached into the drawer and pulled out a box.

Pregnancy test.

Heart beating fast, she turned it over. Unopened, so she hadn't used it yet. Was she worried about pregnancy? Joyful and hopeful?

Frustration bit her. If only she could remember!

Quinn tucked the box back into the drawer.

She moved back into the living room, where her brothers hovered. Helicopter family, she thought, rubbing her head.

The bookshelf held several paperbacks and two rows of snow globes. A shaft of sunlight from the nearby window illuminated them like a spotlight. Quinn picked one up. Most were of pretty ballerinas dancing, but this snow globe held a white carousel horse decorated with pink roses. Pink roses adorned the base. She turned it over and wound the key.

Music played. Quinn wrinkled her brow. It was lovely, and she liked the tune, but it did nothing to trigger her dormant memory.

"Theme song from the musical *Carousel*." West studied her with his intense, dark gaze. "Your favorite Broadway show. We went to a fair two weeks ago and you insisted on riding the carousel horses. I bought that for you as a gift."

It was enormously frustrating to know she'd shared experiences with this man, and he'd been there, in her apartment and she didn't remember any of it.

In the kitchen, plenty of wholesome, organic food had been stocked. She opened another cabinet.

A box of dog biscuits. Rex followed her, sat, his tail wagging.

These weren't items West had stored for Rex while she was in the hospital. Judging from Rex's anticipatory look, he was used to her opening this cabinet.

Accustomed to her giving him a dog biscuit.

She opened the box, held out a biscuit. Rex put up a paw.

Quinn fed him the treat. He gulped it down and wagged his tail.

Tears burned in the back of her throat.

The dog knew her. This dog knew her, and she knew him. Obvious from the treats she'd stored in the cabinet, the worn pillow on the kitchen floor, two well-chewed toys on the carpet.

I can't even remember a dog who shows affection for me.

"What's wrong with me?" she whispered.

Glancing backward into the living room where her brothers paced, she felt West take her hand. "You suffered a horrible injury, Quinn. We're damn lucky you weren't killed. It will get better. I promise."

Somehow she suspected his promise wasn't a platitude like they'd given her at the hospital. Judging from his determined expression, and his gentle demeanor, West truly did care.

But until she regained a glimmer of who she was, and what she was, Quinn didn't want to draw close to this man. Everything felt so unfamiliar and strange. And now she'd agreed to let this big, quiet FBI agent stay in her apartment.

The same agent she'd overheard discussing her on the phone, as if she'd done something wrong.

Disappointment showed on his face as she slid her hand away from his.

Her brothers appeared in the kitchen doorway. "We're taking off," Brayden announced to her, but his gaze riveted to West. "You need anything, call."

When they filed out the door, she sat at the tiny kitchen table, staring out the window at the field beyond the building's back. She'd had an entire life lived here in this home: cooking, cleaning, making love…

And remembered none of it.

West gestured to the stove. "You hungry?"

"No." It hurt too much to shake her head. "Just thirsty."

"I'll make you a cup of tea." He tilted his head. "Unless you'd rather have coffee."

"Tea is nice."

"Later, I'll cook dinner. Do you remember what you like?"

Quinn narrowed her eyes. Silly question. She barely remembered her name. "Why do you ask?"

"I thought I could rustle you up a nice thick steak with a baked potato instead of those sprouts you adore."

Rolling her eyes, she thrust out her hands like a traffic cop. "I may be fresh out of the hospital and fresh out of my memory, but I'm not fresh out of my mind. Red meat is bad news."

West put a hand to his chest and heaved an exaggerated sigh. "I tried. Guess you wouldn't go for a nice bucket of greasy fried chicken, either."

At her horrified expression, he grinned, a crooked, sexy smile that tugged at her insides. Maybe she didn't know this man, but he was certainly charming. And cute.

After the water boiled, he fetched her a cup of chai tea, added a dollop of honey. Quinn inhaled the smell, her tension fleeing a little. "Thank you."

This seemed familiar as well, and soothing.

"I have to get back to work." West jammed his hands into the pockets of his jeans. "The apartment has been checked and there are security cameras, but I hate leaving you alone. I should call someone to stay with you here in the apartment."

"No. I already have one guy standing guard. I need to be alone."

Being alone sounded perfect right now. Maybe quiet time by herself would give her jumbled mind a chance to sort out the details of what had happened to her. Quinn stirred her tea. "I'll be fine. Think I'll take a nap after you're gone. Maybe explore the kitchen."

"When is your appointment with the therapist?"

He *would* remember. She'd wanted to forget. "Tomorrow morning. Austin will drive me there."

West nodded. "I changed the locks, installed an alarm system and double dead bolts. Both up here and down in the store."

Her thoughts went to Noel Larson. "What about my landlord? He has a key."

West snorted. "Not anymore. And if he tries to get inside, he'll have to answer to me and your brothers."

His quiet, intense manner reminded her she still remained vulnerable to whomever had planted the bomb. The suspect was still out there.

"Unsub," she murmured.

West raised his dark brows. "You remember."

Quinn blinked. "I do?"

"*Unsub* is what we at the FBI term an unidentified suspect. Not many civilians use that word. You learned it from being around me."

Hmm. Quinn raised her gaze to his. "What else did I learn from you, Agent Brand?"

Staring at her mouth, he compressed his own, as if fighting an urge to kiss her. "A lot of things we can't do now." West stroked her bottom lip with his thumb, his gentle touch evoking a shiver of pleasure. "Not until you've recuperated. And you learn where the panic button is."

Panic button for sex? But no, he took her around the apartment, showing her the cameras pointed out the windows overlooking the street. West pointed to the video feed from the desktop computer in her bedroom so she could watch the cameras. One in the upstairs hallway and one inside her shop near the entrance. Rex followed, sitting and watching West as he explained everything.

"I set up the feed on your cell, too." He showed her the app for accessing the security cameras through the internet.

Emotion clogged her throat. Maybe this FBI agent had talked about her in the hospital, and investigated her, but she couldn't dismiss his protective nature and caring concern.

She patted Rex's head. He licked her hand. Quinn rubbed behind his ears, the motion soothing and familiar. Perhaps she'd done this very thing before.

Before her world blew up and she lost all sense of herself.

Lost all sense of him as well, this man she'd promised to marry.

West's cell phone rang. He answered it, expression tight, and then hung up. "That was the bomb squad. They blew up the envelope. Standard procedure. Didn't find anything suspicious."

Quinn sighed. "Maybe it was someone who forgot to put their return address. I hope it wasn't a check, because from the sound of things, I could use the money."

"Money's the last thing you'll worry about," he told her. "I will help."

She walked over to the sofa and sat. "Thanks, but one thing I do know. I'm the sort to handle things on my own. I'll get back to speed in no time, get this place running and the bills paid."

Uncertainty clouded his dark eyes. West looked at her, and drew in a deep breath. "Are you sure you'll be okay? I can find someone to stay with you until my shift is over."

"I need alone time. I'll be fine. Go."

He bent over, bringing his face close to hers as if to kiss her, but she jerked away. Heat flooded her cheeks.

She wasn't ready for this. That previous kiss had been a tease, but here in her apartment, her little sanctuary she'd agreed to share with this man? It seemed like an open invitation to do more and she felt too unsteady and insecure.

Hurt flashed on his face, and then he nodded.

"Call me if you need anything. Or text. I'll be in meetings most of the morning." The intense, searing look returned as he studied her. "If you recall anything, anything at all, call me. It's important."

Important to you because you're investigating me? Or important to the investigation? She didn't want to think about the former, because it scared her more. Scared her to think that West Brand, who professed to love her, only wanted to use her.

Still, he was FBI and seemed protective of her. And there was still a person out there who had killed Tia, and would want her dead, as well.

"If I remember anything important, I'll text you," she assured him.

West walked out with Rex. The door locks quietly clicked behind him.

Quinn drank her tea. It soothed her throat and calmed her nerves.

Now she could finally do what she'd itched to do since arriving. Explore.

She went into the bedroom. The dresser was against the wall opposite the windows, and a flat-screen television was mounted on the wall in front of the king-size bed.

She opened the closet. Ordinary enough, with a row of dresses, shirts, pants and stacks of boxes neatly piled atop the wood shelf. Shoes were lined on a rack on the floor.

Quinn combed through her bureau. In the top drawer, buried under a layer of silk panties and lacy bras, she found West's photo.

If they'd kept their relationship hidden from everyone, Quinn suspected she wouldn't openly display his photo. Especially if she had family over, and friends visiting.

Quinn studied the portrait. West stared into the camera, unsmiling and serious. His face dictated endless stories.

It was a strong face, a face filled with expressiveness. Quinn could envision him frustrated, knitting his dark brows together, or infuriated, growing red with rage. Tender with desire and passion, and guarded with secrets.

Secrets he would not share with her.

She wondered how his face would look filled with joy, or the sheer wonder of life's little miracles. Surely there were many. Maybe she couldn't remember them, but Quinn firmly believed in small, important miracles. Her own survival was one.

West hadn't known her for long, perhaps a month or a few weeks. And yet in that time, they'd fallen in love. Or so he said.

He'd shared her bed, pledged his devotion and wanted to share his life with her. West seemed devoted to his job, his duty as an FBI agent. Tucking the photo back into the drawer, she sighed.

Quinn burned the image of his handsome face into her mind. Closing her eyes, she tried to recall anything about him. There, a flicker of memory.

Lying in bed with West's arms around her, watching the television mounted to the wall. He had argued with her, playfully, not really protesting, about her choice of program.

Drawing in a deep breath, she smelled the tang of masculine aftershave, a slight floral scent of women's perfume and the musk of sex. A smile touched her face. This memory made her feel cherished and safe and sated. For a minute she wanted to linger inside it, for it was a square on a cold, impartial blank slate.

They must have made love and then, too restless for sleep, watched television. Quinn picked up the remote on the nightstand, turned on the wide screen.

A cooking show came on. The hostess droned on about mixing spices.

She laughed. Perhaps she couldn't remember what programs she enjoyed, but she'd stayed true to form.

She switched off the remote.

Next she explored the closet. Dresses, all colorful, some polka-dot, some floral. Pretty, not one of them in dull, dreary colors. Shoes… She bent down and examined the shoe rack. A few heels, nothing quite expensive, but smart. Two pairs of flats. Quinn lifted one shoe and looked at the well-worn bottom.

I must wear these while I'm working.

Sinking to the floor, she tossed the leather flat into the closet. Looking at shoes and clothing did nothing to stir dormant memories. Her stomach grumbled with hunger. Quinn pressed a finger against her right temple.

Hot tears burned behind her eyelids. Sitting on the floor, she let them come, surrendering to the sense of utter loss.

She might have survived the explosion, but she'd lost herself.

And Quinn didn't know when she would ever find herself again.

Chapter 10

The warm South Dakota day promised to be fine. It was a time in August for last-minute vacations, fishing and enjoying the weather before the autumn winds blew in the burning colors of changing leaves, leading to the bitter winter snowfalls. The first hint of fall lingered in the cool breeze sweeping along the streets, fluttering the red and blue petunias in the flowerpots.

As he locked the front door to Quinn's shop, checking it twice, West tried to keep his sense of calm. He headed for his truck, nodding politely to the pedestrians passing by, glancing with curiosity at Good Eats. People in town knew what happened to Quinn. A couple stopped, asked after her.

He kept his answers brief and vague. Anyone could pass along information to the unsub.

Hell, anyone could be the unsub, ready to strike again. Delivering death with a bomb intended to inflict as much suffering as possible…

Keys in hand, West went to unlock his truck when a flash of memory slammed into him.

Orange tongues of flame inside his home. Fire, too intense to draw near. Screams echoing in the night, coming from him. *Had to get inside... Save them. Please, someone save them...*

I'm sorry, West. Your parents and your sisters didn't make it.

Closed-casket funerals, wood coffins lined up in a row. A seemingly never-ending parade of his father's fellow cops, friends, neighbors, relatives.

Everyone murmuring sympathy, some weeping as they hugged him. He was a statue, stiff and unyielding. Show no emotion. *Be like Dad, strong, stoic. Make them proud.*

Only much later, after the funeral, and the cars and the hordes of people had left, did he lock himself into the bedroom given to him by his aunt and uncle...and cry. Scream. Rage.

Never again. Never again would anyone he loved die on his watch.

Memories so thick they become noxious, cloying smoke, threatening to squeeze his throat shut. Leaning against the door, he breathed deeply as his therapist taught him. Every male instinct fought to run upstairs, take Quinn into his arms and promise to stick to her until the killer was found.

Leaving Quinn alone, with only a security guard downstairs, made him nervous. He wanted to stay with her, keep her safe. But he had to return to work and analyze the findings on the crime scene.

Not to mention his own findings, and what he'd found at the first blast site.

Work offered solace, a way to deal with the ache of grief fisting in his stomach. Catching the unsub meant others would stay safe. He couldn't bring back his family, or Tia, but he could perform his duty.

You have a clever mind, son. Use it.

Usually the recollection of his father's voice pinched him with sorrow, but today it galvanized him. The memory made him smile a little for the first time in thirteen years. West had been fixing his sweet little Mustang, which had coughed out and died in the driveway. He loved tinkering with the car, but that Sunday, he'd only wanted to drive out to the lake, enjoy the summer sun and hang with friends before heading back to school the next day. His father had come outside to help.

The problem's there. You can find it, his dad had encouraged.

But I can't figure it out. He'd thrown down the wrench in sheer frustration.

His father had glanced down at the tool, then up at him. *You'll never find the solution by throwing away the key to it.*

Ashamed by his outburst, he'd studied the problem again. Analyzed it. Eventually fixed it.

Walking away would have solved nothing.

Find the solution. Use your brain.

Keys. Cabins. Rentals, million-dollar properties left in the balance. Buildings blown up.

West dropped his keys. Picked them up. Jingled them in his palm.

Planning an explosion took effort, time, caution in using delicate materials that could ignite and turn you from a living, breathing human being into shattered bits of bone and blood and flesh. But it was the only way, other than fire, to fully destroy a building.

If the first explosion intended to destroy the abandoned hardware store to test out the TATP explosives used later for Tia's office, what if the second bomb was a cover-up for the real target?

With all the Red Ridge PD concentrating on the explosion in town and Tia's death, resources would be limited.

And a third explosion planned for an expensive vacation spot in Spearfish Canyon, the same property whose sale to the Larson twins fell through, could be rigged to look like a gas leak, garnering much less attention and manpower.

Maybe even covering up the tracks of one Demi Colton, Groom Killer suspect?

Quinn's butterfly compact was found at the first explosion site. She might have hidden Demi at the abandoned hardware store for a day or two, and accidentally left her mirror behind.

Was there a connection between Tia and Demi and Quinn? Could Demi have planted the bomb that killed Tia? And do it at the same time she knew Quinn would deliver lunch? But why kill Tia, whose biggest vices were her greedy nature and short temper?

And more than that, why would Demi want to kill her only sister?

If Demi Colton had found out Quinn and West were together, it could have prodded her into harming her sister. West was FBI. Maybe Demi figured that Quinn would rat her out to her fed boyfriend. Then there was plain old jealousy. Demi had been dumped by her fiancé, so maybe if she found out Quinn was marrying West, she didn't like the idea of her sister getting engaged.

Austin, Quinn's friend, had figured out they were a couple. Chances were that others had, as well. They had been careful, but it only took one time to screw things up.

Planting a bomb took time, money and planning. Shooting Quinn and Tia would have been much easier and less messy.

Unless Demi Colton wanted to hint to people she was still around, still watching and waiting. The two explosions certainly had grabbed the attention of all the townspeople.

Questions swirled in his mind. Keeping an eye out for pedestrians who might overhear, he dialed Mike's number. When she answered, he gave his report.

"Fingerprints at the crime scene belonged to Tia. There were more, but none in the system. Nothing else raised a red flag. If Demi Colton was in the real estate office, we have no clue. The Larson twins are under suspicion for it. We're checking now to see if they were the intended buyers of a prime piece of property Tia planned to sell to them. The sale fell through."

"Murders have been committed for less. But a bomb?" Mike's heavy sigh carried through the phone. "That's a risky way to take out someone you want to kill."

"Unless the unsub used the explosion to cover the murder. Tia was dead before the office blew up. She may have surprised the bomber." Quickly he explained about the autopsy.

"I'm working on another theory," West continued. "The same property, Pine Paradise, is where Quinn took her sister, Demi, once. Demi might have hidden out there." He thought over what he'd found so far. "It's a stretch, but if Tia found out Demi was hiding there and tried blackmailing her, could be motivation for murder. She'd need help, though."

The only way to tell for sure was to trigger Quinn's memory. If Quinn actually saw her sister in the office before the bomb went off…

He swore quietly. Too many unknowns and risky factors in this case.

"Did you share this with the rest of the unit?" Mike asked.

"No. I plan to visit Pine Paradise soon. What about the hair samples and compact I gave you from the first explosion?"

"Lab doesn't have the DNA yet. I'll call soon as I have answers." Mike paused and worry darkened her voice. "West, if Demi Colton is involved, you need to get Quinn to remember. Try anything you can. Have to run."

West thumbed off the cell phone and leaned against his truck, pondering.

The hairs on the back of his neck lifted as he smelled an overpowering, spicy cologne, heard the brisk click of expensive men's shoes on the sidewalk. West looked up, his hand automatically dropping to the butt of his sidearm.

"Larson." His greeting for Noel Larson remained curt. Hostile.

"I heard Quinn was coming home today. Good to know. Home's a good place for her to recover fully." Carrying a leather briefcase, Larson's expression didn't match his words. He looked sly as his gaze flicked up to where Quinn's bedroom window overlooked the street.

All West's instincts fired on alert. Larson was a slick operator, but this kind of crime in town was bad for all the businesses. Unless Larson had a hand in it, and maybe he planned to profit from it?

Still, the man held power over Quinn because the Larsons owned the building and the rent was past due. West gestured to the building. "Quinn gave me a check for the rent."

"It's already paid." Larson didn't even blink. "Her business partner gave me a check for the past due rent, and next month's, as well."

He should have been relieved, but the news made him edgy. As her fiancé, he wanted to help her out. He knew Quinn's pride, too, knew she would not want Austin stepping up to the plate.

"Guess he didn't want Quinn to get evicted." His gaze never left that smirking face.

"Oh, I wouldn't evict her." The smile grew wider. "Too much trouble, when there are alternatives."

A tingle pricked his spine. Alternatives such as getting rid of her for good? "Where were you at noon the day of the explosion?" he demanded.

Larson stared at him and laughed. "You officially questioning me? I don't think so, Brand. None of your damn business."

"I make it my damn business when someone gets killed." West got in the man's face. "I don't know what you're about, Larson. But I'm keeping my eye on you."

Larson blinked. "Keep an eye if you wish, Agent Brand. If you want to question me, you'll have to go through my attorney."

The man strode off.

If Larson had anything to do with the explosion, he'd hang him out to dry. But West realized this wasn't his case. He had to work with the RRPD. No longer could he operate on his own.

With the death of Tia and the close call for Quinn, everything turned around for West.

Barely an hour after West's departure, Quinn grew restless. She had cried and then washed her face, determined to scrub away the tears. Crying accomplished nothing.

Instead, she read a cooking magazine. It contained a few fascinating articles on organic vegetables, but she felt too edgy and distracted to focus.

She tossed the magazine onto the coffee table. Unable to sit still after confined to a hospital bed, she felt restless.

Then there was the matter of that pregnancy test. Quinn headed into the bathroom and took out the box.

Well, she wouldn't find out by standing here.

Minutes after taking the test, she studied the stick. One single line. Not pregnant.

It might be too early. She had no idea of the timing of her cycle.

Quinn tossed out the test and put the box under the cabinet.

Maybe working in the kitchen would jog a memory of her life.

The security guard, reading a book in the store's front, nodded to her as she entered the store. Quinn went into the kitchen. The industrial kitchen was sweet, a chef's dream. Gas burners, all the appliances stainless steel, with plenty of large pots and pans to mix this, and bake and cook that.

She bent down to peer under the table and saw an enormous aluminum bowl, big enough to serve dozens.

A distant memory flashed.

Mayo Fest.

Hand on the table, she let the memory flow.

Mom, working as a server for a catering company. Her careworn, tired face sporting a bright smile solely intended for customers. A big bowl, like this one, filled with... What? Macaroni salad. Lots of mayonnaise.

The caterer had made plenty of salads, cheap and easy recipes, for a company party. Tuna salad. Macaroni salad. Potato salad. Quinn was a teenager, helping her mother serve.

Quinn had called it "Mayo Fest" because of all the white goo in the bowls. Quinn resolved she would own a business some day and serve only healthy, wholesome food.

Wait and see, Mom. I'm going to be a cook, and I'll be the one serving you, only it will be grass-fed beef instead of mayo-clogged tuna, Quinn had bragged.

The memory vanished. Smiling, Quinn stood. Maybe

it wasn't a significant memory, but it was a good start. Others would follow.

More cheerful now, she combed through the row of books on the shelf above the table, she found a notebook and opened it. Strong, bold cursive words were inked on each page of the book. Quinn found a pen, copied one word.

The writing matched. These must be her recipes. Quinn removed the books and found a tattered notebook. Cutouts of fruits and vegetables adorned the front, along with a square of red ribbon. The cursive label penned in gold ink read Recipes.

She opened it.

These were different. Not wholesome ingredients or organic mixtures, but everyday dishes a busy mother might make for her family. Creole chicken. Taco burgers. Noodle supper.

The writing was different as well—more polished, the cursive careful, as if she'd penned this as a soothing meditation exercise. Flour stained some pages, and there were more stains on other pages, smearing the ink.

Her hand rested on the ink stains as a memory jolted her.

Twelve years old. They were fighting again downstairs. Yelling at each other, her mother's shrill voice rising higher and higher. She hated it. Hated this stepdad. Writing would help, block out the voices, make the hurt in her belly go away, the pain of knowing soon her mother would divorce yet again, and they'd have to move...

Butter pecan popcorn. Yummy and perfect for watching movies on television, just her and Mom, settling down to watch what Stepdad number four sneeringly called "chick flicks." Corn syrup was essential, the light kind. Oh, and the pecans, shelled and chopped, so ripe and crunchy she could taste them...

Pulling herself back to the present, she pushed aside the notebook to take upstairs. For now she'd bake a cake.

Feeling more settled, she read over a recipe for organic cranberry-orange cake. Yum.

A batch of colorful bandannas were in a wicker basket near the door. She pulled one over her curls to secure them. Soon she was mixing this and adding that, humming as she worked.

A knock came at the front door.

Drying her hands on a towel, she went into the tiny storefront. Tom came to attention, looked at her.

"Do you want me to tell her the store's closed?" he asked.

Quinn sighed. "She doesn't look threatening." She unlocked the glass door.

The girl looked younger than herself, and had dark eyes and dark hair. She beamed at Quinn.

"Hi, Quinn! I'm so glad you're home again. I'm your cousin Valeria."

The woman ignored the palm Quinn held out, and hugged her instead. Quinn winced.

"Oh dear, that was my fault. I forgot you're probably still hurting." Valeria looked her up and down. "You certainly look like you were in an explosion."

My hair? She went to touch her messy curls, secure under the bandanna. *It looks like you stuck your finger into an electrical outlet*, a voice droned from the past. Who had said that? Her stepfather?

A stepfather.

But Valeria stared at her face. Self-conscious, Quinn touched her bruised cheek.

"Oh, don't worry about it. A little makeup will cover it," Valeria told her.

Quinn gestured to the store. "I'm baking. Come on in."

Tom gestured to the table where he'd been sitting. "I'll be right here, Miss Colton."

West had told her not to leave, but said nothing about inviting in family.

In the kitchen, she resumed mixing cake batter as Valeria perched on a stool and watched, chattering madly, asking questions about how Quinn felt, explaining that she felt awkward visiting the hospital and didn't want to disturb Quinn's rest while she recovered.

Valeria. Pretty name to match the face. Valeria looked as young as Quinn felt old and weary.

Her cousin looked around the kitchen. "I've never been here. I did actually try to visit in the hospital, but Brayden and Shane said no visitors. So here I am!"

Was she ever this young and enthusiastic? Quinn smiled as she continued to find the ingredients. "I'm making cake, if you want to stick around for a snack."

"Can't. I have to get back to the ranch and chores soon." Valeria studied the mixture. "Is it one of your special cakes?"

Everything is special to me now. "Of course."

"Can I tell you a secret?" her cousin asked.

Sure, why not? I probably won't remember it anyway. The thought made her chuckle. "Sure, go ahead."

"I'd planned on getting married. Christmas Eve. I told everyone my engagement to Vincent Gage was off because of the Groom Killer, but we can't wait any longer. I'm tired of living at home and I want to be with him."

The Groom Killer again. Unease pricked her. Had this Groom Killer targeted her because she'd been engaged to West? They'd kept it secret, but her bestie, Austin, had found out. Quinn realized others could, as well.

Valeria heaved a dramatic sigh. "Have you ever been so much in love that it hurts?"

Yes, I believe so. Except I don't remember such a love. All I know is the man who professed to love me could be the agent who's investigating me. How can I trust him? And if you can't trust, how can there ever be true love?

"I can imagine it," she told Valeria. "You're young, in love and impatient. It's natural."

And I'm thirty years old. I must have had relationships, but they came to a dead end. Nothing worked for me. I'm single and it seems up until a few weeks ago, I felt content to stay that way.

What happened with West Brand that she had fallen madly for him? Quinn looked around the kitchen and felt a burst of pride. Maybe the business was floundering, but it was her business, built through hard work and dedication. No one told her what to do, dictated her life to her. She didn't live at home with parents who made demands on her life and her time.

She was free. Independent.

Career had been everything. Quinn stared at the expensive electric mixer. She knew this deep in her heart, that career had been everything to her. She'd wanted to be a success and she had pride in her work.

Her creations. The compulsion to succeed came from never having enough money, enough respect...

Odd how she remembered that from her childhood, and yet remembered nothing of the business that she'd started to overcome those issues.

Quinn checked the oven. Gas. Cooking with gas meant better ability to control temperatures. She remembered that much. A cooking class, perhaps.

Maybe she could control the heat in the kitchen better than the heat in the bedroom. Nothing was certain right now. But those flashes of memory with West indicated they'd had a very good time in that particular room.

"We're thinking of eloping in Las Vegas," Valeria blurted out.

Eloping? Quinn switched off the electric mixer. "That's a big step. Just the two of you, no family with you?"

"Yes. Don't tell anyone?" Valeria made a zipping motion across her mouth.

Quinn offered a faint smile. "Don't worry. I'll probably forget we had this conversation ten minutes after you leave."

The little joke failed to make her cousin smile. Instead, Valeria bit her lip. "I'm sorry, Quinn. I can't imagine what happened to you… It's so terrifying."

"I'm fine," she hastened to assure her.

"Good." Valeria looked around the kitchen. "Did you get my letter with the monogrammed stationary? What did you think?"

"What letter?"

"The one I sent in the mail days ago. There was a red heart on the envelope. It was a sample. I wanted to get your opinion on the stationery."

Laughing, she checked the recipe. "The boys on the bomb squad blew it up."

Valeria's eyes widened. "Blew it up?"

"There was no return address and everyone got suspicious, after what happened at Tia's office."

"There was no return address because everyone in this town, including the postmaster, is nosy. I didn't want anyone but you to see it was from me." Valeria sighed. "Oh well."

"If I were you, I'd hold off on sending any more mail without a return address," Quinn advised.

"Do you think the Groom Killer would still pursue Vincent if we were married?"

The cake batter splashed into the pan. *Glop, glop, glop.* Quinn scraped out the rest with a wide spatula. "Marry, after what happened? I wouldn't. It's too risky, Valeria. Whoever is doing this may not only want grooms dead, but future brides, as well. Look at Tia."

Her cousin frowned. "Tia Linwicki was getting married? I didn't know she dated anyone that seriously."

Quinn pressed two fingers to her head. A dim flash of memory. Phone call. Angry voices.

Marriage made in hell.

You'll never commit.

Was Tia marrying someone, and that's why she'd been killed?

"I don't know." The earlier frustration had returned, leaving her wanting to bang her head against the counter. Maybe that would make everything better.

She wanted to be alone. "Valeria, I'm quite tired and this is my first day home."

Her cousin gave her a quick kiss on the cheek. "All right. But only if you promise to come to our family barbecue this Sunday."

Family gathering? With all those people staring at her, wondering about her? What if the person who did this hid among them?

Wiping her hands on a dish towel, she shook her head. "I don't think so. I'm still recovering."

"It's six days away. You'll feel better by then!"

"Doubt it. I'm not ready."

"Please come," Valeria begged. "It's not going to be a

huge party. Just family, and your cousins will be there. And me. Please, Quinn. I'd love to see you there."

How could she resist such youthful enthusiasm? A small family gathering didn't sound intimidating. How many Coltons could there be in this town, anyway?

"What can I bring?"

Valeria hooked her arm through Quinn's. "You and a date. Or…whoever you wish to bring."

With a wink, she bounded off.

After setting the cake pans into the oven, she returned upstairs, unlocking the door.

In the bathroom, the mirror showed bruises and cuts. She did look like a wreck. Quinn found her makeup. She smeared it on until everything, including her freckles, vanished.

A shiver raced through her. She hardly recognized herself.

Who am I?

Hard work never intimidated West. Neither did cases, because he could turn off his emotions like a water spigot.

Today it had taken all his control to resort to that tactic. Thoughts of Quinn kept pushing through his mind as he analyzed evidence, went over interview notes with interviewees from the most recent bombing, as well as the first one.

Returning to the crime scene to scrutinize it for additional evidence had been pure hell. He could barely get the thought of Quinn, her face bloodied, her body lying so still, out of his mind so he could sift through the rubble once more.

He'd spent an hour interviewing possible witnesses. Broad daylight and no one saw anything. Nothing but

Quinn walking down the street, marching toward Tia's office with the casserole.

Marching toward her possible death.

As he filed his report, his cell rang. West checked the number. Cal Flinders from the ATF.

"What do you have for me?" West asked. "We got the lab results from the powder residue. TATP. What do you know about the bomb itself?"

"Matched the one found at the abandoned hardware store. No signature. Ran the pattern through the database. Nothing came up. Whoever did this wasn't making a statement that he disliked Realtors. Or was protesting development." Cal's voice droned over the phone.

West frowned. Most bombers had signatures, putting certain elements into their work. The typical bomber was male, a loner and involved in criminal activity. They fell into specific categories, such as the terrorist, whose aim was to invoke fear into the general populace. Or a protestor, blowing up a building that opposed his beliefs, such as a real estate office.

"Unless this unsub is new at the game." West leaned back.

"In which case he's lucky to not have blown himself up. He's smart, accurate and organized. He did this to cover Tia's murder and any evidence. Did forensics find anything from Tia's computer?"

"No. It was too damaged."

"Then maybe the computer was the real target. A database. Did she back up to a cloud?"

If Tia did, they could access those records. "She was too insular, distrustful of tech."

Cal sighed. "Sorry, West. If I have anything more for you, I'll call."

He hung up.

By the time he returned to the apartment, West felt emotionally and physically wrung out. He let himself and Rex into the store with his key, and punched in the alarm code once he got upstairs. West unlocked the door, hesitated.

All the previous times he'd been here, Quinn had been whole. Happy. Bubbly. He would anticipate walking through that door, kissing her deeply and relaxing. He knew her habits. Knew her quirks, how she liked to walk around the apartment barefoot and paint her toes bright pink. How she quickly undressed in the morning to prepare for the day and slowly undressed for him with a teasing smile.

And now he was about to enter the home of a total stranger.

Chin up. West opened the door and called out a greeting as Rex ran forward.

Delicious smells of home cooking filled the air. His stomach rumbled, reminding him he'd skipped lunch. The apartment was slightly warm, but a cooling breeze came through the open living room window, billowing the curtains. West frowned. Even a second-story open window presented a threat. An unsub could lob an explosive, tearing through the screen, blowing up the place…

He shut the window as Quinn came out of the kitchen, drying her hands on a dish towel. "Hi."

Her voice sounded hoarse still, uncertain. This was so awkward, coming home to someone who had no memory of him. The same someone who would greet him with a soul-searing kiss, whose warm concern would erase the gritty memories of ugliness that came with the job.

"Hi." She petted Rex.

"Hi." West gestured to the window. "Don't leave it open unless I'm home."

Halfway expecting her to argue, as the old Quinn might,

he was surprised to see her nod. "All right. Did you have a good day?"

Ordinary small talk, common to ordinary relationships. "It was all right." West jammed his hands into his jeans pockets as Rex looked up and whined.

His dog sensed his tension. West followed Quinn into the kitchen. The drop leaf table had been set with plates and silverware. Meatballs bubbled in a skillet filled with red sauce.

"I made whole-wheat linguini with tomatoes, peppers, scallions and cilantro. I also cooked some he-man meat for you. Found some lean ground beef in the freezer and I made meatballs in case the froufrou food doesn't appeal to you."

The cutest little frown dented her brow. "I wonder where that term came from? It sounds familiar."

His shoulders relaxed their rigid stance. West grinned. He-man, now that sounded more like the old Quinn. Considering, he scratched his chest and affected a lazy drawl. "Well, I dunno, little lady. He-man balls in red sauce sounds mighty wimpy to me without the proper he-man juice. Got a beer to go with it?"

Quinn stared.

Okay, that tanked. West shifted his weight, uncomfortable with her scrutiny. Hell, this was harder than he'd ever imagined, trying to crack a joke with a woman who used to laugh at everything.

A woman who used to share intimacies with him as easily as she made delicious dinners.

She turned and left. He heard her heading downstairs.

His heart sank. Damn. Now he'd driven her off. West rubbed his face, knowing he should go after her.

A minute later, she returned, six bottles of beer in her arms. Now it was his turn to stare.

Quinn dumped them onto the table. A saucy smile, the one he adored, lit her face. "Will this do for your manliness or do you need some homemade moonshine from the still out yonder in back?"

The grin returned as he picked up a bottle. "No need for a moonshine chaser, little lady. Thanks."

"I may be little, but I bet I could drink you under the table, on top of the table and sideways. And many other positions, doing many other things other than drinking."

Now his grin widened. "I like the sound of that."

How many times had she told him that in the past few weeks? And then they'd ended in bed, tangling together in the sheets, the food and liquor forgotten?

Quinn's smile faded. She tilted her head and frowned. "Did I actually say that? Is that something I've said before?"

Whoa, this was new turf. West set down the beer. "You have. It'll come back to you."

Because she looked so woebegone and lost, he didn't pursue it. Here he'd been so worried about forging new connections with her, and she must feel as uncertain and uncomfortable as a teenager at her first dance.

"I am hungry," he told her. "Your dinner smells delicious, but you don't have to wait for me to come home, or feed me, Quinn."

Coming closer, she rested her palm upon his chest, over his heart. "Yes, I do. Someone has to take care of you to make sure your arteries don't harden to concrete before you're forty."

His gaze remained steady, though his heart pounded a little harder. Quinn always had the ability to throw him off guard, make him feel alive and aware.

And sexually responsive. West stepped back a pace. It was warm in there, and not only from the heat generated by the stove. *Easy. Now is not the time to kiss her, follow up on your feelings. Let her set the pace.*

"I'll go wash up," he muttered.

When he returned to the kitchen—his gun locked in the case he'd brought over, his hair damp from a quick scrubbing—West wore clean chinos, a green polo shirt and socks with hamburgers all over them. Maybe the socks would nudge her into remembering.

But she didn't even glance at his feet, only bustled around the kitchen to bring the food to the table. He tried to help, and she shooed him away.

As they sat, he forked a generous portion of her linguini, added some meatballs. "This is special. Thank you. But don't feel like you have to wait on me, Quinn. I work late and I would rather have you rest and recover."

She spun linguini around on her fork. "I needed to make dinner, West. I need to feel useful again, not like an invalid."

"You're not an invalid, honey." He sipped some cold beer. "You're recovering."

"I did manage to make dessert, too. I was downstairs, baking a cake, trying to get back to some kind of routine in hopes it jogged my memory." She sighed. "I didn't remember much."

Something was different about her. West dug into his meal with gusto, talking about Red Ridge, the cops on the force, the funny story he'd heard about her father's bar. He talked more than he had all day.

And yet that damnable blank look still rested on her face, as if he'd chattered on about a city that she'd never visited and people she'd never met.

Her own father. Well, Rusty Colton was a loser. Not worth remembering him. But right now, he'd even settle for Quinn recalling Rusty.

West set down his fork, realizing what was wrong with Quinn's expression. "What did you do to your face?"

She touched her cheek. "It's makeup."

Suppressing a groan, he gave her a level look. "Remove it."

She bristled. "Why? It's my face."

Okay, the old Quinn had returned. West got up, bent down by her chair, cupping her cheek with one hand. "Don't cover up your freckles. They're gorgeous."

"And I'm ugly. The cuts—"

"Will heal. And the bruises." He stroked a thumb over her cheek gently. "You never wore makeup before. All natural. It's what drew me to you. Why now?"

As he listened to her talk about Valeria's visit and reaction to seeing Quinn, he felt his anger rise.

West returned to his seat, drank more beer. Hell, the way this night was going, he might just need all six bottles, even though he seldom drank more than one a night, even on weekends.

Getting drunk meant lowering his guard, losing control.

Losing control meant something could slip past him, hurt those he loved.

He pushed back the beer. Water would suffice. "Valeria may mean well, but she's young and impulsive."

"She invited me to a family barbecue this Sunday. I told her no, but she was persistent." Quinn's gaze looked troubled. "Do you think it's safe for me to go? Will you go with me?"

West's heart beat a little faster. Maybe he was a stranger to her, but she trusted him a little. "Of course. I'm sure Brayden will be there, and your cousin Finn, Valeria's brother."

They finished dinner and he insisted on cleaning up, telling her to go into the living room while he made her a cup of tea. She didn't protest, which indicated she was more exhausted than she'd let on.

When he brought out the tea, he sat next to her on the sofa. Quinn pushed over to the sofa's opposite side. West clenched his gut. Once, she would have all but been in his lap.

He patted Rex's head as the dog came over with a chew toy. West tossed it into the far corner. Rex grabbed it and lay on the floor, happily gnawing.

"This party, there will be a lot of police there?" Quinn asked.

"Maybe a few. Does that bother you?"

"No, it makes me feel safe." She looked at his belt. "Where's your gun?"

"Locked in the gun case in your nightstand drawer. You always insist I lock my sidearm when I come over."

"I don't like guns. But knowing you have one makes me feel safe."

She curled her feet underneath herself, a move he recognized as pure Quinn. Flexible. So flexible. He tried not to think of exactly how flexible she'd been when they'd been naked together...

"I know. I tried to take you to the range to shoot, but you nixed that idea." West's mouth quirked. "You told me if an intruder came in, you'd beat him over the head with your cast-iron skillet."

"What else do I like to do besides cooking? What did we enjoy together?"

The question startled him. He considered. "There's things I had yet to discover about you. But you and I enjoyed horseback riding, shopping at flea markets and yard sales, seeing movies. Mostly just talking and relaxing together."

And sex, yeah, the sex was amazing, but you won't even sit next to me, as if you're afraid of me. Damn, that hurts.

"Was I a chatterbox? The type to never stop talking? My cousin Valeria seems that way. She's sweet, but she goes on and on."

"Not you. You would have made a terrific bartender."

She gave him an incredulous look. "Because I know how to pour beer?"

West's chest tightened. "No. Because you know how to listen. You're good at it, Quinn. It's what drew me to you. Rarely do you find someone willing to truly pay attention and listen to you, someone who doesn't finish your sentences for you because they're eager to talk about their own troubles."

Fingers curled tightly around the teacup. Quinn stared into the cup as if trying to divine the future. Or the past. "I don't know if I can be that woman again. I don't know who I am, or what I am, West. All I know is someone nearly killed me. And I need to find myself again, before whoever did this finds me first."

Couldn't help it. He pushed over to where she sat, her lower lip wobbling tremulously. Brave Quinn, strong and stubborn.

"I won't let that happen, honey. I'm doing everything in my power, and so is the entire Red Ridge PD, to find the unsub."

He slid a hand around her neck, staring into eyes that once sparkled with life and now flashed with fear. Quinn glanced at him, nodded. Then she pulled away.

"I'm really tired. I'm going to bed now. I found a soft mattress topper downstairs, put it by the sofa for you."

Before vanishing into the hallway, she paused. "Thank you, West. I'm sorry. I know this must be hard on you."

"Good night," he said quietly, his body aching to hold her, his mind screaming with the need of it.

Discipline and focus had seen him through the FBI academy. He needed both now.

West waited until hearing her bedroom door close. Then he headed for the bathroom.

He brushed and flossed. West went to throw out the floss and saw a white stick in the trash. His heart skipped a beat as he fished it out.

Pregnancy test.

Staring at the test's single line, he sat on the tub's lip, his head spinning. Quinn must have thought herself pregnant and bought it before the bombing. But it was negative.

They'd been careless, yeah, but the timing had been on their side.

West replaced the test in the trash and splashed cold water on his face. Then he prepared for bed and collapsed onto the sofa, Rex on a pillow on the floor. Sleep proved elusive. For the longest time he remained awake, staring at the ceiling.

Wondering if he would ever get to share a bed again with Quinn Colton.

Chapter 11

The day after her release from the hospital, Quinn's appointment with the therapist made her more frustrated than ever.

Her doctor had suggested therapy would help recover her memory. Quinn would do anything to trigger recollections of the past.

Maybe her expectations were too high, and her patience too low, but she found the session boring. Especially the part where the doctor suggested she envision her past by creating a vision board.

"I want you to mentally relax, think of pictures you like and paste them on this board." Dr. Ross handed her a piece of twenty-by-thirty foam board. "Instead of creating a vision for what you wish for your future, this will help you to recover the past."

Studying the board, she saw only the bits and pieces from a childhood anyone would wish to forget. Oh, it wasn't a terrible life. Her mother loved her, but with the revolving door of stepfathers drifting in and out, Quinn distrusted the idea of marriage.

Her mother had relied on men to help pay the bills and support her emotionally and financially. Seeing how frail and dependent she was on men only strengthened Quinn's resolve for independence. Standards became higher, expectations, as well.

She was thirty years old, never married. Probably happy on her own. Successful. And then came West Brand.

What is it about West that I would agree to marriage? He must be quite special. Did we plan on a large wedding? Elopement? Her thoughts drifted to images of pink roses and white freesia bouquets, cute flower girls traipsing down a carpeted aisle, a tuxedo-clad West Brand waiting at the altar for her.

And Rusty, the father who others said was the town lowlife, escorting her down the aisle? The vision shattered like a hammer on glass.

"Quinn? Are you remembering something?" Dr. Ross asked.

She blinked, loath to share personal information. "I do remember my mother hating to be alone. She got married a lot."

And then their time was up. Quinn made an appointment for the following week, walked into the lobby to see Austin, who'd offered to accompany her, talking quietly on the phone. He hung up and smiled upon seeing her.

"Ready?"

Quinn got into the elevator and eyed his phone. "Who were you talking to?"

"Oh, a client. He needs soy fettucine Alfredo and roasted-vegetable salad for fifteen by this afternoon. He's hosting a small dinner for clients at his house."

Good. Work would help more than cutting and pasting pictures from a magazine of someone else's life.

Austin pointed at the board as they reached his car. "What's that?"

Outside, she took the board and tossed it into the back of Austin's little sedan. "It's a waste of time."

Her partner sighed. "Give it a chance, Quinn. You went through a lot and need rest."

What I need is action, not vision. "What other orders do we have for catering?"

Austin drove out of the parking lot, his hands tight on the wheel. "A few. Nothing I can't handle by myself."

She put a hand on his arm. "Hey, this is a partnership. I'll do my part. Tell me what you need and I'll prepare the meals."

"You couldn't even remember who I am, and you can recall how to make roasted vegetable salad?"

That hurt. Quinn fisted her hands. "Have you ever heard of a recipe book? I went through those books yesterday. I may have lost my memory, but I know I can cook, damn it."

He gave her a sideways glance. "Wow, I've never heard you swear before."

"Get used to it. I'm going to turn the air blue if you dare push me out of my kitchen."

A small smile touched his mouth. "Okay. When we get back, I'll get started on the veggies, and you boil the noodles."

That was more like it.

He stopped at a light and frowned. "You know, Quinn, maybe you should get out of town for a few days. Go someplace else."

Quinn closed her eyes, trying to relax. Everyone seemed to be hammering at her to rest, recover. As if she were bedridden.

Staying in bed terrified her. She had to keep moving, and scrape together the shards of her shattered life.

Quinn resolved to make the best meals ever this afternoon for the client's dinner party.

She had to make it right. Because if she failed at this, she wasn't sure anyone would trust her to resume being the old Quinn Colton again.

By the time the Colton barbecue arrived, Quinn felt no more confident than she had after talking to her cousin Valeria.

All week, she'd spent time in her shop, making meals for Austin to fill catering orders. The orders were small, consistent. Quinn suspected people in town felt sorry for her and wanted to help, and decided this was the best way.

Instead of bringing her food, they asked her to cook for them.

The cooking soothed her, and she fell into a familiar pattern. As she made the recipes, spurts of memories surfaced. Recollections of baking cookies with her mother, testing out her own creations.

As a child, she and her mother had spent most of their time together in the kitchen, especially after yet another stepfather decided to dump her mother and take off for parts unknown.

If that was her past, no wonder she had stayed single so long. It made Quinn curious about West Brand. Surely he had to be quite special for her to agree to marriage.

She'd met a few people, only when Austin was in the shop. Not knowing who to trust meant she took no chances.

But she did tell the security guards to leave. Quinn was tired of having them babysit her. She'd pointed out to her brothers and West that security cameras would pick up anything suspicious. Finally they agreed, as long as she always had someone with her in the store.

Today's party was a welcome break from the tension she'd felt all week, especially around West. He didn't share with her any information gathered in the investigation. West was tight-lipped. She wondered if it had to do with him investigating her, or his personality.

Quinn wasn't sure about this deal with the devil she'd made.

West sleeping in her apartment.

No memory of him. Only flashes of recollections from a childhood she suspected she didn't want to remember.

Today she needed fresh air. The barbecue sounded like a fine escape. And so did a drive.

Quinn searched the kitchen for the keys to the small sedan Finn had told her she owned. After opening and searching each drawer, frustration filled her.

A jingling caught her attention. She whirled to see West standing in the doorway, keys dangling from one finger.

"Looking for these?"

"Yes." She slammed the drawer shut. "I'm driving to the barbecue. Give them to me."

"No, you're not."

"I can drive."

"Doesn't matter." West pocketed the keys.

Quinn scowled. "I'm perfectly fine. The doctor released me."

"Medically, yes. You'll get your memory back." West leaned against the doorway, hooking his thumbs through the belt loops of his jeans. He looked more like a cowboy, ready to ride for miles, than a rugged FBI agent.

"Then why are you shadowing me? I don't need help."

"Sweetheart, get used to it. I'm not leaving your side." West came closer until he nearly backed her up to the wall. "Too many unknowns. The unsub might have been after Tia…"

"Of course he was. She's dead."

"We don't know that for certain yet. He could have targeted Tia. Or he could have planned to kill you. Or both of you. And you may be a witness, the only witness, to what happened before the explosion. Until you get your memory back, we can't be sure."

West caged her with his arms, leaning close. "I almost lost you, Quinn. Not going to take any chances or give the unsub a chance to finish what he started."

"My brothers—" she started.

"Are not responsible for you. Only one person is, and you're looking at him."

She stared up into his dark, intense gaze. The sad recollections of her broken, hard childhood indicated she'd had to learn to fend for herself from an early age. She'd been an independent soul, and didn't like handing control over to another person, especially with her personal life. But West had a good point. Frustrated as she was with the lack of memory of the blast, it was little compared to what could have happened. Still, she didn't like relying on someone else to care for her. "What gives you the right to tell me what I can or can't do in my own home?"

West touched her left hand, the finger missing a ring. "This. And this."

He lowered his head and kissed her. As kisses went, it was brief, but the passion behind it made her toes curl and her belly clench tight.

Before releasing her, he gave her bottom lip a brief nip, as if claiming her in a different manner than mere words. West pulled away, his gaze smoldering and dark. He rested his hands on her shoulders, his body not touching hers, but there was possessive intent in the manner in which he touched her.

Quinn licked her lips. "That's a mighty fine kiss, cowboy, but you'll have to do better than that. I need a reason why you're being so stubborn."

"I couldn't bear losing you to that bastard who nearly took you away from me, Quinn. And if that means tying you to my side while I do my job, I'll do it. Until we catch this son of a bitch, I won't stop worrying about you."

His quiet tone and the shadow of vulnerability in his expression assured Quinn of West's sincerity. He wasn't being a dominating he-man, but a man who wanted to keep her safe.

So she let him drive, Rex riding happily in the back seat of West's truck.

West pulled up to the ranch house, walked around his truck to let her out. Quinn carried a container of raspberry-cream cake. The ranching crowd here would be meat lovers, so she'd made a special sweet dessert. Rex bounded out of the back seat, barking happily.

The sharp blue skies and burning sunshine promised a hot day, broken by an occasional cooling breeze that tousled her curls and played with the hem of her floral dress. Gently sloping land stretched for endless miles. This was a good land, where one could raise cattle, horses and children in relative peace, far from the crime-ridden cities.

She'd been here before to mingle with her Colton cousins. Quinn didn't remember when or why, but her senses tingled.

She'd always been a city girl. Quinn halted a moment, stricken with another flash of memory. Mom, struggling to hold down a series of dead-end jobs, yet always managing to pay the bills. Quinn had learned to cook for herself at an early age when the double shifts meant Mom didn't get home until midnight.

West stopped as well, studying her. "What's wrong?"

Shoulders lifted. "Nothing. It's pretty here."

Loath to share the memory with West, because she didn't want him quizzing her, she pushed on. When they entered the backyard, Quinn jerked to an abrupt halt.

If this was a small gathering, she'd hate to think of what constituted a large one.

People crowded the yard in back of the big ranch house. Laughing, talking, gathered in small groups and larger clusters. Smells of grilling meat and barbecue sauce filled the air, mingling with the earthy scent of horses and hay. A gaunt woman in a black uniform and white apron lingered in the crowd, serving a silver tray of small canapés.

Her stomach lurched. If these people were family, she remembered none of them. And then a familiar face popped up in the crowd. Brayden, her brother.

Half brother. But at least there was one face she recognized.

As if sensing her anxiety, West stopped. Looked down at her. "You sure you're ready to go through with this?"

Maybe seeing some of these faces would help her remember. Quinn knew that hiding in her apartment wouldn't solve anything.

"Let's do it." Shoulders thrown back, she strode forward as Rex ran ahead of them.

A group of people talking saw them, turned. None of them looked unfriendly; rather, they were curious.

Still, it made her feel like a sideshow act. West gave them an abrupt nod and took her elbow, steering her past them.

"Let's say hello to your cousin Finn," he murmured.

Grateful for West, she walked over to a dark-haired,

good-looking man she did remember from the hospital. Finn Colton. Police chief. Her cousin.

Finn's face lit up upon seeing them.

"Brand," he greeted. He gave Quinn a warm peck on the cheek. "Glad you made it."

She thrust the dish at him. "Dessert. I found it among my recipes."

"Smells fantastic."

They followed him over to a canopy where a large table had been set with several tempting desserts. At the bar, Finn fetched a beer for West and a bottle of green tea for her.

Surprised at his thoughtfulness, she thanked him. "How did you know?"

His look was grave. "Everyone knows you're a green tea drinker, Quinn. You got Valeria started on the kick and a few others, as well."

News to her. She wondered if she would enjoy the same things she had before losing all sense of time and place.

Finn held a bottle of beer and gestured to the crowd with it. "The food will be ready in about thirty minutes. Let me introduce you around, Quinn. Some of the Colton clan you've met before."

Pasting a bright smile on her face, she followed him as he made introductions.

People greeted them, but they were strangers. They gave second looks at West, who stuck to her side.

Then friendly, pretty Valeria bounced over. She hugged Quinn. "Oh, I'm so glad you could come!"

Valeria studied West. "Hi. Nice to see you again."

He nodded at Valeria, and then his expression softened for Quinn. "I see Brayden over there. Have to talk shop about the training center for a few minutes. Will you be okay?"

"She'll be fine. I'll take care of her." Valeria made a shooing gesture. "Go talk your testosterone stuff."

Amused, Quinn let Valeria lead her over to a group of people whom she didn't know. Earlier, she'd decided to overcome her fear of meeting those she didn't remember by asking them questions about their interests. It was a good way to deflect attention from herself and to the person.

Everyone loved talking about themselves.

Everyone but West Brand.

These strangers were friendly and were talking about horses. Riding. She liked horses. Or did she?

At any rate, it was ordinary. Normal. Ranching talk. Holding her bottle of green tea, she smiled, nodded, listened. Asked questions when someone turned to her, as if wanting to know more about her.

Quinn didn't want to talk about herself. Not even about her business because she feared she lacked the right answers.

Valeria excused herself to attend to the barbecue. When the talk switched to cooking and more glances flicked to her, she scanned the crowd for an escape. *Please don't ask me about my bestselling recipe for vegan or something else you liked. I have no clue. Right now I'm lucky I remembered to make dessert.*

Smile and nod. She could do that much. But every few minutes, when it felt as if her face would crack, she scanned the crowd for West, needing reassurance. As long as his tall, muscled form was nearby, she felt confident enough in this first public outing since the explosion.

And then suddenly, she could not find him.

West's specialty as an FBI wasn't only investigating bomb sites with his canine partner, but good old-fashioned police work.

Most people, he'd learned, never truly listened to what someone else said. While the other person talked, they were already forming in their head a response. Or even interrupting.

Today at the barbecue, he had a perfect opportunity to listen to Shane, Brayden and Finn, his three targets on the Red Ridge police force. His FBI boss, Mike, felt certain the Coltons knew something about where Demi was, and were covering up the information to protect her.

Much as he hated leaving Quinn alone, he had his duties. Here in the informal atmosphere of food, family and fresh air, he brought up the subject.

One or two beers also helped to loosen tongues. West sipped his as he stood in a semicircle with the three Coltons near the fence.

He mentioned something about the Groom Killer going quiet since the bombing. That led to talk about the killer, and the victims. Then West focused on the Colton most likely to defend Demi. In the locker room recently, Brayden had muttered his sister was innocent and being framed.

Of all the Colton siblings, Brayden was the only one who believed in Demi's innocence. "Do you think Demi is guilty?" he asked Brayden.

That was all it took. He shut up, and the three Coltons began to discuss the case. West said nothing, but watched their faces. Shane had received a text message a couple of months ago from Demi. He wished he knew her whereabouts.

"She's alone with a baby. She can't take care of a newborn on the run," Shane muttered. "I wish she'd turn herself in, and we could help her."

"She didn't do it. Demi's too smart for that," Brayden countered.

West gestured with his beer. "What do you think, Chief?"

Finn Colton gazed into the distance, his expression thoughtful. "Demi's smart. I don't know if she did it. We can only discern that once she's found and questioned. At this point, I want this case solved. We have too much to lose."

"More grooms," Shane cut in.

"Don't forget the funding for the center," Brayden added.

West sipped his beer. The chief was proud of the K-9 training center and the team. He needed Fenwick Colton's funding to keep the unit operational.

The trio kept talking about the Groom Killer, then talk switched to the recent bombing and Quinn. He made noncommittal answers when they questioned him about Quinn's recovery.

Doubts filled him. Mike might suspect the Coltons of harboring information, but the more time he spent with them, the less he believed his boss's assertions.

He mulled the information over in his head. Carson and Danica Gage had believed Demi killed their brother, Bo, the first victim, and the other grooms—until they themselves had gotten romantically involved with Coltons who professed Demi's innocence. Maybe deep down, though, the Gages still believed Demi had murdered their brother.

Mike suspected the Coltons were withholding information because they were family and evidence pointed to Demi as the suspect.

Could the FBI have been dragged into an old family feud, with the Gage family pointing fingers at the Coltons because of past grievances? Mike was smarter than that, but he knew his boss's ruthless abilities. Mike was as zealous as West when it came to delivering justice.

But he'd been hanging with the Coltons for barely a month, and saw no justification for Mike's beliefs.

The main reasons?

The Coltons might have a famous feud with the Gage family, but they were dedicated to the job. Single-minded— a trait he shared with them.

And all three—Finn, Shane and Brayden—had steady female companions of their own, even if they weren't obvious about it. He'd seen Shane around Danica Gage.

He saw the way Finn Colton gazed at Darby Gage when they'd passed each other on the street.

They hadn't said anything, but West would bet his shield that the men were damn serious about those women. Even if they tried to keep those relationships secret.

Serious enough to marry.

And no one dared to get married in this town until the Groom Killer was caught.

They wanted the Groom Killer caught.

Making a mental note to dig further, he walked with Brayden over to watch the horses in the pasture. Of all the Coltons, Brayden was the one who most believed in Demi's innocence.

Brayden was the one with the most to hide…

Quinn tried not to panic. West was someplace in the crowd. He wouldn't abandon her. Surely he had a good reason to walk out of view.

She needed a respite. Some place to sit, relax and decompress because she felt as if she were swimming through a vat of Jell-O.

A dark-haired man turned, saw her, his hard gaze fixed to her. Smoke wreathed his head from the cigar dangling from his thin lips.

That look…cold as ice…

Smoke.

Quinn froze. An enormous buzzing seared her ears, as if the air compressed and the world went dark. The green tea bottle spilled from her hand, crashing onto the patio.

In the distance a locomotive wailed, the eerie blast of horn echoing across the rolling plains. It sounded like a cry.

A scream for help from a woman.

"I remember…" Quinn gasped.

A man's face, a flash of dark hair, but that expression. Cruel, ruthless. She vowed she'd never forget it.

And she had not. Because it came back to her like a jolt of electricity.

People crowded around her, asking questions, but their voices became a jumbled buzz of sound. West. She needed West. Where was he? Frantic, she whipped her head around, the people pressing closer, suffocating her…

Quinn fumbled for her cell phone. Fingers shaking, she pressed the speed dial for his number, the number he'd urged her to call if she got scared.

West spotted her. His expression dropped. He raced to her side. "Back off. Everyone get back," he commanded in his strong, authoritative voice.

The crush of people eased a little and she could breathe. West gently gripped her shoulders.

"Quinn, honey, what is it?"

"That man, that man… I know. I remember." Throat dry, she could barely form the words. "I remember what happened right before the bomb went off."

West went still. Then he scanned the crowd. "Is he here?"

She looked around. The dark-haired man with the hard eyes had drawn closer, but his chin was all wrong and his hairline receding, unlike the man she'd seen before the explosion. He looked the ruthless type, but seeing him close made her realize the resemblance had been in his expression.

"No. I just…remembered."

"Quinn, this is imperative. Write down all the details you remember about the man, what you saw."

West guided her to a nearby picnic table. Valeria raced into the house, returned with a yellow legal pad and pen. Hand trembling, she penned the snatches of memory coming to her like a blinking light. That profile, the jeering smile that had looked as if he enjoyed inflicting pain, the cheap business suit.

Cheap because the cuffs came halfway down his hand. Ill fitted, not tailored as the one Noel Larson had worn. His hair inky black.

When she finished, her stomach knotted in tension. Finn Colton, sitting across from her, studied the list.

"We need to sit you down with the sketch artist. Because if this is what I suspect, you've just remembered the last person in Tia's office," Finn told her.

She looked at West, her rock of stability right now. "The last person? The one who set off the bomb?"

His jaw tensed beneath the slight beard stubble. "Yes. Tia's killer."

Chapter 12

The police station at Red Ridge felt impersonal, brisk, filled with efficiency. Yet it was quieter and less suffocating than the atmosphere at the Colton ranch.

Finn had sequestered her in a small conference room while he went to find the sketch artist. West accompanied him.

She was alone with her thoughts. Memories.

Heart racing, she closed her eyes, trying to recall every last detail of the killer's face, what he'd been doing the day her world blew up and killed Tia. Smells helped, as well. She could recall the delicious fragrance of the casserole she'd held, hoping it would please Tia. Such a difficult client.

Always demanding.

Cigar smoke.

Snatches of argument... No, that was the previous day.

Tia, on the phone, yelling at someone as Quinn quietly walked into the office.

You'll never have it, Larson! And I'll never partner with you. That would be a marriage made in hell!

Hold on to the image of the killer...that smirk as if he owned the world, the cowlick in front sticking out, she reminded herself.

The door opened and Finn walked inside with West and a tall, lanky man bearing an artist's pad. The lanky man introduced himself as Derek, the police sketch artist.

Quinn told West and Finn what she remembered of the conversation. She gave an anxious glance to the artist. "Are you certain this will work?"

He gave an encouraging smile. "I'm going to ask a series of questions, and you answer them as best as you can."

West sat at her side, holding her hand. His palm was warm, strong and comforting as she haltingly explained the man's features. Round chin. Thin mouth, smirking. That cowlick.

"I remember the hair because of mine." Quinn pointed to her curls. "It looked like he'd had a bad hair day."

During the process, her brothers Shane and Brayden walked in. She barely noticed them, for all her concentration centered on the memory regained.

Thirty minutes later, a stranger stared at her from the sketch pad.

"I've never seen him before the bombing, not that I remember and by now I would remember him," Quinn told him. "But that's the man who was there in Tia's office before the bomb went off."

"I have no idea who he is." Finn glanced at West. "Do you?"

"No. I'll send this through the facial recognition database, see if we get a hit," West said. "Then once the DNA analysis is complete, we'll run it through CODIS."

"What's CODIS?" she asked.

"The FBI's DNA database for violent offenders." West's expression tightened. "We could be looking at someone with no priors."

Finn nodded. "Which will make him harder to ID. I'll bet he's not local. I'll make a copy, get this on the wire."

"I'll show it around to my contacts," Shane offered, following him out.

Derek went with them, leaving her with Brayden and West.

West's expression darkened. "He's probably connected some way to the Larson brothers. My gut tells me they had something to do with Tia's death."

"Probably," Brayden agreed. "At least this is something that can't be pinned on Demi. She didn't do this."

Tension curled in her stomach as West's expression narrowed. She didn't know what Demi was capable of, but everyone seemed to blame her for everything.

"How do you know, Brayden?" West asked.

"My sister doesn't know anything about making bombs," Brayden shot back.

"Demi's far from innocent. Until she's found, and those hiding her are found, Quinn's not safe." West leaned on the table. "Do you know where she is?"

Brayden scowled. "Of course not!"

"Really?"

"Are you calling me a liar, Brand?"

"Do you have something to lie about, Colton?" West challenged.

He locked gazes with Brayden. Neither man backed down.

Quinn threw up her arms. "Enough! Can we end this? I'm really tired and I want to go home."

Brayden looked apologetic, but West did not. He looked intense. Focused. Driven.

Which made her wonder… Why was West Brand really in Red Ridge? To help the department by filling in for the injured Dean Landon?

Or was he hiding a secret of his own?

The whole experience at the police station left her shaky. Quinn fought to keep her hands from trembling as West drove her home.

"Why did you say that about my sister, Demi?" she asked him.

Knuckles white on the steering wheel, West stared at the road. "Because your sister could not only be the Groom Killer, but she might have targeted you, Quinn. If she found out about our engagement, she may have wanted you dead, as well."

"That's ridiculous. If she is killing grooms, she'd be after you, not me."

"Unless she changed her methodology, and her motivations changed, as well. Her only sister, getting married, while Demi's own engagement was broken, the man she loved jilting her to marry another. Jealousy is a strong motivation."

"You said no one knew we were engaged."

West reached over, picked up her hand and gently squeezed it. "Austin figured out we're engaged. That means others can, sooner or later. People have a habit around here of finding out secrets, much as they have a habit of keeping them."

"Do you think Brayden is keeping one? Is that why you jumped all over him?"

West dropped her hand, his jaw tensing. "He could be.

And I didn't jump all over him, Quinn. It's called questioning. Don't worry about it."

No, she had more than her brother's secrets to concern her. West's secrets were more bothersome.

"Aren't you supposed to be working with him and the others on the squad? Why are you antagonizing him? He wouldn't hide anything to do with Demi."

"Oh? She's his sister. He might want to protect her."

"And she's my sister, as well. Maybe you don't believe me, either." Quinn watched his face. "Or maybe you think I know something, or did know, before the explosion. Do you?"

West said nothing.

Silence, when she needed answers. *I'm not giving up.* "West, do you think I know something?"

A quick, sideways glance. "Not now, Quinn."

Some answer. Ambiguous. "Not now" meaning he wanted to drop the conversation? Or "not now" meaning he didn't think she knew anything now because she'd lost her memory?

Too exhausted and mentally drained, she dropped the topic and they rode in silence the rest of the way.

He escorted her up the stairs to her apartment. Giving her the usual grave look, he made a cup of tea and set it on the kitchen table. Rex gulped down water from the bowl she'd set for him in the corner, then sat, panting.

She fetched him a dog biscuit. He ate it in one gulp and then pushed his cold, wet nose against her leg. Tears burned in the back of her throat. Dogs were so loyal and good. They weren't suspicious and didn't have ulterior motives.

People, such as the man whom she'd identified to the police sketch artist, were not good.

West seemed like one of the good guys. He'd demonstrated concern the entire time since she'd been awake. And yet the cold, calculating way he'd interrogated her brother at the station indicated West Brand wasn't all he seemed. And he'd failed to answer her question.

If only he hadn't made that phone call in her hospital room! Better to be safe and wary of him, than caught off guard like before.

West rubbed a hand over the slight bristles on his high cheekbones.

"I have to get back to work and I'll be working late now that we have a suspect. Are you certain you'll be all right on your own?"

Quinn stirred the tea with a desultory gesture. "I'm fine. Go. Go find the bastard who did this. The sooner you catch him, the safer I am."

He bent his head, gave her a quick, smooth kiss on the cheek. "Wish I could leave Rex here, but we have to get to the training center. Don't leave the apartment unless you take someone with you. Stay here, watch those movies you love. I'll try to make it back around midnight."

With a last look around the kitchen, he left.

Quinn sipped her tea. Hard to watch movies when she didn't remember what she enjoyed.

Taking a nap might help.

She fell asleep as soon as her head hit the pillow. Dreams danced in her head, a cruel-faced, dark-haired man turning as he bent over Tia.

"You're next," he whispered.

She awoke in a start. Sweat dampened the mattress beneath her. Quinn released the fistful of sheet she'd grabbed in her sleep.

Her nostrils twitched as she smelled peppermint, sharp and sweet, as if someone munched on strong breath mints. Odd.

And then she heard it.

A slight, but audible cough, coming from inside her closet. Bone-chilling fear curdled in her stomach. Quinn gripped the sheets tighter.

Someone was in her closet. Hiding. Watching her through the slats as she slept...

Waiting to pounce on her.

Don't be a sissy. There's nothing there. Remember West's security cameras? No one can break inside, not without the security cameras recording it.

Still, she wondered if she had imagined that cough. Was her mind that muzzy still?

Only one way to find out. Quinn opened the door.

Nothing.

With a shaky laugh, she pushed the curls out of her face. Now she was imagining monsters hiding in her closet. What was next, checking under the bed?

She padded into the kitchen for another cup of tea. Hunger grumbled in her stomach, reminding her she'd skipped lunch at the barbecue.

After heating and eating leftover pasta, she felt restless again. Caged. The killer was out there, and no one had an idea who it was. But her brother and West agreed on one thing. The man would be gone by now, knowing police were searching for him.

It had been a long day. Suddenly she felt an urgent need to get out, get free, explore. There was a cozy, cute-looking bar she'd noticed earlier. It looked safe and friendly, a neighborhood bar where one could grab a sandwich and a beer. Nothing pretentious.

Surely West couldn't force her to stay here all day and night while he worked. She wasn't a child.

Walking over to the window, she looked down at Main

Street. A throng of pedestrians hurried along the sidewalk. So normal. Ordinary.

Safe.

Now that flashes of her memory had returned, she needed to be around other people, hear the laughter of good times, the animated chatter of interesting conversation. Find out what happened to this town.

Find out what happened to her sister, Demi.

And in doing so, find out where she stood in the midst of it. Answers wouldn't come knocking at her door.

Quinn looked through the closet, found a cute coral-pink sweater with glass beads and slid it on.

After grabbing her keys and a purse with some money, Quinn checked her appearance in the hallway mirror. Eyes too big for her face, a few cuts and big purple bruises on her cheek and neck.

I look like I've been in a bar fight.

She found makeup in the bathroom, touched up the bruises, lessening their impact. West liked her without cosmetics. He wasn't here.

Well, it was dark. Maybe no one would notice. Then again, the entire town seemed to know what had happened to her, so what did it matter? She donned a lightweight jacket and took her keys and then locked the apartment.

West ordered her not to leave, but a walk in the fresh air would clear her head, maybe lift this horrid fog. It was barely dark, the streetlamps blazed and no one would dare stalk her in the busy downtown area.

After locking the downstairs shop door behind her, she emerged out onto the sidewalk. The night was cool, crisp air blowing from the west. Quinn jammed her hands into the pockets of her jacket, enjoying the feel of the breeze against her heated cheeks. Streetlights illuminated the sidewalk, circular pools of protection from the dark.

Red Ridge was a cozy small town where everyone knew each other. The cards and letters penned in crayon offering her good wishes and a speedy recovery had led her to believe the townspeople cared about what happened to her.

Maybe she didn't know her own history in Red Ridge, but the support she'd received while hospitalized showed her that she had a history. A good one.

Her short heels clicking on the sidewalk, she passed several storefronts, all dark now that night had fallen. Quinn hurried along. The streets were deserted, as if everyone had abandoned downtown when the lights came on. Only a group of people two blocks away were mingling in front of the bar she'd seen earlier.

As she started to walk faster, wishing her legs were longer and could eat up space like West's stride did, Quinn felt a prick of unease. Shadows dappled the sidewalks, and not even a car passed by on the street.

The bar seemed closer. She walked faster, but her body was still healing and felt sore, too sore to move quickly.

Footsteps echoed behind her. Quinn's heart galloped.

Probably nothing. Another pedestrian trying to get home, or out to dinner…

The steps came quicker. Harder. More forceful. Glancing over her shoulder, not stopping, she made a mental note of the person following.

A man, sticking to the shadows close to the shops, wearing a heavy coat and hat. Hard to make out his face. She drew in a lungful of air and stumbled.

The smells assaulted her memory. Cigar smoke wreathing a man's head as he smoked, his gaze hard in the dimly lit room…the office stank of it.

The smoker was Tia's killer.

And he was right behind her.

Panic iced her veins, but Quinn forced herself to keep

walking briskly. It could be an innocent man. But he followed her too closely.

An alleyway lurked to her right, shadowed and long. A perfect place to pull someone in for an attack.

I may be short, but I can pack a punch.

The memory burst back like a firecracker. She knew self-defense, knew how to free herself from danger.

Defending herself had caught West's attention. He'd always dismissed her as a frail, fragile female in need of protection.

The first time she'd thrown him to the ground had caught him off guard, sputtering in anger and surprise. Then he'd laughed.

And since, he'd taught her a few more moves certain to aid her in danger.

Krav Maga self-defense. It was all about energy, realizing how your attacker came at you. Just as she'd been taught to turn into a curve when her car swerved to one side, Quinn remembered to use her own energy against this assailant.

Just as she increased her pace, she felt him move.

He grabbed her mouth, and wrapped his fingers around her upper arm. The man began dragging her toward the alley.

"Don't scream," he muttered. "I'll kill you."

The hell with that. She had her left arm free and he couldn't use both arms to restrain her. *Use the attacker's energy. Step with him.*

Quinn curled her thumb tight to her right fist, knowing her left, weak wrist was almost useless. *Stab at the face as a distraction. Turn your body in the direction he's pulling you instead of fighting the force.*

She brought her right fist up, using her thumb like a

knife, and jabbed at her assailant's face. A howl of pain ensued and the arm left her mouth.

Quinn pulled free and ran, screaming and screaming. Not "Help," as her instincts urged, but "Fire!"

People were more likely to respond to a scream of fire than a cry for help.

The group chattering and laughing far down the street stopped, turned. Quinn ran toward them, zigging and zagging, screaming and screaming.

Winded, her side aching, her wrist throbbing from where she'd jerked it away from her attacker, she wheezed and bent over, too worn to go on. And then people were coming toward her, shouts of alarm and concern, and lights shining, blessed, strong lights cutting through the dark that covered men who grabbed women in the night and dragged them away to harm them.

Quinn sank to her knees, wrapping her arms around her stomach. "Call…9-1-1. I—I've been attacked."

A woman crouched down, rubbed her back. Questions asked. Was she hurt? Did she need an ambulance? But all Quinn could do was tremble and gulp down air, blessed air. That arm around her throat, the hand cutting off her scream, her flow of oxygen…

Someone helped her to stand and led her over to a park bench in front of a storefront. She collapsed onto the wood seat, moaning and rocking back and forth.

Was any place safe from her attacker? Who wanted her dead?

Someone must have seen, or heard, that she'd remembered elements of the person who'd blown up Tia. Someone clearly wanted to remain anonymous and saw Quinn as a threat.

A liability to be eliminated.

Wailing sirens cut through the air, lights flashing, making

her close her eyes and wish she were still back in her apartment, away from men who wanted to hurt her. The EMTs arrived, checked her over and took her pulse. Quinn waved them away. "I'm okay."

And then West was there, strong, capable West. He knelt down and looked at her, his expression taut with worry. Rex trotted up to her, licked her face.

Quinn fisted her hands to hide their shaking.

No matter what he thought of her role with her sister, West cared about her.

But he was FBI and he needed information, needed to know about her attacker. Quinn gripped his arm. "He was taller than me, about six inches."

West gestured to the detective hovering nearby, who started writing in his notebook.

"What else, Quinn? Did you see his face?" West asked.

"No, he grabbed me from behind. He wore boots, I think. The heels clicked on the pavement, but they were heavy, thudding like cowboy boots. Wool coat or something scratchy, I felt it against my neck and cheek. Cigar smoke. It smelled like burned coffee. Disgusting. I smelled it before he grabbed me. He choked me, dragged me off. I was so scared, but I remembered the moves you taught me…"

Babbling now, she talked too fast.

Gently, he cupped her face. "Quinn, honey, slow down. It's okay. You're safe now. You're safe."

Shaking, she fell into his arms. He held her tight, stroking her hair. "You're safe now," he repeated, and a hard note entered his voice. "That bastard is not getting to you again. I promise. No matter what it takes, you'll be safe."

She clung to him in sheer desperation. West promised to keep her safe from her attacker. But every day she felt herself slipping further away from the life she'd known and loved.

Every day, she walked closer to danger, toward a killer who would leave no witnesses behind this time.

Her life was eroding away before her eyes, and she didn't know how to stop it.

Chapter 13

Enough of this.

One attempt on Quinn's life was too many. And now with the attack, West felt certain Tia's killer would try again soon as she was alone.

Outside Finn Colton's office the following morning, West paced with restless energy. Right now her business partner was Quinn-sitting until West got home. He refused to take chances and leave her alone.

Taking Quinn away meant she'd be safe. He planned to stick to her constantly and take her to visit Pine Paradise. With Tia's death, the cabins were empty and the property in dispute with Tia's heirs.

If he took Quinn there, perhaps it would jar her into remembering.

The door opened and Finn Colton gestured. "Come in, Brand."

Once inside, Colton pointed to one of two chairs set before the desk. "Sit."

I'm not my dog. But he sat, hands folded on his lap, waiting. Watching.

What the hell did Colton know? Did Quinn and Demi's cousin, the police chief of Red Ridge, hide knowledge of Demi's whereabouts?

His boss, Mike, thought as much. The Coltons in town were thick, she'd told him. But after living in Red Ridge for more than a month, he knew better. Rusty Colton barely spoke to his offspring and Rusty was considered the low-life in town. Finn Colton might be related to Demi, but the man had honor.

He studied the desktop. Clean, neat, photos in frames. Not too many. Files piled to one side, pencil cup holding several pens and pencils. An American flag standing beside the credenza behind the desk.

Colton's office was functional, no real hint of the steely personality.

Colton might be his temporary boss, but when it came to Quinn's personal welfare, West had decided he was in charge. And he would not tolerate interference.

"I need three days off. I'm taking Quinn out of town." West tightened his jaw. "She's not safe here and unless she's with me 24/7, she's in danger. Whoever attacked her will try again, and this time, he won't stop until he finishes the job."

"Let me talk some sense into you." Colton began to walk around. Brand knew the maneuver, had done it several times himself.

Circled the subject, tossed him off guard, made him sweat, wonder what your next move was.

Moved so he couldn't read your expression. Power play.

Colton stopped. "Let's say you do take Quinn away to

protect her. In the meantime, you're not doing your job.
You're a top-notch field investigator, Brand. You came
highly recommended by your district supervisor. That
means for every day you have away from the crime scene,
away from the office, protecting my cousin, it's another
day the killer has to slip further away."

He'd already prepared for that question.

"Jogging her memory so Quinn remembers everything
is pertinent. She's our only witness. Last night's attack
caused her to remember the unsub smoked cigars that
smelled like burned coffee and spice. Details like that are
critical."

Finn said nothing, only kept pacing. Finally he stopped,
turned.

"I need to know exactly where you're headed. Name,
contact information."

Fair enough. "A friend owns a cabin in the canyon,
near Pine Paradise Cabins. Secluded, ingress and egress
limited from the main road. And there's an electric fence
around the property." West did not smile. "Problems with
poachers on the land."

Colton's mouth thinned. "This isn't a field trip merely
to hide Quinn. You're going to take a second look at Pine
Paradise while you're there. We already checked out the
property. You think it's worth a second look?"

"Yes. A much more thorough look." He watched his
boss, saw Colton mentally size up the idea.

"You don't have a search warrant. I could get you a
bench warrant, but there's no need." Colton considered.
"I'll talk to the attorney handling the estate, who gave us
the keys to the cabins, have it on the QT that you're headed
there and get you the keys."

The rigid tension gripping him eased a little. "Do any

of her relatives know why the sale to the Larson brothers went south?"

"They didn't even know Tia was selling the property. Tia had two brothers, both Realtors in Colorado. They'd planned to stay there for a week in September and do some fishing." Finn considered. "The property's been in the family for generations. They were shocked she even considered selling. Her grandfather left it to her in his will because she spent all her summers there growing up."

And yet Tia was willing to sell it for a fast buck. Tia kept secrets of her own, it seemed. "How well did the Larsons and Tia get along? Other than romantically?"

Finn walked over to the desk, leaned against it. "Not well. They were competitors in a sense. Maybe why Noel Larson started dating her, figured he'd marry the competition. But Tia was too smart for that. I didn't know her well, only her reputation. She was a shark."

A shark in a pool infested with bigger sharks.

The phone on the desk rang. Finn picked it up. "Send him in."

West raised his brows.

"I asked Shane Colton to join us." Finn folded his arms across his chest. "I've asked him to check deeper into Tia's history and talk with her clients and contacts. That angle you mentioned the other day about Pine Paradise is all we have to go on for motive right now."

Shane came in, sat in the chair near West. "I got more dirt on Tia Linwicki."

They waited.

"She wasn't selling Pine Paradise for two million," Shane told him. "She *wanted* to sell it for two million. The Larsons told her they'd give her three."

Stunned, West reeled back in his chair. "They offered more money than the asking price?"

"Too much. The land is valuable, but not that valuable. Cabins need updating, renovating." Shane drummed his fingers on the armrest.

West's mind clicked over the new facts. Too much money for a real estate transaction meant one thing. "The Larsons needed to dump cash and quick. Money laundering."

Shane and Finn exchanged glances. "Yeah," Shane said. "Except we can't prove it. They may have even wanted the place for cooking heroin. Cabins are off the beaten path, no one would investigate. They could renovate, say they were remodeling and close the place down for a long time."

"Or instead of cooking heroin, they could want to make bombs for another attack. It's secluded and remote, and no one would know. No nosy neighbors to make inquiries." West leaned back in his chair.

The tentacles of the investigation got longer. West thought in patterns, because human behavior could be quite predictable. An unsub's motivations, methodology tied to the victim of the crime not in straight lines. More like building blocks intersecting. And at the foundation was a crime organization run by twin brothers no one had managed to pin anything on.

Yet.

Finn frowned. "If something shady is going on at Pine Paradise, you shouldn't investigate on your own, Brand. I'll send backup with you."

"No. Too many people will jar Quinn." He gave his boss a level look. "I'm taking her to Pine Paradise to see if she can remember anything. Being in Red Ridge hasn't worked. Going back to a place she loved to stay may work."

"All right, but I don't feel comfortable about this. Don't take any chances." Finn frowned. "I've already lost one good man on this force to injury. I don't want to have to drag you home in a body bag."

"I'm not taking any chances with Quinn. Rex and I will check it out first before she gets near the property. And you have nothing to worry about. I'm the best. If there are explosives anywhere near Pine Paradise, Rex will find them."

Three days in a forest in a secluded cabin sounded like heaven to Quinn. After the latest attack, she didn't feel safe in her own apartment.

She'd kept checking the windows, the locks, and staring out to see who came close to her shop. Nerves shattered, she felt like a poster child for paranoia.

West was mainly silent on the long drive south. Quinn stared out the window, wondering when her memories would return. She'd lived in Red Ridge a long time, but nothing looked familiar.

She shot a quick glance over at the grim-faced West. "Where is your friend's cabin?"

"West of Rapid City. But I have another intention, Quinn. We're also visiting a place where you once stayed. In fact, Tia gave you a key to stay there when the cabin was vacant." West inclined his head to the cup holder, where a key rested. "I got a key from the lawyer in charge of the property. I'm hoping visiting it will trigger your memory."

Quinn tilted her head at him. "Is this a place where we once stayed together?"

He drew in a deep breath. "You mentioned it before the explosion. It was the most serene, peaceful feeling you had in a long time. It's a place where you can forget yourself, and all your troubles."

"Sounds like some place over the rainbow." She began humming a few bars, stopped. Quinn pressed her fingers to her right temple. "How can I remember a song from a movie I watched as a child, and I can't even recall my own brothers?"

"It'll come back to you. You had quite a nasty blow to the head, sweetheart." He slid his hand over to touch hers, but she pulled away.

"I'm sorry," she told him. "I just...can't."

West gave an abrupt nod. Quinn rubbed her hands together, wishing she didn't have to hurt him this way. She could only imagine what he must think—having a girlfriend/ fiancée who held no memory of being with him.

Now was a good time to ask, without her brothers hovering. "How long ago did we get engaged?"

"One day, before you..."

He fell silent, as if talking about the explosion proved too painful.

A secret engagement that was practically nonexistent. She didn't know West Brand, didn't remember anything about him. But those flashes of memory—teasing and seductive— of having amazing sex...

Surely that was West. Because Quinn felt certain she was a one-relationship kind of woman.

Maybe if she got this taciturn man to talk about his past, his childhood, it would trigger a memory of their own relationship. Because surely West Brand had a better childhood than the one she recalled—a flurry of stepfathers blowing in and out of her life, her mother desperately searching for the one man who would make her happy, fulfill all her dreams.

Quinn was pretty sure that a man wasn't the answer to fulfilling dreams. She remembered even telling her mother that at one point. Not that her mother had listened. A flash of memory surfaced—a pretty, but faded brunette woman looking at her with hurt eyes, and then shrugging as she applied lipstick, picked up a short jacket and told her to get into bed by nine o'clock.

A lump formed in her throat. There seemed to be more of those memories, along with the smell of cheap beer and wine and cigarettes, than there were of her mother tucking her in at night, reading to her, hanging her childish artwork on the refrigerator.

"What was your childhood like? Do you have sisters and brothers? Are your parents still together?"

West stiffened. Every muscle in his body seemed to turn to stone. His grip on the steering wheel became white-knuckle.

"Why are you asking?"

His voice was low and gravelly, carrying a hint of anger.

Quinn tensed, as well. "I thought…it was something we'd talked about before."

He turned the truck left onto a dirt road, stopped and shifted the gears so the truck was in four-wheel drive. One hand on the wheel, West turned toward her.

"We didn't. And I never talk about my family. They're dead. An accident."

Quinn felt a surge of horror and pity. This time she was the one putting her hand over his. "I'm sorry for asking. I didn't know… I don't remember."

He gave a curt nod. "No problem."

As they climbed upward, she struggled to come up with conversation that wouldn't involve families, friends or delicate subjects. It was so hard. Quinn felt as if she treaded on emotional land mines—his and hers.

She gazed out the window. Weather and scenery seemed safe enough. "It's very pretty here," she noted, looking at the sweep of tall pines, white birch and cottonwood trees.

Odd how she could remember the types of trees, but couldn't remember her own fiancé.

West nodded. "I used to come out here sometimes, relax and do some fly-fishing."

Another memory struck her—sitting in flannel polka-dot pajamas before a stone fireplace, the flames flickering, as she dealt a deck of cards out on the floor. There was a redhead there, whose smile seemed strained.

"I have been in this area before," she murmured, closing her eyes. "Maybe a year ago."

When she opened her eyes, West parked the truck in a gravel recess between two pine trees. He shut off the engine. "Here we are."

Rex gave an approving bark from the back seat.

The pine-log cabin looked less rustic than she'd anticipated. Colorful pots of geraniums decorated a front porch, and pink and purple petunias filled a small planter set near the entrance. Inside, she examined the living room with its satellite television, comfortable sofa and chairs set before a rock fireplace, and the kitchen with a gas stove, refrigerator and microwave. There was a dining table for four, and the bathroom and bedroom looked remodeled.

As West dragged their suitcases into the cabin, she folded her arms. "This is how guys rough it?"

He grinned. "My friend's idea of roughing it includes heat and hockey games."

After they unpacked, they sat on the sofa, looking at the view from the floor-to-ceiling window. Rock canyon walls and pine trees surrounded them.

Rex nosed around the living room and jumped onto the sofa between them, wagging his tail.

"Off," Quinn ordered.

West shrugged. "My friend won't mind."

"I wasn't talking about the dog. I meant you, West."

For a moment, she feared he'd take her seriously. And

then he laughed, a deep sound that rumbled out of his chest. It sounded sexy and earthy and all natural.

"Did I used to make you do that before? Laugh?" she asked.

West studied her. "All the time. It's one of your charms."

His voice deepened. "It's why I fell in love with you, Quinn Colton. You make me laugh when there's too much damn sadness and suffering in my world."

For a long moment, he said nothing, only studied her with such intensity, her breath hitched. Quinn stared at the sensual curve of his lower lip, wondering what it felt like to kiss him. Do more than kiss him...

West Brand had strong, masculine features, a face that could crinkle with laughter one moment, and go dead serious the next. Penetrating dark eyes that seemed to sear through to her soul. He looked like the kind of man who would pull no stops to protect those under his care, a man who could be thoughtful and gentle with the woman he loved, but ruthless with those he deemed a threat to both family and country.

Perhaps it sounded old-fashioned, but she liked the idea of a man caring for her, a man who respected her and treated her with courtesy as an equal out of bed, but wasn't afraid to be dominant in it.

Quinn licked her mouth, feeling a flush heat her body.

Arousal rushed through her. Maybe she had no sense of the past, but the present looked like a mighty fine place to start something.

He drew in a shuddering breath. "Rex needs exercise after that long walk. Let's go into town for groceries, and then come back and hike before it gets dark."

This could be much tougher than he'd ever anticipated. Alone with Quinn in a cabin, no brothers to drop by, no business partner to dash upstairs and ask about catering orders.

No interruptions.

Nothing but privacy.

Every bone in his body ached to kiss her senseless, hold her tight and make love to her.

They drove back to town and bought groceries and provisions. After the truck was loaded, Quinn saw an arts and crafts shop. While she went inside, he ducked into a drugstore and bought a box of condoms. No way would he push her into sex, but if she was ready, he'd be ready, too.

Maybe a long, slow bout of lovemaking would trigger memories of him.

Back at the cabin, they put away the groceries. West fetched the gift he'd purchased for her before leaving Red Ridge.

Quinn studied it. "What is it?"

"You don't like guns. You never did want to learn to fire one, so I bought you a Taser."

They went outside.

"Next time someone attacks you, use this and it will give you time to get away." He showed her how to trigger the switch and then gave her the belt and holster he'd also purchased. "Especially when you're alone in the store, Quinn. You're too vulnerable there."

West watched her practice removing it from the holster for the next few minutes. Quinn handled the Taser well. She turned it over in her hands.

"You're really protective, Agent Brand."

West flashed a brief smile. He touched her cheek, longing to kiss her again. "Always."

They went for a walk on the path snaking through the woods. A few minutes later, they set out on a narrow trail cutting through the woods, up the mountain. Rex bounded ahead of them, sniffing out the rabbits and squirrels hiding in the undergrowth.

In worn jeans and a soft sweater, Quinn walked alongside him as they hiked the path. Birds chirped in the overhead trees, and he heard a faint rustle in the underbrush. West clasped her arm to halt her. A black snake slithered away.

"Oh, that's nothing." Quinn shrugged. "Bull snake. They get big, but they won't hurt you. Not like rattlers. My father taught me that."

"Rusty actually knows the difference between a bull snake and a rattler? I thought he had a hard time differentiating between light beer and regular."

Quinn laughed, her first real laugh in days. It felt good to hear it from her.

He lifted a branch out of her way. "It's good to hear you laugh again, sweetheart. I've missed that sound."

"I'll make a note to do it more often." She took his hand as he helped her climb over a fallen tree limb. Her palm was soft, smooth, and a shudder raced through him as he recalled the feel of her hands stroking his naked body...

Easy now.

He kept a close eye on Quinn as she climbed over rocks and used the stick to playfully poke at the brush.

"Careful, you'll upset the rattlesnakes."

She turned, her eyes wide. "You've seen them?"

West chuckled and she mock scowled, swatting him with the stick. "You're teasing me."

"They'll let you know when you get close."

"They rattle."

Quinn laughed. Man, he adored that sound of her low, sexy laugh, loved making her smile. His own smile dropped. He had a job to do—get her to remember anything and everything, especially about Demi.

"Do you remember that song?" he asked. "Our first dance?"

Confusion wrinkled her brow. "No. I'm sorry I don't. But I'd like to remember. Tell me."

His chest ached as he told her how he spotted her at the bar and asked her for a dance.

She'd told him she didn't dance and he'd replied that all she had to do was follow his lead.

The country-and-western band had struck up that song and they danced nice and slow. Quinn only stepped on his toes twice, and he'd been wearing boots. They fitted together just fine and he'd wanted to stay in her arms for much longer than the song. As it ended, Quinn had lifted her head to him and told him, *Hey, cowboy, don't think that just because we shared a dance that this means we're in love.*

He'd looked down at her and said, *I'll settle for a steak dinner, rare, without sprouts.*

She'd laughed. *You'd stand a better chance of me learning to salsa than cooking you something that moos, Agent Brand.*

From that moment on, she grabbed his heart and held on. Because Quinn Colton wasn't into playing games as some women did. She was open and honest, unwilling to change just to please a man. She was true to herself. After dating a series of women who were not, West found her deeply refreshing.

He told her this as they navigated the pathway winding up to a splendid view of the canyon cliffs. Quinn stopped and looked at him.

The little frown dented her brow. "You're good with animals. You treat them well and love them. I remember that now. I remember thinking that a man whom animals trusted was a man I could trust, as well."

Pleased she'd recalled even a sliver of a memory, West touched her arm. He craved the connection between them, needing it as much as he needed to find Demi Colton.

"You can trust me, sweetheart," he said in a low voice made husky by desire and sheer need. "I aim to keep you safe, and care for you the rest of your life."

But Quinn only looked away. She flicked a hand upward. "If there's a place up there with a bench, let's stop. I need to rest."

He didn't want her pushing herself. West struggled between the need to care for her and the urgent need to get her to remember every damn thing about what she'd seen before the world exploded and nearly took her with it.

Because if a killer stalked her, he had to know who it was. He couldn't keep an eye on her every waking moment.

At the plateau, there was a simple bench made from a log. Rex joined them as Quinn sat, her breath heaving in and out. West uncapped his water bottle and handed it to her.

He watched her drink, the little beads of sweat rolling down her temple.

Removing the collapsible cup from his jacket, he set it down and filled it for Rex, who gulped down the water.

"Feels like I haven't exercised like that in a long time. But it feels good to get outside, breathe in the fresh air again." Quinn peered at the cliffs. "So pretty up here. We're far away from Red Ridge."

"Town's that way. Up north." He felt an ache of regret. She didn't remember her little saying, either.

You're my West, she'd told him much later. *And my north, south and east.*

She was his entire world.

You have a job to do. Concentrate on finding out where Demi Colton is and what Quinn knows.

But he also needed his Quinn back, the woman who gave him slow, deep kisses with fire in her heart, the woman who made him feel like he was more than the job, and could do anything he wanted. West was beginning to tire of the Bureau. He enjoyed his job, and Mike was a damn good boss, but the politics had gotten to him. Being a canine officer limited his career choices in the Bureau.

West was good with dogs, and liked them more than people at times. Being a canine cop had saved his sanity during the times when he couldn't take the chatter and games people played. You could trust dogs. They were loyal and honest, letting you know what they wanted.

They harbored no secrets. Not like people. Quinn liked dogs for the same reasons.

Did she know where Demi hid?

West drank from the same bottle and then tucked it into his backpack. For a moment they sat in companionable silence, listening to the birds sing in the trees, the wind rustling through the pine boughs and the distant gurgle of water gushing far below in the canyon.

"North, south, east, west." She turned to him, a glimmer of something in her pretty eyes. Recognition at last? "You're my West."

Relief filled him. Finally. "You remember that."

Quinn's excitement died. "I remember that, but nothing else. Why can't I recall any time with you?"

Unable to help it, he slid close and put his arm around her. "I don't know."

But, hell, it was a start and he'd take it.

When she scrambled to her feet, ready to hike again, he was at her side. Quinn didn't object when he put a hand on her elbow to steady her as they climbed up the dirt trail. Switchbacks made the ascent easier, but he could tell she was tiring fast. So he turned around, and when she protested she could make it, insisted they could try again to-morrow.

He talked about the canyon, and how the Badlands got its name from the pioneers and Native Americans who forged lives in this land. "Weather here gets unpredictable, too. Temperatures drop into the forties in summer."

"Sounds divine after cooking all day. Sometimes I would get so hot I'd dream of the winter, and then when winter came, I'd be glad for the heat of the ovens." Quinn stopped on the trail, her stick held aloft. "I do love to cook. I think I started my own business because my mother left me on my own a lot, and I had to fend for myself. She was always searching for a new guy to marry. My mother... She didn't like being single."

Something new he didn't know about his Quinn, now that memories of her childhood surged. West ached for the little girl whose mother was too busy to care for her, more concerned with her own personal life than her daughter.

"Did your mom like to cook?" Quinn asked.

An innocent question, one that caused the familiar guilt to surface. But if talking about his childhood helped Quinn recover her memory, he'd go down that painful path.

"My father said my mother could burn water." He smiled, the memory not quite so painful now. "When they got married, he did all the cooking. Later, when the job meant he'd work long hours, she took classes so she could have a hot meal waiting for him when he got home. Mom taught me to cook, and my sisters. She said a man should learn to make meals and not rely on a woman to do it for him. And then Dad would wink at me and say that he didn't marry Mom for her talent in the kitchen, and he could still turn out a better rump roast than she did."

Quinn laughed. "Your parents sound wonderful." Her expression turned sad. "I'm sorry you lost your family.

Even though it feels like I've lost mine as well because I can't remember them, I can't imagine how horrible it is to lose all of them in an accident."

An accident. West rubbed his chest, remembering the flames, the sirens, the horrified looks of neighbors as his home, his family and his life went up in flames.

"Let's get back. Going to be dark soon." He stood, offered his hand, which she took, giving him a puzzled glance.

Damn, he was not ready to discuss his own past, his life. Too busy trying to live in the present, trying to reconcile himself with the only woman he vowed to love for the rest of his life.

A woman who had no memory of him, but trusted him enough to come here alone. Her level of trust astounded him. Quinn's values hadn't changed. She'd always been optimistic, determined to see the best in everyone.

Even a cynical FBI agent who shied away from most people, devoting himself to his work and his canine.

West Brand was a total enigma. She'd tried to coax out details of his past, his childhood, and he'd shut down like a machine.

Maybe he didn't have a nice childhood and didn't want to discuss it. But it couldn't have been as hectic and unsettled as hers, always moving from one home to another, a nomadic lifestyle she detested.

Moving until she'd gone off on her own, determined to settle in one place, find one special man to love and marry.

She'd agreed to settle down with West before the explosion. Maybe it was time to see what kind of man he really was.

Clearing her throat, she pointed at his cell. "Does that even work out here?"

West thumbed through his phone, put it away. "Sometimes. More of a habit than anything."

"Good. No more phone time. I need your help." Quinn looked at the oven. "Special Agent Brand, I'm going to make you a special dinner."

West's nose wrinkled. "Tofu again?"

She grinned. "No. I'm setting aside my usual vegetarian preferences for tonight. But I'll need you to make another trip into the grocery store. And I do hope you like bacon."

His dark eyes lit up. "Real bacon? Not that fake stuff?"

"Real bacon." She handed him a list. "Be prepared to exercise tomorrow 'cause, honey, you won't want to stop eating."

While he took the truck into town, she took her journal from the suitcase and began jotting notes. Bits of memory, slices of childhood.

Nothing from the present.

Now was not the time to recall her attacker's hot breath on her neck, the hissing words he spat at her, the ill-concealed fury in his rough hand as he clapped it over her mouth...

As if sensing her distress, Rex pushed his nose into her lap. Quinn patted his head. The dog proved himself an excellent caretaker and guardian. Almost as nurturing as West himself.

Needing to stay busy, she started gathering the pots, pans and mixing bowls she needed for dinner. The cabin was surprisingly stocked, but West had mentioned his friend rented it out sometimes during the summer to vacationing families.

By the time West returned, her aplomb had, as well. Rex greeted him at the screen door with a happy woof and wagging tail.

West unpacked the bag, set down the bacon, spices and

okra, and put the chicken in the refrigerator. "Can't I get some idea of what you're making?"

"Creole chicken." Quinn pointed to a handwritten recipe. "My special mixture I made when I was a teen."

"Can I help?"

She liked this about him. He didn't nose around the kitchen, like Rex was doing, but offered. "Start slicing the okra after you wash it. And then get a cookie sheet. I bake my okra. Makes it less gooey."

Soon they stood side by side in the kitchen, working in a comfortable rhythm as bacon sizzled in the big cast-iron skillet on the stove. She washed and cut the chicken into smaller slices, dried them with a paper towel and rubbed the garlic clove onto the skin.

Cooking soothed her, and she needed something familiar after being alone in this big cabin with West. No need to instruct him either, for he was turning the bacon, making sure it didn't burn.

Next, he finished slicing the okra. She told him to set it on the cookie sheet, sprinkle it with salt and pepper, and add a little olive oil.

After he did, West slid it into the oven. He watched her work, his gaze thoughtful. "You never did tell me when and why you fell into catering."

Funny, that was a memory she did recall.

"I started cooking to nurture my mother." Quinn crumbled the bacon and added it to the chicken, tomatoes and Tabasco. She sprinkled in parsley. "I remember parts of my childhood. She worked hard and came home so exhausted. Food was my outlet, my way of telling her I cared. She'd sit, eat a few bites, and her whole face would light up. That meant the world to me."

"You put your love, your caring, into your creations."

West slid his arms around her midsection. Quinn stiffened but did not pull away.

She kept working. "Those were the good times, in between all the steps."

West kissed the top of her head. "Steps?"

"Stepfathers. One after another. Mom was a single mother, and she wanted to settle, find a good man to care for her, and me. It never worked out. So I kept cooking. Each time I heard her fighting with a new step downstairs, I'd climb out of bed, scribble in my journal. Not my emotions, but recipes. Ways to make a new dish fun, exciting. I'd close my eyes and remember the aroma of freshly roasted peppers or the fragrance of blueberries bubbling in a pie. Hear the sizzle of bacon-wrapped asparagus. It was my way of self-soothing."

"Most kids that age turn to alcohol, drugs or worse," he murmured.

"I had enough of that with my father, seeing how people regarded him. I needed something more, something that I could claim myself. Cooking taught me patience. You can't be in a hurry if you want to create something wonderful for someone you care about."

When dinner was ready, they set the table together. West fed Rex and then sat at the table, doling out a portion of chicken for her, and helped himself to a larger one.

When he tasted it, his dark eyes sparkled. "Wow. This is really tasty." He chewed some more, looked hopeful. "Can we make another recipe like this tomorrow night?"

Quinn laughed. "Why do I get the feeling you don't like what I usually make for customers?"

"I'm a guy. Meat and potatoes. He-man chow." West winked at her.

She found him utterly charming. *No wonder I fell in love with you. I wish I could remember that.*

"Maybe I'll let you cook tomorrow night. All those he-man genes must mean you carry the dominant Grill Man gene, as well."

A quick, knowing grin. "There is a nice gas grill out back. I bought some ribs, and the sauce I make will turn you back into a carnivore for good."

Quinn forked another piece of chicken. "You can try."

She needed to know more about their life, their relationship, before the explosion. "Did we set a wedding date yet?"

West's dark gaze fell on her bare left hand. "We didn't plan yet because of the Groom Killer and we'd only just become engaged. We had agreed to keep our relationship secret."

"Too bad. No wedding cake talk, flowers, dresses. That romantic stuff brides love." Quinn fluttered her lashes and heaved an exaggerated sigh.

But instead of laughing, he looked solemn. "If it made you happy, Quinn, I'd have invited the whole damn town. All that mattered to me, still does, is making you happy."

Such devotional talk warmed her, and made her uncomfortable because she couldn't demonstrate the same to him. "Why did you ask me out in the first place?"

Maybe a memory of their dating would surface. She could hope.

"Your personality and being genuine. You say what's on your mind and what you want, instead of what you think I want. You're not ostentatious. You care more about what's inside a person than the outer shell. It's one trait that attracted me to you."

Such quiet admiration in his voice. "I must have some negative traits that you dislike. No woman can live on a pedestal."

West speared a forkful of chicken, lifted it to regard it

thoughtfully. "Your vegan cooking. But after this, wow, I may have to put you back on your pedestal."

She laughed.

They talked about cooking for a while. West made a gesture with his fork and she saw the unmistakable sign of scar tissue. Nasty burn. She had a few minor ones on her right arm, but nothing like his.

"How did you get that?" She pointed to his right hand. "Was that something that happened while we dated?"

She doubted it. But maybe he'd open up about his family.

West barely glanced down. "It was a long time ago, when I was a teenager. Say, this is really good with the flavoring. Not too spicy, but tasty. Did you have other recipes with Tabasco?"

So it was cooking talk. Safer, not the morass of the past. Quinn let it slide and told him about the composition book and the recipes she'd collected.

He sipped the water they'd drawn straight from the tap. Cold, refreshing. Nothing bottled here. "Tomorrow, we'll go fishing. Before we leave, I'm taking you to Pine Paradise, the vacation spot you once stayed at with your sister."

A cold shiver raced down her spine, not caused by the chilly breeze blowing in from the open living room windows. "Is it safe enough, after what happened to Tia?"

His gaze met hers. "I won't let anything happen to you, honey. That's a promise."

A promise he intended to keep.

Doubts had flickered on her face. West didn't know what hurt more, her failure to trust him fully, or the memories she'd kicked up with her questions about his childhood.

And his burned palm.

He'd hoped being alone out here would ease her back

into the relationship they once shared. Instead, no memories surfaced. It was starting all over again, with Quinn getting to know him, except for his faint, deep fear that she'd change her mind.

Decide she didn't want to get married, decide she never wanted to see him again. West didn't want her to know about his family, the circumstances surrounding their deaths.

Not now. Those wounds ran too deep and Quinn had wounds of her own to heal.

And once she discovered his true assignment in Red Ridge?

Would she kick him to the curb, or forgive him for hiding the truth from her?

West felt confident the old Quinn would lean toward forgiveness. This Quinn, who hardly knew him, might not be so merciful.

After dinner, she headed into the bedroom. West washed up, thinking of this area, these woods that could hide Demi Colton herself.

He finished washing the dishes and went into the bedroom. West ground to a halt, seeing Quinn stretched out on the bed in her fleece pajamas.

She looked defenseless, young and vulnerable in her sleep. For a moment he felt tempted to bend over, kiss her awake. Like Prince Charming to Sleeping Beauty.

This was no fairy tale, and he needed to remember Quinn had a long recuperation period ahead of her. She required rest, not long, loving kisses.

No matter how passionate those kisses were.

West covered her with a thick wool blanket. Sighing, he headed into the living room to resign himself to another night sleeping on the sofa.

First, he went outside, taking Rex with him. The Lab

bounded off toward a tree. Bracing his hands on the porch railing, West relaxed. The woods always comforted him, solitude never bothered him. He preferred to be alone. Until Quinn had come along.

Sounds of the night greeted him, insects humming in the nearby field, an owl hooting close by…

Gunfire.

He listened.

Far off in the distance came another series of shots. Large caliber, perhaps a rifle. Gunfire in these mountains wasn't unusual. Probably some drunk taking potshots at a tree trunk.

But the gunfire came from the direction of Pine Paradise Cabins.

West circled around the cabin, checked the property. Phone lines and electrical were underground and protected by ridges of razor wire, and couldn't be easily cut by intruders. It was why he'd elected to stay here with Quinn. Security was tight.

Still, unease pricked his skin. West whistled for Rex, who came running, and then locked the dead bolt after they went inside. He shut and locked all the windows, checking the bolts.

Before getting ready for bed, he took his pistol, made sure it was loaded and set it on the end table by the sofa.

If someone found out Quinn was here and came after her, that bastard would have to go through him first.

Chapter 14

Sunshine dappled the canyon and the birds chirped over-head in outstretched pine boughs as he hiked with Quinn the next day. She'd protested that she needed exercise, so they set out to stretch their legs.

They took a break after two miles, resting on a boul-der alongside the path. West drank some water, wiped his mouth with the back of one hand. He nodded at her left wrist, which she rubbed.

The bandage had been removed a few days ago, but she kept touching it, as if the sprain still hurt.

"You okay?"

"Habit." Quinn dangled her legs over the boulder, drank some water.

"Did Demi like hiking in the woods?" West touched her right wrist, feeling her pulse beat steady.

Quinn didn't take the bait. "How should I know? I told

you, I have a memory of barely knowing her. We weren't close."

Each question he asked about her sister met with a shrug or a change of subject.

They resumed hiking again, until reaching a bluff overlooking the canyon below. He sat on the park bench, patted the space beside him. Quinn joined him, sighing with pleasure.

"So lovely. Peaceful. Places like this are great for getting away from work pressure. I bet your buddy knew this and that's why he bought it."

He grunted.

"What's one of the worst cases you've ever had?" She curled up her legs beneath her.

West didn't want to talk about it. Talking about his work had been off-limits for them both. Bringing home the ugliness of his job.

"They're all bad."

"How do you handle the pressure of seeing these things?" Quinn studied her injured wrist. "The cruelty that others inflict?"

"Takes time. I have an internal switch that I click on when I'm investigating."

"But there must have been one case that got to you."

West leaned against the bench.

"It was back East, before I moved to South Dakota. Someone had been cooking meth in an apartment complex and a mother and child were caught in the explosion and killed. I was assigned to search the third quadrant, where they lived. Rowan, the dog I had at the time, searched every inch of that bedroom and then we found it."

The doll had been burned in the explosion, but not destroyed. Blackened, partly melted face, one eye missing, the hair half turned to cinders. Scorch marks on the pink-

and-white dress. He'd held the doll in his gloved hands for a long time, thinking about the little girl who once held that doll. Once held tea parties and hugged her doll, and slept with her at night until a killer erased her off this planet.

The old scar tissue on his right hand ached like a phantom limb.

"This was somebody's life and they were just gone, in a matter of seconds. That one got to me."

"Why?"

Maybe it was time he told her. Reveal a secret. Get her to trust him again. West studied his burned hand. No. Not now.

"Because the doll reminded me of the innocence of childhood. My sisters… They died when they were barely out of childhood."

Quinn snuggled closer to him. "I keep feeling as if you're not leveling with me, West. So thank you for sharing that. It helps me to get to know you all over again."

He kissed the top of her head, inhaling the scent of apple shampoo. "I don't like bringing work home with me, Quinn. There's too much ugliness in the job. I switch it off when I get home."

They headed back to the cabin. Once there, Rex settled on the porch, lying down as he and Quinn took to the wicker love seat overlooking the canyon. For a few minutes they sat in companionable silence.

Finally she looked at him. "How can you do your job? I don't know how you manage to face all that, seeing the bodies, the crime scenes." She gave a delicate shiver.

"The others, you go into automatic. Recovering evidence, doing field investigations and you can't get personally involved because emotions prevent you from doing the job to the best of your ability."

"What happens when you do get personally involved? When it's someone you know, like me?"

He looked her square on. "That's the worst."

She took his hand, turning it over to examine the scar tissue. West stiffened but did not pull away.

"That's how you got this," she said softly. "It happened when they died. Talk to me, West. I loved you enough to agree to marry you. Can you love me enough, and trust me, to share with me what happened to your family?"

Ever since they'd met, West wanted to erase his past, start over again. Quinn would be his new beginning. But the explosion had sent them both hurling backward—Quinn because she lost her memory, and West because he'd nearly lost her.

"Not now. Someday, I promise."

She gave him a searching look. "Can you tell me how you got that scar?"

Once she'd asked him the same question and he'd clammed up. Now, here in the wildness and the cool air, he felt ready to share. Maybe because after seeing her lying so pale and still, he didn't want to spend another minute regretting his choices. If he expected Quinn to be honest with him as she regained all her memories, then he should reciprocate.

West fisted his hands and slowly forced his fingers to open. He stared at his hands. His mother used to say that he had beautiful hands, like those of a pianist. Or a surgeon. She'd wanted so much more for him, a profession where he wouldn't walk into danger every day and she'd have to wait up, wondering if he'd survived yet another day. Waiting for the terrible phone call that something happened, that the man you married was never coming home.

In the end, it wasn't his mother who got that phone call.

"Burn. I was trying to get into a house on fire, and burned it."

Quinn watched him, but he was no longer with her in the forest, in the clear, crisp South Dakota air. He was seventeen again, arrogant, confident and ready for a night of sex with his girlfriend.

A night he figured he'd always remember.

A night, as it turned out, he longed to forget.

She lifted his hand to her cheek, rubbing against it, cat-like. Soothing him. Suddenly he needed her in a way he never had. Telling her had ripped open his heart, and he bled all over again.

West curled his other arm around her waist and held her tight, resting his cheek upon her head. Inhaling the scent of her, all woman and apples. Quinn smelled like home, cider and pie, where smiling mothers greeted you at day's end with admonitions to wipe your feet, dinner would be ready soon, *Are you going out again tonight, West?*

He'd lost so damn much as a teenager. Turning to a career as an FBI agent fed him purpose, but he hadn't really lived.

Not until meeting Quinn, and daring to risk love again.

West lifted his head, took her face into his hands. "I love you, Quinn Colton. I think I loved you from the moment you sassed me back at your store. I don't know what will happen to us, to this…but I'm not letting go. Ever."

He lowered his mouth to hers and kissed her. West moved his lips over hers, teasing and light, letting her grow accustomed to him. Letting her set the pace. God, he did not want her scared, not of him. He wanted her willing, pliant and eager. To Quinn, he was all but a stranger.

To him, she was his heart, his reason for breathing and for life to be truly lived. Not living to work, to spend all his time hunting down killers and psychopaths who devalued human life. But to come home each night, knowing she was there, knowing her sparkling gaze would lift his weary spirits, her bubbling laughter would erase the horror of body parts and burns and death, and her warm, soft body would chase away the ice shield he threw up to keep others away.

Quinn Colton had penetrated his outer armor, and he'd let her. Only Quinn saw him as he really was—not a heroic FBI agent dedicated to the job and catching the bad guys, but a wounded teenager who fought each day to find renewed purpose in his own shattered life.

Quinn opened her mouth beneath his, darted her tongue out to lick him. She slid her arms around his neck, drawing him closer.

She looked up into his darkened gaze. West's breath hitched. "You sure about this?"

Quinn moved West's hand to cover her right breast. "Absolutely. Make love to me, West. I don't care about anything else right now."

Quinn had never felt more certain of anything in her life. She couldn't recall much about her time with West, but now that didn't matter. She only wanted to be with him. She didn't care that he was an FBI agent.

They were only a man and a woman, with this burning need between them.

He took her into the bedroom, snapped on a light. West tugged the shirt over his head and shed his boots and pants. Breath caught in her throat.

He looked up with a grin as he kicked his clothing aside. Dark hair covered his chest, stretching from nipple to nipple. Muscles layered his flat abdomen, his biceps. She glanced down at his genitals. His thick shaft was long and erect.

* * *

The thought of taking his hardness into her body filled her with anticipation. His muscles quivered beneath as she touched him, then he shuddered as she kissed his neck, tasting the salt of his skin.

Heat smoldered in his gaze. Never had anyone looked at her with such fire, such stark craving.

"Undress for me," he said softly.

Slowly she removed her clothes. Her body tingled with arousal, hungering for the contact between them. She was naked, shivering as cool air caressed her breasts.

"You're so beautiful."

Tremendous heat suffused her beneath the warmth of his gaze. Quinn arched beneath his touch as West thumbed her cresting nipples. When he bent his head and took one into his mouth, she clung to him, dizzy with need, her core growing wet and throbbing. He swirled his tongue over the taut peak, then suckled her. She was growing hotter now, a fire stoking inside her as the sweet tension braced her body.

They fell onto the bed, as he kept kissing her breasts. She whimpered, her hips rising and falling, driven by instincts of her own.

"Soon," he soothed her.

Gathering her close, he ran a hand over her silky skin, marveling at her softness. West kissed her deeply, his hand drifting over her belly, down to her feminine curls. It felt wonderful and erotic as he kissed her, sliding a finger across her wet cleft.

Quinn gripped his wide shoulders as he began playing with her. Somewhere in the back of her mind flickered a memory of moments like this—West bringing her to the brink, then easing her back and building the pleasure again. Whispering to her that she was his and his alone, and how very much he loved her and wanted to spend the rest of his life showing her exactly how much he cared about her.

His whispers forged a connection between them her mind could not fully recall, but her body did.

It was consuming, setting her on fire, her body crying out for something more. Quinn strained toward him as he teased and stroked, his hands sure and skillful. The ache between her legs intensified and she pumped her hips upward, desperate for something she didn't understand. Every stroke and whorl sucked air from her lungs until she gasped for breath, ready to burst out of her skin. Tension heightened, spiraling her upward and upward. And then the feeling between her legs exploded. Quinn screamed, crying out his name as she dug her nails into his wide shoulders.

Her eyes fluttered as she fell back to the bed, spent and dazed.

Finally, her breathing eased and she lifted her head. A hint of untamed danger lurked in his eyes. Then he gave a dangerous smile. "Again," West told her.

He dropped to his knees as she lay on the bed, breathing heavily. "Now, lie back and just relax."

West splayed her thighs wide-open with his hands. Then he put his mouth on her.

The first touch of his warm tongue made her jerk backward in delighted shock. He slid his tongue between her folds in slow, steady strokes.

The orgasm slammed into her, making her cry out. West stayed with her, kissing her gently. Then he looked up with a small smile, backhanding his mouth. He opened the drawer and withdrew the condoms he'd placed there and sheathed himself.

Quinn held out her arms to him.

"I want to take it slow," he whispered to her. "I need you to remember this, remember me."

He kissed her. Over and over, his tongue stroking her inside, imitating what was to come with his body. Nudging his hips between her legs, he braced himself on his hands.

"Look at me," he commanded.

Slowly he pushed slightly inside her. Trust filled her. She needed this tenderness and loving, but most of all, she needed him.

She needed to know that he loved her, and this was more than mere sex.

West laced his fingers through hers. Slowly he pushed into her. He pulled back and began to stroke inside her. His muscles contracted as he thrust, powerful shoulders flexing and back arching.

Quinn drew him close as they moved together. This was West, who said he cared for her, who wanted her to recover. She needed this, needed him.

The delicious friction was wonderful, the closeness of his body to hers, his tangy scent filling her nostrils. She pumped her hips, as he taught her the rhythm, feeling the silky slide of the hair on his legs. He began to move faster, his gaze holding hers.

She could fall in love with him all over again, and that memory would not flee. Emotions crowded her chest as she gripped his hard shoulders. It felt as if he locked her spirit in his.

His thrusts became more urgent. Close, so close… She writhed and reached for it, the tension growing until she felt ready to explode.

Screaming his name, she came again, squeezing him tightly as she arched nearly off the bed. He threw his head back with a hoarse shout. Collapsing atop her, he pillowed his head next to hers.

For a few minutes they lay tangled together, the sheets damp with perspiration, the cool night air sweeping over their bodies. Then he rolled off.

West gathered her close. It felt right, being with him like this. She wanted to be held by him all night, reassured that he did care.

He ran a hand through her tousled curls and smiled. West curled his big body next to her and draped a muscled arm about her waist.

She snuggled against him with a tiny sigh of pure contentment.

West's deep voice rumbled into her ear.

"You're mine, Quinn. And I always take care of my own."

Then his words became a haze as she drifted to sleep.

"I only wish you would remember how much I love you."

Chapter 15

She woke up the next morning to the sound of birds singing in the trees outside their window. A cool breeze blew into the bedroom, making her snuggle deeper under the covers. Beside her West still slept, one arm flung above his head.

He looked relaxed in sleep, as if it were the only time he truly could relax.

Well, maybe not. There was one activity guaranteed to make this man unwind. Quinn traced a line up the ridges of his rippling abdomen, circling one small brown nipple.

Yawning, he rolled over, faced her. His hand smoothed down her hair.

"No regrets," he murmured.

"None."

West found another condom, put it on and kissed her neck. He rolled atop her and they began the rhythm she recognized. Slow and deep, as if they had all the time in the world. She moved with him, smooth as water, and stared up into his face. Fierce passion filled his dark eyes, but he smiled down at her.

Maybe she had no memory of their romance, their engagement, but her heart assured her that this man was hers, and she belonged to him. He would never do anything to hurt her, and she could trust him. Quinn wrapped her legs around his hips and urged him to go faster.

His pace increased and she met it as an equal. The feeling blossomed in her loins and they came together in a shattering climax, West groaning her name as she hugged him tightly to her.

They dozed off, drowsing in each other's arms. And then West sat up, pushing a hand through his hair.

"Breakfast, and then I'm taking you on that fishing expedition I promised, before we go to Pine Paradise and then back to town."

Her nose wrinkled. "Do you mind cleaning the fish I catch?"

The sexy grin he gave her melted her all over again. "So confident. If you catch one, I'll clean it and you can cook it."

He gave her a quick kiss and then padded naked out of bed to the bathroom. Sounds of the shower soon followed.

Quinn lay in bed, the bliss from lovemaking fading as the sun crept higher into the sky. Something nagged at her, a faint buzz like the hum of a mosquito. If she loved West and he loved her, and they were engaged, why did she suspect he was investigating her and her family? Was this all a farce so he could get closer to uncloak secrets?

Thirty minutes later, freshly showered and dressed, she joined him on the porch as they ate oatmeal and fresh fruit.

"You told me about your family. It's time I told you about mine. About Demi and our relationship."

West stiffened, the coffee mug halfway to his mouth. "Go on."

"I wanted to be close to her, but our mothers weren't exactly friends. Demi was an ideal for me."

"Why?" He set down his mug, studied her with his dark, intense gaze. It felt as if he scrutinized her, wanted answers to questions that went far beyond her childhood. Quinn fiddled with her fork.

"I thought if I had a sister, even a half sister, that my family life would be complete. A sister would keep me company when my mom worked late, or dumped me with my grandparents when she jetted off to Vegas to marry again.

"Demi really wasn't interested in being my friend. And that hurt. But I learned to live with it." She stretched out her hands, studying the bruises and scrapes.

"I always wanted to have a large family, kids all gathered around the dinner table, around the tree at Christmas. Siblings to play with, fight with, anything to escape the constant fear that I wasn't good enough for the steps in my life."

"Stepfathers," he said quietly.

Her childhood hadn't been rosy, filled with lemonade stands and dolls and playtime. More like loneliness, of waiting for a mother to come home from work, or fearing that the new stepfather would not like her.

An endless parade of dads, like steps in a ladder, only leading nowhere.

Quinn stretched out her hands, showing the rough spots, the calluses, the broken nails.

"Look at me, West. I'm not glamorous. I don't remember everything about my life, but I know I was poor. I came from the wrong side of the tracks. Everything I have, I've worked hard and long to keep. I may not have much, but what little I do have is important to me. It's not easy being a woman business owner in a man's world. Even more so being a respectable businesswoman when you've been stigmatized for having a father who's a lowlife."

He waited, watching her. She pressed on.

"I remember this—there were times I wanted to give up because it seemed so overwhelming. It was a dream to own Good Eats, a silly dream when I could have made money working for someone else. But I needed my business, needed to prove to myself and others I could do this. I'm not rich, in fact, I can barely pay the rent. But even though I've lost most of my memory, I know who I am."

Quinn drew in a breath. "I'm Quinn Colton, a woman who fights to the end and doesn't surrender. I'm not giving in to this amnesia and I'm not giving in to whoever attacked me. They will not win."

West reached over, cupped her cheek. "No, they will not."

A fierce pride and longing filled her. "And I'm not losing you, either. You may have secrets a foot deep, but if I cared about you enough to agree to marry you before all this happened, then this Quinn, the new Quinn, accepts that love. Even if she can't remember it."

Her mouth was warm and soft beneath his own as he bent his head and kissed her. West smoothed away an errant curl from her face. "Let's take a break and go fishing."

Her nose wrinkled. "You were serious about that?"

"Absolutely."

West found two fishing poles in the closet and a tackle box filled with lures, and a battered khaki hat with hooks stuck in the band. He plopped it on her curls.

"Perfect fit," he teased.

"I can't believe you're going to take me fishing."

"Of course. We made a deal about dinner, and I am always serious about fishing."

Fishing provided a way to relax and free the mind. West hoped it would help Quinn remember.

An hour later, both of them wearing waders and flannel shirts, they arrived at the creek he knew to be prime fishing territory.

Standing at the creek's edge, he showed her how to fly cast, sending the lure upstream so it floated downward. Fat speckled trout swam lazily in the current, but none bothered to nibble at the lures. Sunshine warmed his face as he reeled in the lure, and the cooling breeze from the canyon made it a perfect August day. Back in Red Ridge, the temps would be climbing past the high eighties, but here was paradise.

Quinn cast her line, reeling it in too fast. Rex barked at a daring trout that swam close to shore and began frisking in the icy water.

"Rex! Stop scaring the fish," West ordered. "Go find. Squirrel!"

The dog bounded off into the woods. Quinn laughed. "You seriously taught him to hunt squirrels?"

He grinned. "If we don't catch dinner, I hope you know how to cook squirrel."

"You're teasing."

"Huh." West dipped his head and gave her a brief, but sizzling kiss. "Maybe we should skip dinner and go to bed early."

"Woman cannot live on love alone," she quipped. "She needs tofu, too."

Quinn laughed at his crestfallen expression.

He showed her how to fly cast once more, and let the lure wriggle to attract the trout. And then her line tugged.

"I got one!" Quinn spun the reel, her face alight with pleasure.

"Great job! I'm cooking dinner tonight." West fetched the net.

It felt wonderful to be there with her, no problems, no one pestering them. Before leaving, they would explore Pine Paradise. But for now, he'd remain in this snug illusion that all was well.

Although in his heart, he knew it was not.

Chapter 16

After packing their luggage, they drove to Pine Paradise Cabins. Quinn's stomach churned with anxiety. Maybe regaining her memory wasn't such a terrific idea.

She might discover things about herself she didn't like. Or her mysterious sister, Demi.

As the truck bumped and bounced over the gravel road, Quinn recalled another memory. A car with springs that squeaked and balding tires. Her mother always scrimping and scraping together enough money for them to live. Never enough for extras, like new clothing for school or toys. Quinn once thought her middle name was Secondhand.

He turned onto a steep gravel road barred by a yellow steel gate. The gate was padlocked.

After putting the truck into Park, he turned to her. "Rex and I are doing a quick sweep of the property, and then I'll drive up to the cabin you stayed at with Demi. Stay here."

While they were inspecting the area, Quinn thought about West and all he'd done for her, and the fierce passion of his lovemaking.

West taking time to help her remember struck her as something very sweet and unselfish.

He returned fifteen minutes later and unlocked the gate. Quinn took a deep breath as he let Rex into the back seat and then climbed back into the truck. "West, I'm scared."

He turned, leather creaking beneath his jeans. "Why, honey?"

"What if I remember something nasty? Something that will make you think less of me?" She bit her lip. "Make me think less of myself? Not having any recollection of my past feels horrid, but in a way, it's a clean slate. I can re-create myself."

Long dark lashes swept down as he gazed at his scarred hand. "I understand. And I get that you're scared. I'm scared, as well. I'm terrified that you won't remember anything about us, and I'll lose you."

Her heart turned over. "You want to keep me? Battered and bruises and all."

No smile. "You're the best damn thing that ever happened to me, Quinn. Before I met you, I seldom smiled. Hardly ever laughed. You make life outside the job worth living again."

Mouth wobbling, she reached over and touched his arm. "Thank you. I had started to think I was a hot mess and always would be. If you aren't my future husband, I almost wish you were."

That earned her a quiet smile. "I'm glad you said that," he murmured.

When they drove through the gate, up the gravel road, she stared at the cabins peppering the roadside. Rough-hewn, with purple and pink petunias in flower boxes at each window, but nothing looked familiar.

They arrived at cabin seven. Narrow porch, one story. Dark wood, green shutters. He took the key, jingled them in his hand as they got out of the truck.

"I looked for the key you said you had, couldn't find it, so I got this key from Tia's brother. I need to check out the cabin first, Quinn. Just in case."

In case there is a threat. She read it in his eyes.

West opened the glove box, withdrew a revolver. He handed it to her. "I know you hate guns, but if you get scared or see something fishy, fire it. I'll come running."

Quinn touched her purse, where her Taser rested. "I can use the Taser." She picked up the weapon gingerly. "I don't remember how to shoot."

He showed her the safety and how to click it off. "Just point and fire. Except try not to aim it at me." A crooked, sexy grin. "You never did learn how to shoot, hon, so that's not something you forgot."

Quinn watched him whistle to Rex. "Rex, find!"

It was fascinating to watch him work. She suspected she'd never seen this part of Agent West Brand. Driven and focused, concentrating on searching the perimeter of the cabin and the roadside, his brown eyes hard and purposeful.

A few minutes later, he returned, locked the revolver in the glove box. Then West held out his hand. "All clear."

"Good to know." She let him help her out of the truck. West grabbed a flashlight from the glove box.

The gun at his lean hip assured her she'd be well protected.

Rex bounded out of the truck, loped up the porch steps.

"Tia's relatives said the power was turned off about a month ago. That was the time around when she was supposed to sell the property and she would have closed the account so the new owner could open his own," West told her.

Using his key, he opened the door.

"Take your time," he told her in his deep, soothing voice.

Quinn walked around the living room. The stone fireplace was cold, no evidence of the fire that once crackled there merrily. Rug mats were strewed about the pine floor, and the sofa was brown. Her memory flickered. A redheaded woman, sitting on the couch, making a face.

"Puke green. The sofa here was green. We called it puke green," she told him. "It was like pea soup."

West didn't pepper her with questions or say anything. He simply waited.

"I know this place." Quinn frowned, trying to remember. "I came here once, a long time ago. Isn't it odd how I can remember things in spurts?"

"The doctor said that's normal. It will return to you," he assured her. "Who was with you?"

She pressed a hand to her temple, thinking. "Demi."

She closed her eyes, inhaling the stale air, exhaling the memories.

Quinn had been in this very cabin, or at least this area, with Demi Colton. One night with the sister she'd longed to connect with, longed to befriend, but had never really known.

Demi had collared a felon who skipped bail, but the case had turned ugly. Demi had needed a place to retreat, get away from the ugly side of life. Quinn had booked this cabin for a short vacation, invited Demi. Just the two of them, trying to forge bonds they'd never had growing up.

Quinn always wanted a sister, the kind you could swap stories with of boys you thought were cute, brush each other's hair and borrow each other's clothing. It had been one night where they'd both reached out, tried to make it work.

Quinn had been so eager and Demi cautious. In the end, Demi left early. Demi hadn't shed her private side, hadn't wanted to share secrets or swap stories or do any of the things Quinn imagined.

But she had been in this cabin.

West didn't pressure her, only remained quiet. Quinn was glad of the silence. Too many people had been pounding at her like a jackhammer, trying to get her memory triggered. Finn, with his attention to duty, to find a suspect in Tia's death. Brayden and Shane.

West hadn't nagged or prodded. He simply waited, watched, and she sensed he worried about her safety, especially now. Quinn realized it was part of his personality, like a big wolf always on guard against predators wishing to harm the pack.

"She seemed a little secretive. I remember that. I hate secrets," she muttered. "People keep things from me, like my mom did, trying to hide how broke we were, trying to hide the fact that she was marrying yet another loser so I'd have a stepfather."

The bedroom had a queen bed and two nightstands. Quinn went into the bedroom, touching the blue-and-green comforter. The cabin had a slightly musty air of disuse, and a pang of sadness struck her.

"What was the deal with this cabin?" she asked West.

"Tia was planning to sell, and the sale fell through and the property was closed." His fingers rested on the gun's hilt. "Sale was to the Larson brothers. Two million, but they offered three mil."

Anxiety pinched her insides. "Too much money. They wanted it badly. Are they suspects?"

A shoulder shrug. "Always are with everything, but there's no evidence."

Quinn returned to the living room and peered outside the windows at the surrounding canyon walls, the sweep of pine and oak trees ringing the wood porch. She went outside, touched one of the two wooden rockers. The sound was soothing. *Creak*, back. *Crick*, up.

Another memory surfaced. A laughing redhead, rocking back and forth, teasing Quinn about her being the older sister, the first one who would be an *old lady rocking in a chair like this, knitting socks for the grandbabies*.

"She sat here," Quinn mused. "Demi. She said I'd be the first to be a grandmother, and she would take advice from me. I told her I'd make sure my grandchildren ate all their vegetables and I would not be a grandmother who spoiled them. Then Demi said I'd probably serve them kale cake instead of chocolate."

A slight smile tugged her mouth upward, and then it faded. One hand went to her abdomen. "She was pregnant when she vanished."

West nodded. "Yes."

"And she went someplace, alone, to have her baby. I can't bear to think of her being alone, with a baby to care for, no one to help her."

Throat closing tight, she stared down at the rocker. She knew she and Demi never shared much, but how she wished she could be there for her little sister now. Tears burned the backs of her eyelids. Then she felt two strong arms encircle her waist from behind, and West laid his cheek against her head.

"It's okay, sweetheart. You'll get your memory back."

For a moment she rested against him. Maybe she couldn't remember anything about her relationship with this big, strong man, but he had only been considerate and tender with her since the moment she'd seen him in the hospital.

Quinn pulled away to face him. "Why is it so important that I remember being here with Demi?"

Gaze steady, he studied her. "Any memory you regain is helpful. This property is central to the bombing investigation. The Larson brothers itched to purchase this property. They wanted it for something, and it didn't have to do with planting pansies or relaxing on porch rockers."

If being in this cabin helped kick-start her memory, then she'd comb through every square inch. Quinn returned inside to the bedroom.

The king-size bed was neatly made, the room spotless, though the musty air of disuse lingered. West pulled open the closet door.

He went very still and very quiet.

"What's wrong?" she asked.

Quinn peered into the closet. A sleeping bag, stashed in the corner, along with a packet of disposable diapers, a box of energy bars and a battery-operated lantern.

But that was not what caught West's attention. He took a leather jacket off a hanger and turned, the jacket dangling from two fingers.

His expression turned grim.

"Quinn, you want to tell me about this?" West's voice deepened. "You told me this jacket was hanging in your closet. Then why is Demi's motorcycle jacket here?"

Chapter 17

West ushered Quinn outside while Rex remained on the porch. Phone to his ear, West made the call.

"Finn? I'm at Pine Paradise. Cabin number seven, where Quinn stayed last year with her sister. I found a jacket belonging to Demi Colton."

West's stomach lurched at Finn's next words.

"We got a tip today from an anonymous caller, anonymous for now, who gave us very specific information on cabin seven. He said he saw Demi there a few days ago when he was making a delivery to a resort in the area. I'll send a team straightaway."

He thumbed off the phone.

West turned to his fiancée, the woman he loved. The woman who at this moment could have helped to harbor a fugitive from the law.

"Finn told me someone called in a tip. Demi was seen in this area."

Quinn's gaze widened. "My sister was here?"

"The jacket and those items in the closet seem to indicate so. Why is Demi's jacket here, Quinn?"

"I don't know." Her voice rose slightly. "I can't remember anything, West. Why would Demi be here?"

It's a good place to hide out and if she had a hand in planting that bomb...

If he'd thought Quinn was innocent of hiding information on the whereabouts of her sister, seeing Demi's jacket changed his mind.

Eyes wide, Quinn shook her head. "I have no idea how it got there!"

"You lost your memory and you wouldn't remember. Not now," he told her. "But think. Does this cabin trigger anything to you? Anything Demi said to you that would lead her back here to hide out?"

Quinn bit her lip. "No."

They walked to the truck to wait for the Red Ridge police officers. Quinn was trembling, so he removed his windbreaker jacket and put it over her shoulders. Getting her agitated would not solve anything.

West started talking about the fishing trips he'd taken, to calm her frazzled nerves. Get her to relax. But Quinn remained staring at the cabin, huddled into his jacket.

Finally a convoy of police cars arrived. He briefed Finn on what he'd found as crime scene techs began dusting the doorknob for prints. He took a pair of latex gloves to cover his hands and preserve any additional evidence found.

West returned to his truck and a visibly upset Quinn. "Stay here," he told her. "I'll finish soon and take you back."

With all the police swarming over the cabin, he knew Demi wouldn't return. Nor would anyone threaten Quinn.

But it wasn't looking good for her. If only her memory

would return, he could question her, watch her face to see if she told the truth.

The cabin smelled musty with disuse. Yet his gut told him someone had been here, holing up and making bombs in the woods.

Frustrated, West looked around the living room as the other officers began working the scene.

He had more questions than answers, but at least a starting place.

Whoever had been here had left it clean. No dirt on the wood floor, not a speck of dust on the table. Bathroom was clean as well, with fresh towels hanging on the rack and no water droplets in the sink or shower.

It made sense that Demi would use the cabin as a hiding place, since she'd been here with Quinn previously. If she had informed her brothers, they wouldn't have told him.

He went into the bedroom where Demi's jacket had hung in the closet. Crime scene techs were dusting everything. The cabin, isolated and hidden from the main road, made a perfect hiding place.

West swept his flashlight over the room as the techs worked in the closet. He went to the bureau by the window and opened drawers.

Empty, except for the top one that contained a hairbrush.

West picked up the brush, which bore strands of long red hair. He knew of only one woman purported to have hair that color. A woman on the run.

Demi Colton.

He returned to the living room and watched Brayden comb through the cabin, he studied the man to see if his fellow officer hid evidence. He didn't trust the Coltons.

The only Colton he did trust was Quinn. But Brayden was shadowed by a fellow K-9 officer West trusted.

West glanced at Rex. "Too crowded in here. Let's head outside."

Rex wagged his tail.

If the unsub used this cabin, Rex would detect even the smallest amount of explosive residue left behind. As Rex sniffed the ground, West searched the ground for inorganic evidence. Something as simple as a cigarette butt contained DNA evidence.

One of the officers came forward. "Found this. What do you make of it?"

Sunlight glinted off the object. Foil, looked like a gum wrapper twisted into something. He smelled it. Interesting. Fruity.

"Bag it as evidence," he told the officer.

Might be nothing, only a litterbug's discards.

Or it could be something.

He ordered Rex to find as they searched the perimeter of the cabin once more.

West smelled the redolent odor of pine, fresh mountain air and little else. But Rex, with his keen sense of smell, could pick up days-old traces of gunpowder.

After a few minutes, when the dog had not stopped, West began thinking he'd been too cautious. Suddenly Rex lifted his head and stared in the direction of the woods. West immediately went on alert.

"Find," he ordered, and the dog bolted.

West followed. Nose to the ground, Rex kept loping along a narrow trail cutting through the forest leading down to the creek. Leaves crunched beneath West's boot soles as he scanned the area. Ferns and bushes brushed at the legs of his jeans. The trail was little used and barely visible, but for the flattened stalks of plants.

Someone had been here recently.

Could be the cabin's occupant used this trail to access the creek to fish. Or something else…something that caught Rex's attention.

Rex clambered down a few rocks and then hooked a left around the bend. Leaves rustled overhead in the breeze and he could hear the gurgling of Pine Creek.

West climbed down the rocks, saw the sparkle of sunlight upon the rushing water tumbling over rocks. Beneath a recess in the cliff wall, Rex sat. The rock alcove looked natural, carved out by nature. Part of the wall had eroded, leaving a flat ledge big enough to accommodate two people. Hidden by thick brush, the recess wasn't visible until you rounded the corner.

Made a great place for nature lovers to share romantic moments with each other…or for an unsub to make a bomb.

"Good boy," he murmured, giving Rex his favorite treat. West crouched down to study the remains of what would look like a campfire to most people.

Taking out his penknife from a back pocket, West stirred the ashes on the ground. This location next to the creek was ideal for anyone wanting to make bombs. Close enough to water in case of an *oops*. Far enough away from prying eyes and ears. One could set off a small explosion, and even with the sound echoing off the canyon cliffs, it would be mistaken for gunfire, something not unusual in these parts, just like the gunshots he'd heard the other night. Plenty of people in South Dakota owned guns. They just didn't advertise it like some folks did.

He sniffed the residue on his penknife. Oh yeah. The same distinctive bleach odor indicating a bomb.

West found a small cylinder. Whoever had done this was probably the bomber. He couldn't be certain if the residue was fresh, not without lab tests. Maybe he'd rented the cabin in the past. And although Tia might have records of that transaction, the papers had been destroyed in the explosion. The computer had been blown apart.

With extreme care, West dug up the residue and deposited it into a plastic baggie. More evidence for the FBI lab.

Demi Colton could have used the cabin, and possibly made explosives here, down by the creek, washing her hands in the cold water to dispose of residue.

But Rex would have picked up the slightest bit of explosive residue in the cabin. He had not. The dog's nose was so sensitive, Rex could discern a teaspoon of sugar placed into a swimming pool.

So why was Demi's jacket in cabin seven?

Checking his cell phone, he saw a good signal. And Mike had left a voice mail.

He dialed her number.

As usual, his boss didn't waste time. "DNA on the butterfly compact matched the hair sample you gave me of Quinn Colton. It's definitely hers. We didn't find any other DNA on it and the fingerprints were too smudged."

Fingers tightened on the cell phone. He wanted to ask if she was certain, or if there had been a mistake. He knew better. DNA was conclusive.

Damn, the evidence was stacking against Quinn, placing her in the first bomb site. He closed his eyes, wishing he'd been wrong. But he'd known all along the compact was hers. She needed to regain her memory.

Maybe there was a legitimate reason she'd been at the first bomb site. Right. Quinn had been there delivering meals to her sister, the Groom Killer.

She's innocent until proven guilty. There's no proof of anything.

"Where are you?" Mike asked. "I called the station. They told me you took a few days off."

"I'm out at Pine Paradise Cabins, the property Tia was selling." He paused. "I went there with Quinn to trigger her memory since she stayed here last year. I found Demi's jacket inside."

West took a deep breath. Damn, this was hard, accusing his fiancée, but he had his duty. "The same jacket that had been in Quinn's closet recently."

"Which means either Quinn used it to visit the cabin herself, or Demi stole it back, or she gave her sister back the jacket. More than likely it's the last," Mike said in her dry voice.

"I'm near the creek with Rex. He alerted to explosive powder. Found remains of materials for a TATP bomb in a rock alcove. But no alerts on the cabin itself. Nothing."

"So if Demi made the bomb, she could have washed herself clean of residue."

West frowned. "I doubt it. Rex is too trained and sensitive. He would have found something in the cabin."

"Has Quinn remembered anything?" Mike asked.

"Bits and pieces from childhood. Nothing concrete, except she did recall the unsub's face before the building blew."

"Huh."

Not caring for that "Huh," he paced. "Get to the point, Mike."

"Odd that Quinn remembered the unsub and remembers nothing else. Mighty strange. Maybe that memory is one she made up, to throw you off, lead all you ganders on a wild-goose chase to throw off suspicion from Quinn's sister."

"That is the stupidest idea you've had in a long time, Mike. Did she let herself get blown up, too?"

"I'll let that slide, West, because you're stressed. But you're not separating yourself from this case. You're too close to the players and not thinking clearly. I sent you there to get friendly with the people in town, investigate Demi Colton's relatives on the police force, and now you're too involved."

"Get off my back, Mike. I do my job." He struggled with his temper. "They're sending the evidence to our lab for analysis."

"I'm coming there."

West's heart dropped to his stomach. Aw hell no. "Not a good idea. People will talk."

"The way they're now talking about you and Quinn Colton?"

He glanced around. "Who's talking?"

"Everyone, West. I paid a little visit to Red Ridge a few days ago on my way back from Casper, hung out in Rusty's bar…"

West felt his heart kick harder against his ribs. "Checking up on me? You should have given me a heads-up."

"Why? So you would have a chance to pretend there was nothing between you two?"

"No, so I could have invited you over for dinner, had you and Quinn do your nails, let her hear from you how I'm here to secretly investigate her family. You know, girl talk."

Silence on the other end. He didn't give a damn. Everything had gone south since the day Quinn walked into Tia's office. Each day he struggled between his personal feelings for Quinn and his dedication to getting the job done.

Seeing justice delivered.

Mike sighed. "Sarcasm doesn't suit you, West. You're too taciturn."

"Not anymore. I'm a real chatterbox these days, Mike."

"A chatterbox in bed? Pillow talk goes both ways, West."

Good thing Mike wasn't in the room, because he wanted to throttle her. Right now he was ready to climb through the phone. "I never bring home the job. And that's not why I fell in love with Quinn Colton."

There, he'd said it aloud. Why not? Best to clear the air with Mike. Level with her.

"I fell in love with her, but the job didn't come between us. I haven't told her why I'm really in Red Ridge because I'm not one hundred percent certain she doesn't know where her sister is hiding. And now that we know her DNA was on the compact powder puff, and the compact was hers or she did use it, I need to grill her harder. But until she gets her damn memory back, that's not possible!"

He told her about the attack on Quinn, and the reason for taking her to hide in the cabin.

"There's a good chance being out here, where she came before, will trigger her memory."

"You'd better hope she does remember soon. And not only because someone is after her, West. Because if Quinn Colton is hiding her sister, you need to find out. I know you care about her...but the job comes first."

"The day I stop doing my job is the day I'll personally hand you my shield, Mike."

A heavy sigh came over the phone. "I know you, West. That's why I stopped at the bar, to hear the town gossips to confirm what I already know. I study behavior for kicks and giggles, and you're a classic case of 'West Brand is clearly bonkers over a woman.'"

"I'm not bonkers. I love her—" he dragged in a deep breath "—but my head is clear."

"Regardless, I'm coming there to see for myself."

Nothing would deter Mike. Woman was like a hound dog. He told her and then hung up.

He made another call, informed Finn what he'd found. Minutes later, techs swarmed over the scene. West gripped Rex's leash as he led the dog around the trail, but Rex found no other residue, except for a small spot near the creek.

The unsub had clearly washed off. He left the others to secure the scene and returned with Quinn to their cabin. They didn't talk on the drive over. West was too busy mulling over troubling thoughts.

Was Demi firing her gun at someone? Was that the gunfire he'd heard?

An intruder? Or killing game to survive? Did Quinn aid her fugitive sister? Or was it the bomber?

Until Quinn retrieved her memory, they were clueless. But there was still the security footage at her apartment.

If Quinn had taken the jacket out to give to her sister, they'd have a digital record of it.

But as he pulled in front of the cabin, Quinn finally spoke. "Am I under arrest?"

West drew in a deep breath. "No. But I will tell you, it doesn't look good for you."

"What's going to happen to me, West?"

He slid his palm over hers. "Nothing. Not for now. They'll take the evidence to the lab, work it over. See what they find."

Once inside, he worked on his laptop as Quinn cut photos from magazines for her vision board.

Was Quinn lying to him about Demi? Did she distrust him, wanted to throw him off Demi's trail? What if she had returned the jacket to Demi—cold, alone and on the run? Somehow it had made its way into the cabin.

Yet the items he found didn't paint a complete picture.

If Demi had stayed there with her new baby, why were there only diapers and no other baby items? Unless she'd fled in a hurry and took everything with her.

After an hour, he closed his laptop. Quinn sat at the table, studying the board.

"Dr. Ross said to create a vision board of what little past I can remember. Why do I keep adding him?"

She pointed to the faces creating the collage on the poster board. West's blood ran cold.

Each photo bore a strong resemblance to the same identifying characteristics as the man Quinn had described to the police sketch artist. All were scowling, angry. The therapist encouraged her to create a board linking her to the past.

Maybe Quinn's subconscious couldn't erase the dark-haired man. Or he had a greater significance, one she couldn't yet place.

"What do you remember of him? Close your eyes and tell me." *Don't push her. Don't scare her.*

"Smoke, thick, gagging. Nasty look to him, as if he wanted to hurt people. He scared me a little. I…had to get to Tia."

"Why? Why did he scare you, Quinn? What was he doing to Tia that made you open that door to go inside, instead of turning and calling the police?"

"I—I don't know!"

Scraps of paper littered the table. A small frown dented her brow as she opened her eyes. "West, what's wrong with me? Will I ever get my life together?"

The whispered plea tore at him. "It will take time. You have to believe your memory will return, honey."

The frown deepened. "I don't know."

"Don't stress about it."

"No. I mean, I didn't know." She pointed to the photos on the board. "I remember thinking that I'd seen him before, but couldn't recall where. And then I opened the door and *pow*!"

West considered himself a good judge of character. He'd undergone behavioral analysis training at Quantico, knew how to watch a subject to see if the pulse jumped, the eyes darted, or stiffened, rubbed his eyes or nose.

He knew Quinn, at least he thought he did. Guile wasn't in Quinn's personality. She embraced honesty and directness.

"Quinn, do you know where Demi is? Have you been helping her hide?"

Her eyes widened. "No. I—I don't think so. How could you even ask me that?"

"Because you said you wished to get closer to her. If she asked you to help her, would you? Or turn her over to the police?"

Quinn's mouth wobbled precariously. "Honestly, I don't know what I would have done before, West. Maybe. I don't know how her jacket got in the cabin. All I know is I remember wanting to get closer to her, and failing. So what does that make me? A suspect?"

West's heart jumped as his pragmatic side reeled in emotions. "I don't know. That would be determined after you recover your memory."

A wry smile touched her lips. "Sounds like a good reason not to fully recover." Quinn sighed. "But I'll face whatever I must. I don't care. I only want to get better, West."

He had no more answers than before.

A car lumbered up the roadway. Quinn frowned. "Does anyone know we're here? Besides your friend?"

"Mike." He felt his stomach lurch with hard anxiety. "Mike is my boss with the FBI."

"Your boss. Mike is the one you were talking with in the hospital room when you thought I was asleep."

Aw damn. West fisted his hands. "Why didn't you tell me?"

"Why didn't you tell me, West? What's going on that you're so secretive? I overheard you talking with someone named Mike about getting closer to me to find out what I know about my sister's disappearance."

Stomach knotting, he waited for her to finish. That damn phone call in the hospital...

Quinn dropped the scissors. "Did Mike tell you to check on me? Instruct you to get close, try to get information on my sister?"

Maybe it was time he leveled with her. Hell, a little, anyway. "Mike authorized my being on loan to the RRPD."

"You said something about waiting for me to wake up and remember where Demi was." She came closer, until she could see the darkness in his eyes. "I kept drifting in and out of sleep, but I know you didn't intend for me to overhear that conversation."

Her voice quavered. "I guess it's a safe assumption I'm not the only Colton you're investigating."

Clever Quinn. Too smart.

Quinn kept twisting her hands on her lap. "I hate secrets. Not knowing. Keeping secrets from me isn't the way to get me to fall for you, West. It won't get me to open up, either."

"Neither will hiding from the facts, Quinn."

"I'm not hiding. I want to remember! But you have plenty to hide. You've been hiding from the moment you set foot in Red Ridge. Do you know what my brothers would do if they knew you were investigating them?"

His jaw tightened. "My job is to help catch the killer. This town needs help, Quinn. They need me. And Rex. You have a killer slaying grooms, and all weddings have ceased. There's no joy, no future here. Until the unsub is caught, no one can feel safe. What if the unsub changes his methodology? Decides to begin killing brides? Or friends of brides?"

West looked outside as the car parked. "Until this person is caught, no one is truly safe."

And until the bomber who killed Tia was caught, Quinn wasn't safe, either.

Chapter 18

Quinn felt her world shattering as they went outside.

Mousy brown hair. Short. Thin, and horn-rimmed glasses. Didn't bother to knock. The woman lounging on the porch rocker looked professional. Too sharp to be at home here in the outdoors, doing things West liked.

They went outside. Arms folded, Quinn stopped and locked gazes with him.

"Quinn, meet Mike. My boss. Mikayla. Mike, this is Quinn Colton."

The owner of the cabin. The person ordering him to spy on Quinn.

Words failed her. Later, she'd talk with West, but for now, she was caught in a hard place.

West put a hand on the small of her back as he escorted her forward. Quinn gritted her teeth, controlling her wild impulse to march back into the cabin, pack her bag and leave.

Mouth dry, her heart aching, she watched the woman stand. Felt her quietly assess her, sum her up in a quick glance. Rex greeted the woman by pushing his nose into her outstretched hand.

Mike patted his head.

"Rex, go lie down." West pointed to the porch.

Whatever else Mike was, she wasn't stupid. A gleaming intelligence lurked behind those glasses. Quinn looked at Mike, then at the cabin. Something told her Mike disguised herself with the outfit and glasses, hiding her true self.

Quinn understood about hiding. Knew how it felt to be a woman struggling to make a stand in a world dominated by powerful men.

Mike nodded at Quinn. "Miss Colton. I've been curious to meet you."

"Here I am. Anything you want to know? My favorite color? Favorite food? Where I've hidden my sister?"

The barest twitch of those thin lips. "Where your sister is hiding is much more interesting than talking about food. Do you know where she is?"

Small talk. West's boss was direct and blunt. In another life, they might have been friends.

Not now. Not with this huge sword of accusations and suspicions dangling over her head. Mike remained the enemy.

So did West, the man who'd professed to love her. Cherish her.

Reported to this Mike that he'd investigate her.

"If I did, why would I tell you?" Quinn challenged.

Mike's gaze flicked to West. "Oh, I doubt you'd tell me, a stranger. But West here, you might have given him a clue, since it was his job to investigate you."

West closed his eyes. Quinn's heart dropped to her

stomach. She'd known. But hearing the confirmation from this woman hurt deeply.

Who could she trust? Not these two, who wanted to find Demi, perhaps arrest her. And they'd do anything to achieve that.

"I don't know." Quinn's gaze locked onto the woman. "I have no memory before the explosion. But I'm sure West already informed you. I'm sure he told you everything about me, since that's the reason why he came to Red Ridge. He probably told you what kind of shampoo I use, what soap I prefer, as well. Everything personal about me."

She lowered her voice. "Did you also order him to sleep with me?"

"Hold on a minute, Quinn," West snapped.

Something sparked in Mike's gaze. "No. I didn't even know how close you'd become to him. In fact, he told me very little personal information about you. Only recently did I conclude you were lovers."

Mike glanced backward at the cabin. "Though if I let myself inside, I'm sure I'd find evidence of that."

"Breaking and entering?" Quinn asked sweetly. "Then why wait for us?"

Another twitch of Mike's lips. "Not exactly B and E, since I do own the cabin."

More shock. Quinn turned to West. "You said this cabin belonged to a good friend. So she's the friend? What kind of relationship do you have with Mike? The same kind? What, do you have a lover in every city?"

West's dark gaze snapped. "Mike's my supervisor. A friend. Nothing more. The cabin was convenient, safe, and I knew you'd be protected."

From others, but not from West Brand. Agent West Brand, whose foremost concern was spying on Quinn and her brothers.

"I don't know where my sister is. Neither do my brothers. I'm sure if one of them knew, they'd have told me, knowing I worried about Demi."

West's mouth narrowed to a thin slash. "But you do know where her jacket is, Quinn."

"I told you, I don't remember!"

His gaze remained even. "Did Demi walk into your apartment, take her jacket and walk out without your knowledge?"

Suddenly weary, she sank into the second rocker. "What do you want, West?"

"I want you to tell me the truth. As far as you remember, did you return Demi's jacket?"

"I don't know! I don't know anything." She rocked back and forth, hugging herself. This was a true nightmare. No memory to defend herself from such horrid accusations.

Her knight in shining Kevlar was now looking at her as if she were in a police lineup. She knew West was ruthless. Dedicated.

Now she knew what it felt like to be subjected to that brutal focus.

Mike stood, paced the porch. "Miss Colton, this will go easier on you if you tell us what exactly you were doing at the first bomb site."

First bomb site? Quinn pressed two fingers to her head. "What?"

"I found a butterfly compact that looked like the one you said you had. It was in the rubble at the old hardware store after the first bomb went off." Unsmiling, West regarded her. "I want to believe you, Quinn. I want to believe you are innocent. Do you remember anything—anything—about meeting anyone there at that building?"

Tension knotted her stomach. "Maybe I was catering an event there."

Mike and West exchanged knowing glances, sealing themselves inside that tight little FBI bubble. Sealing her out.

"Catering an event at an abandoned building?"

It didn't matter. Until she got her memory back, she couldn't tell them a thing. Nor could she provide a suitable defense for herself.

Nausea gripped her, but she raised her chin and gave West a cool look. "Am I under arrest? Do I need to call a lawyer?"

"No," he replied, not even glancing at Mike.

But Quinn watched Mike. Something flickered in her gaze. Uncertainty, perhaps.

"Agent Brand, I need to talk with you alone." Mike jerked a thumb at the door.

"Wait out here, Quinn. This won't take long," West told her.

Rocking back and forth, she considered her options. Taking the truck and returning to town alone. But if they planned to haul her in for questioning, she'd be in more trouble.

Whatever happened, she could no longer stay here. At her side, Rex whined as if sensing the tension.

A lump formed in her throat. "I'm sorry, Rex." She patted his head. "You're such a good boy. Your owner is not."

Fishing her cell phone out of her jeans pocket, she looked at the screen. Barely a signal. Quinn walked off the porch, circled around the cabin until she got two bars.

Inside, she heard raised voices. Mike and West arguing about her? Or a lovers' quarrel? Didn't matter. It was over.

Austin answered on the third ring, sounding breathless. "Quinn! Everything okay? West hauled you away so suddenly. I didn't know where you went. All I saw was that note left on the counter."

"I'm in Spearfish Canyon at a private cabin. Can you come get me?"

His voice dropped to a whisper. "Quinn, what happened? Where are you?"

Suddenly the dam of emotions let loose. Quinn struggled to speak through her tears. "Austin, I really need you now. I know it's a lot to ask…but I need to come home and I don't want West to take me."

A pause, and then he said, "Where are you?"

"The cabin, I'll look up directions on my phone. It's remote, but not far from Pine Paradise, the property Tia owned and talked about selling."

Austin sighed. "I wish I could. I'm prepping an order for tonight in Red Ridge. I sure could use your help. Can you call an Uber?"

Austin had always been there for her, far as she knew. Now even he was far too busy to help her.

Business came first. *It's all falling apart. He's trying to save Good Eats, so don't blame him.*

"I'll get home, and when I do, I'll help you." Quinn ended the call.

West and Mike finally emerged from the cabin. Quinn waited.

"Mike's going to stay here for the night. We're driving back to Red Ridge." West didn't look at his boss, only her.

Fine with her. Quinn went inside and packed in minutes.

When they were in his truck, headed back to town, she kept silent.

West remained tight-lipped. Finally she couldn't stand it anymore.

"I heard you both fighting. About what?"

"We argued about you. Before arriving here, Mike

wanted to pull me off the case. Said I was too personally involved." His fingers tightened on the steering wheel. "And then she changed her mind after meeting you."

Struggling to rein in her temper, she glanced at him. "Why?"

"Because she thinks you're not involved."

"And she could tell from one brief meeting with me? Is she psychic?"

"No. She thinks…you're too much in love with me to hide information about your sister. Mike said you're the type of woman who'd confess to her lover."

That stung. Quinn gripped her hands. "You mean I'm a lovesick silly woman."

"I didn't say that," West grated out.

"But she did. She's a hard person, this Mike you work for. So you agreed with her?"

"I told Mike that you were smart and we were in love, but you detested secrets."

You got that right.

She'd been stupid. Memory loss or not, thinking that West Brand loved her. Cared enough about her to spend a lifetime together. All those childhood memories proved something. Men weren't reliable. They slept with you, married you and, when they got tired of using you like a dishrag, disposed of you.

She'd thought West Brand was different from the succession of stepfathers in her life. Maybe he seemed more honorable, loyal and dependable, but in the end, he was not.

"What else did you discuss about me? That sleeping with a suspect makes for good interrogation tactics? Pillow talk reveals secrets?" Quinn stared at the road. "Too bad this suspect doesn't have any memory of the person you're hunting."

"You're not a suspect, Quinn. I was assigned to uncover any information Chief Colton, and your brothers, may have hidden on Demi." He exhaled sharply. "But it makes it damn suspicious that a jacket once hanging in your closet turned up in a hiding place that has Demi Colton's stamp all over it."

"I told you, I didn't give it to her. Far as I remember. What is definite is that you used me, Agent Brand. You used me to gather information on my sister, my brothers." Her voice quavered. "You told me you loved me."

"I do love you."

Love was a cheap four-letter word men used to make women like her mother, and herself, go starry-eyed and forget all common sense.

It had worked in the past.

Not anymore.

Finally they reached Red Ridge. West pulled up before Good Eats. He retrieved her suitcase and placed it on the sidewalk, as Rex poked his head out the back window. Quinn couldn't even bear to pet the dog.

It took everything she had to control herself.

"Don't bother coming inside. I'll have your things delivered to your place."

"Quinn, let's talk—"

"No. No more talking. You, Agent Brand," she said, struggling with her emotions. "I never want to see you again."

Chapter 19

West had never felt this low before. He couldn't remember being gut punched, as if someone kicked him and didn't stop.

Even after his family died in the bomb blast, he'd been in shock. Too stricken and numb to feel.

Oh, he felt now. Felt every single bit of guilt, grief and longing since Quinn struck him out of her life.

Two days after she broke up with him, he saw her on every street corner, heard her gurgling laughter each time he left his shoebox apartment. Remembered the soft feel of her warm body as he held her in bed, the eagerness with which she turned to him as they made love.

Rubbing his chest, he climbed out of his truck. Look at him, love struck and pining for a woman who wanted nothing to do with him.

So love struck he left Rex at the tiny apartment he'd rented before meeting Quinn, and hauled his sorry ass to her father's seedy bar.

Just to forge some kind of weak connection. West told himself it was to gather information from Rusty about Quinn's enemies. But deep inside, he knew it was an excuse.

Yesterday he'd returned to Quinn's apartment to look over every inch of security footage, not daring to turn the digital tapes over to the chief or her brothers. Quinn had left for the day to deliver an order with Austin.

West had found nothing. How the hell Demi's jacket had gotten into the cabin, he hadn't a clue. Unless Quinn had turned it over to her sister, or brought it to Pine Paradise before her accident.

Though it was barely 1 p.m., five cars were parked before the building. Dark, dimly lit, he paused for a moment at the entrance, struggling to adjust his eyesight. Old cigarette smoke and sour beer punched his senses. Not a bar he'd ordinarily frequent.

West enjoyed a beer or two, but seldom drank more. Not since that night he'd lost his entire family.

Felt weird being here in broad daylight. But he wanted answers and Rusty might provide them. The old man had been reticent when West questioned him in official police capacity.

Maybe he'd open up now to a customer.

West sat on a stool at the counter. It was clean, at least. At the pool table near the back, a customer aimed his cue at a fresh rack. The hard clack of pool balls breaking grated on his nerves. A few other customers sat at the bar, drinking beer.

Smoke wreathed the head of Pool Guy as he puffed away on his cigarette. Terrific. West sighed. If he didn't die in the line of duty, maybe he'd get lung cancer.

Rusty came out from the back and West immediately sensed the other man's wariness. Rusty Colton might be drunk many times, but he had the sharp senses of the street.

West ordered a draft, watched Rusty pour. The bar owner slapped it on the counter.

"Run a tab?" Rusty sneered at him.

"Maybe." West sipped. "Depends on how drunk I want to get. How much I owe now?"

That stunned the old man. *Good. Keep him off guard.*

"Four bucks."

For him. West knew the draft beers were $2.99 on special. A sign said so in crooked letters on the mirror emblazoned with a beer logo. He didn't complain. Instead, he pulled out a wad of bills, peeled off a ten, laid it on the counter.

"Keep the change," he told Rusty.

Rusty snatched the bill, stashed it in the drawer. "Never seen you around here much."

Alexander Hamilton worked his magic. Rusty wanted to talk, be friendly. Rusty came from behind the counter to sit next to him.

"Been busy working 24/7, trying to catch the bomber. West Brand," he told Rusty.

"Rusty Colton."

West shook the man's hand, marveling that this sleazy bar owner had managed to father Quinn, who seldom drank, stayed classy during hard times and had a laugh sweeter than chocolate.

"I'm trying to find out who planted the bomb that killed Tia Linwicki and hurt Quinn."

"Yeah." Rusty looked around. "Bad thing. Bad for business."

Of course, the man only thought in dollars and cents. Still West pressed on. Surely Rusty had to have some paternal instinct floating in his alcohol-laden brain.

"Do you know anyone who would want to hurt your

daughter? Have you heard anything about someone complaining about Quinn? Complaining enough to seriously injure her?"

Rusty shook his head.

"What about Tia Linwicki?"

"Tia. That broad always had her nose in the air."

"Was she close to Quinn?" West wanted to shake the man. This was a bar. Gossip abounded, unless Rusty had been too drunk to pay attention.

"I don't know. Quinn's an odd sort. Kid's always kept to herself. Never shared money with her old man." Rusty leaned on the bar, the greed shining in his eyes discernible even in this low light. "You sweet on her?"

Odd, hearing Rusty say that old-fashioned term. West shrugged. "We dated. Broke it off. Just wondering if she said anything to you."

"No. I barely talk to her." Rusty frowned. "Too bad. You're better off. Quinn can be a bitch, just like her mother."

That was it. "No one calls my Quinn a bitch," West snapped.

West stood up, and slugged the man. Rusty fell off the stool, his arm sweeping over his beer mug, spilling it to the floor.

Standing over him, fists clenched, he was ready to deliver another punch when someone grabbed him.

West started to shrug him off.

"Easy, big guy. Whoa, Agent Brand."

Recognizing the voice, he calmed a little.

"Let's take it outside," Brayden said. The K-9 officer gripped West's arm and dragged him away. "Not here. Not with my father. Not worth it. C'mon."

Outside, West gulped down fresh air, glad to get the stink of smoke and beer out of his lungs.

He glanced at the other man. "What the hell are you doing here?"

Brayden's expression flattened. "Same as you. Trying to get information, find out anything about the person who killed Tia. Shane hasn't been able to dig up anything and the bar can be a good source for information."

"But not lately." West dragged in another deep breath.

"No. Too many people are scared these days after that bomb." Brayden released West.

They walked out to the parking lot.

"Sorry for decking your old man," West told Brayden.

The K-9 officer grinned. "No problem. I want to deck him myself at times. Maybe I'll deck your old man and we'll call it even."

West felt the familiar, unpleasant tug in his chest. "He's dead."

Brayden blinked. "Sorry. When?"

"Years ago." He didn't want to talk about it, never had, except with Quinn.

Fortunately, Brayden didn't press him. At West's truck, the other officer turned, shoved his hands into his pants pockets. "You love my sister."

A statement from Brayden. West stared at the ground, too miserable to answer. He felt like a total heel.

Weak.

West couldn't afford to be weak. Men who let their guard down allowed murderers to creep inside their homes, destroy their entire families. A family who had relied on his dad to keep them safe.

"I figured something happened with the both of you."

"She broke it off with me." West looked him in the eye, man-to-man. "I did something I'm not proud of, but it was part of my job. It's her prerogative to tell you, if she wishes."

Brayden nodded. He glanced at the bar. "It isn't easy having Rusty for a dad. I'm sure Quinn has her moments, as well. Know I do. My old man isn't a pillar of society. He's not so bad at times. But when he gets drunk, he gets mean. Like having two personalities."

"Did you get any information from Rusty? From anyone?" West asked.

Brayden shook his head. "It's like the guy who did this simply vanished into thin air."

But West suspected he had not. He'd stuck around to attack Quinn again. And some unsubs liked to hover. They'd keep trophies from their vics, or return to the crime scene to admire their handiwork. Red Ridge wasn't a big city, and it wouldn't be as easy to blend. You'd almost have to be in disguise...

Two personalities.

West rubbed his sore knuckles, his thoughts in a maelstrom. All this time he'd been focusing on Quinn and Tia, not the first bombing. There could have been something he totally missed.

Something so subtle and yet obvious, it passed him by.

"You going back to the station? Want to grab lunch someplace else?" Brayden asked.

"Thanks," he said, meaning it. "Another time. There's something I need to check out first."

He returned home, walked Rex and grabbed an energy bar for lunch.

Then with Rex, he returned to the site of Tia's office.

The crime scene had been released to Tia's family, but they were feuding over her will. So the bomb site remained, the ghostly ashes and wreckage a grim reminder of a violent death.

West stood outside the building once more, not to find evidence, but refresh his memory.

Thirty minutes later, he sat at his desk at the Red Ridge Police Department, Rex lying on the floor beside him. West scribbled notes on a pad, jotting down recollections experienced while rummaging through the building. Sensory ones.

He'd focused on connecting the bombing with the Groom Killer. But everything pointed to the explosions being separate, a means to kill Tia.

That cigar stump he'd found at the scene… Quinn reported her attacker on the street reeked of cigar smoke.

Tia's killer may have indulged in a smoke before murdering her. He needed the DNA report on that evidence. Mike had assured him he'd have it today.

West leaned back in his chair, studying the artist's rendering of the man Quinn had remembered. Something about the shape of his chin…

He made a phone call to Derek, the police artist. An hour later, they were seated before a computer screen, the digitized sketch on the screen. The software program they used would enable him to adjust the sketch.

West tapped on the suspect's hair. "Make his hair greasy, get rid of the cowlick."

Derek adjusted the image.

"Cheeks fatter, nose more bulbous with a few broken veins, green eyes instead of brown, eyebrows thicker and blacker," West instructed.

When they were finished, Derek whistled. "Do you know this guy?"

The man on the screen only slightly resembled the one pulled from Quinn's scrambled memories. But he knew this man. He'd interviewed him.

Cotton in the cheeks made lean cheeks fuller, darker

eyebrows, green contact lenses, a body suit to appear fatter than the unsub truly was…

His heart dropped to his stomach. How the hell could they have missed this?

"Email it to me and I'll run it through our facial recognition database."

Back at his computer, he logged on to the database and began running the program with the new sketch. The Bureau had more than four hundred million images in the database, but he narrowed the parameters.

Mike called him a few minutes later.

"Hey, how are you doing, champ? How's Quinn?" Her voice was soft, but he wasn't buying it.

"I'm fine. Guess she is, as well."

"I'm sorry, West. It's a bitch trying to keep a relationship thriving with this job. I hope it works out for you."

Too personal. "What do you have for me?"

"DNA evidence at the second crime scene turned up inconclusive. Vic's DNA, and nothing else flagged." Mike paused. "But we found something interesting from the first bomb site."

His heart skipped a beat. West gripped the phone receiver. "What?"

"The cigarette you bagged."

West frowned. And then he remembered. "Oh. I must have tossed that in with the evidence I gave you. A witness tossed it on the ground."

"Good thing you bagged and tagged it."

He listened to what Mike told him.

When she finished, he steeled himself. "Mike, I'm coming clean with the Coltons."

Silence.

"There's no evidence they're hiding their sister, or have

destroyed any leads linking her to the Groom Killer. I'm tired of working on the outside."

A heavy sigh. "Your call, West. Pack it in, and soon as Dean Landon returns to duty at Red Ridge, you're back in Sioux Falls."

She hung up.

Sioux Falls. Once he would have jumped at the chance to return to the field office, leave behind the camaraderie of working closely with other officers.

Not any longer. Maybe he'd make other changes, as well.

Next he called Quinn. Her voice was soft, hesitant as she answered, "Hi, West."

First names. Maybe she had forgiven him a little. "Hi. I really need to talk with you, Quinn." He swallowed his pride. "Please. There's something you need to know."

"I can't. I have a client stopping by at six thirty to pick up an order for a dinner party." She sighed. "Maybe tomorrow we can meet at the store."

Had to keep her on the phone. "What kind of dinner? What are you making?"

"Mexican vegetarian. Enchiladas, burritos… The guy is Hispanic, a salesman on his way back from Cheyenne, entertaining corporate clients."

"Sounds good. Even if it's meatless. What does he sell?"

"Aluminum siding, I think."

West paused, gripped the phone tight. "I miss you."

"I miss you, too," she whispered. "Have to run. Bye."

The line clicked off.

Encouraged, he focused on the job before him. West read over all his notes from the first bombing. He began rearranging words on paper. And then everything clicked.

By 5:30 p.m., he organized his notes, printed out the report Mike emailed and called Finn Colton, asking for

Brayden and Shane to attend the meeting. Then he found an energy bar at his desk and ate it while waiting for the chief.

West studied the report Mike had sent over. It was time to have a little talk with Finn, Shane and Brayden.

Taking the report, he headed to the chief's office. Finn Colton was at his computer. He glanced up as West strode inside.

Chief Colton scrutinized his expression. "Want to tell me what this is about?"

When both were seated at the conference table in the office, West sat where he had all three within easy view. Then he tossed the fax in front of Finn.

"Lab report on the sleeping bag found at cabin seven in Pine Paradise. Nothing was in it. It was brand-new. All the items there, including the baby diapers, had no prints on them. Demi could have used gloves, but it's not winter."

Finn blinked. "And her jacket?"

"Her prints were all over the jacket. Quinn's, as well. She could have been there. Could be Demi is in league with the bomber. Or someone stole her jacket, but that's doubtful since the security cameras would have picked up anyone entering or exiting Quinn's apartment."

If Brayden knew where she was, the man might trip now, blurt out a clue in his fierce defense of Demi.

"My sister is innocent."

"We don't know if she is," Finn said slowly. "We can't be certain until she's found."

Shane spoke out, his tone milder than his brother's. "And knowing Demi, she's good at hiding."

West leaned forward. "Do you know where she is?"

As he spoke, he studied the three Coltons. None looked away, even Brayden. They made eye contact, and no one tensed up.

Quiet relief filled him. All his instincts told him they didn't know any more than he did. At least these Coltons on the force had no clue of her whereabouts. West rubbed the back of his neck. "The hairs on the brush aren't human."

"Synthetic," Finn murmured. "A wig."

West nodded. "Nothing else there except food wrappers, a sleeping bag in a bedroom with a bed that wasn't slept in and the hairbrush. No fingerprints on anything. Not even the brush."

Finn leaned back in his chair. "Someone's trying to frame Demi."

"Not so much framing her as trying to make us believe she was there so they could collect on Devlin Harrington's reward. Who was the person who called in the tip?" West locked gazes with the chief, who shook his head.

"It was a man. Didn't leave a name, said he'd call back with details soon. Knew that reward was a bad idea," Finn muttered.

"The lack of fingerprints, of real clear evidence, points to someone wanting us to believe she was there. No biological fluids, no prints anywhere in the cabin. No skin cells." West drummed his fingers on the armrest.

West knew, as they did, that you always shed skin cells when you slept. Microscopic skin cells should have been present inside the sleeping bag. Even if Demi slept fully clothed, there would be cells present.

"The only real evidence pointing to Demi was the jacket. Maybe the unsub planted it there to throw us off," Brayden mused.

"Or the unsub used the property while he experimented with making the TATP bomb. He just didn't stay. And he's long gone by now."

Shane frowned. "Then where is he?"

West narrowed his eyes. "In town. Right under our noses."

He pulled out the report and pointed to the new sketch. "DNA on a cigarette stub at the first bombing belongs to Aston Reston, accessory to a car bombing in Kanas City eight years ago. Sentenced for ten to twenty, served four years. Released in February for good behavior, skipped parole. He probably headed to South Dakota. His mother still lives in Sioux Falls."

"First bombing?" Finn leaned forward. "The cigarette was found in the rubble?"

West explained how he had bagged the stub to throw out and included it in his evidence to submit to the FBI lab, along with the butterfly compact.

The chief's expression hardened. "I don't recall a woman's compact logged as evidence from the first scene."

He locked gazes with the other man. "Because I didn't include it. I sent it separately to my field supervisor to run the DNA. I'll explain later. Right now you need to read this report."

Finn studied the papers. "Aston Reston is related to Noel and Evan Larson. Second cousin. Damn, this was under our noses all this time?"

"More than under our noses. In our faces! He was a witness. *Santo Nestor* is an anagram for *Aston Reston*. Nestor is the man I interviewed at the first crime scene. He changed his name after violating his parole. Changed his appearance, as well."

Chief Colton went very still. "We've found our bomber."

West clenched his fists. "Yes. And he's still in town, after Quinn, the only witness who can identify him."

"Well, I'll send a team over to alert her. Keep an eye out for this Santo/Aston and put an APB on him."

West headed for his truck, Rex trotting behind him. He opened the door, and the Lab jumped inside.

For a moment he sat, trying to collect his thoughts. Santo. Hispanic. Aluminum siding. Witness.

"Damn, Rex," he said, his heart banging hard. "Her new client."

West dialed Quinn's phone. It went to voice mail. He left a message, then raced to his desk to collect his keys.

He started the engine, praying he could reach her on time.

Because the bomber who killed Tia had a six-thirty appointment with Quinn.

Chapter 20

Quinn walked around the kitchen in a daze. She picked up a bottle of seasoning, set it down. Picked it up again.

Everything inside hurt as if someone had sliced her open. Backing up against the wall, she slid downward until she sat on the floor. Quinn buried her face into her hands.

How could this have happened? She didn't remember her life with West, but everything indicated they'd been happy. He'd loved her, cared for her. Quinn had been alone for most of her adult life, never finding that right man she wanted to marry.

And now she'd pushed him out of her life and she was alone once more.

How could he lie to her? What was wrong with her that everyone left her?

There's nothing wrong with you, a little voice inside whispered. *You're fine. It's the other people who have a problem.*

Her father. Her mother, and the parade of stepfathers roaming in and out of her childhood. Even Demi, who had never wanted to get close.

And West.

But maybe it wasn't always them. Not West, who had been kind and thoughtful and staunchly always there for her.

Maybe it's you.

It hurt to acknowledge she was partly at fault.

If you hadn't shut him out, shut him down, jumped all over him when he told you the truth, he'd still be here.

She hated secrets. Secrets damaged people, they seldom could be kept for long. Most of all, she hated being the target of one.

And yet West merely did his job. He hadn't come to Red Ridge for her, but to find the Groom Killer, and discern if Demi's relatives knew her hiding places.

All her life, she'd felt like a second-class citizen, the Colton from the wrong side of the tracks. She'd struggled to build her business, build respectability.

No one would ever ignore her or make her feel rejected and unwanted again. The only people who drew close were those who wanted something from her.

That's the real reason I drove West off. All those memories from the past, the people who I thought cared and didn't. I thought he was the same. He kept a secret from me. But other than hiding his real purpose here, what crime has he committed?

Did he ignore you as your mother did? Sneer at you and tell you to "get lost, kid," as your second stepdad did?

Invite you to parties as that one Colton cousin did, and then laugh, saying, "Mistake. You aren't invited, after all."

No, he's been nothing like that. Don't screw up, Quinn. Don't toss him into the garbage pail of all your past hurt memories and paint him with that brush because you're afraid of getting hurt again.

Afraid of being rejected like you were all those times from your stepdads, and your own mother.

Quinn lifted her head and hugged her knees. There was a killer on the loose and Agent West Brand vowed to keep her safe. He kept that promise.

She'd made a promise, too, to marry him. To trust that the old Quinn would love him enough to commit the rest of her life with him. Because for her, marriage wasn't like shopping at a grocery store as it had been with her mom.

It was the real deal, a one-stop, no-more-shop event. The old Quinn would have worked hard at marriage the same way she'd done with her catering business. It didn't matter what others in town thought of her.

What mattered the most was how she thought of herself.

The oven timer dinged. Quinn walked over to the industrial oven to check on the cream cheese enchiladas. Steam misted from the bubbling dish. Using heavy mitts, she pulled it out and set it on a metal trivet.

It smelled delicious, but she had no appetite.

She found a box to pack the foil containers and keep them warm. Everything was ready. Except Austin wasn't here. Her business partner had muttered something about getting sales from a client preparing an end-of-summer party in another city.

Ordinarily she wouldn't mind, because she loved to cook and focus on her creations. Today the quiet bothered her. Too much swimming through her brain. Not memories she desperately needed to recall, but images of West.

How could he have kept such a drastic secret from her? She didn't know what was real and what was not. Trusting her partner was important. How could they have any kind of relationship, let alone a marriage, if he lied?

A tinkling sounded from the storefront. West had installed a small silver bell to alert her of customers. At the thought of West, her throat closed up.

Quinn pasted a bright smile on her face and wiped her hands on a dish towel, then went to greet the client.

He lounged by the pastry case, but studied the room and not the treats inside the glass. Lanky, his hair slicked back, he didn't look like a polished salesman.

"Hi. I'm Quinn Colton, owner of Good Eats. You're Mr. Nestor?"

"Yeah." His dark gaze crawled up and down her dress and widened at her belt. "Nice flashlight."

Her smile was terse. "It's a Taser. My boyfriend taught me how to use it for when I was alone."

Ex-boyfriend, but Nestor didn't need to know that.

"Good thinking. Is the order ready?"

He kept staring at her boldly. Quinn shifted her weight, uncomfortable with the scrutiny. She glanced at the sign West had installed, indicating the security cameras were operational and anyone entering the store would be recorded.

The cameras provided her a small amount of reassurance. That and the weapon.

"I received your deposit into my bank account, and I have the order ready. Do you need help loading it into your vehicle?"

"Nah." The man handed her a check.

Right amount, right date. Gooseflesh crawled over her bare arms. Something about the man nagged at her. With his skinny-fit chinos, short-sleeved plaid shirt and sneakers, he dressed too casually for an important corporate party.

Doused in cologne, the man couldn't hide the fact

that the stench of smoke clung to his clothing. Her nose wrinkled.

Scolding herself for judging—*hey, the guy could be changing after delivering the dinner*—she started for the kitchen.

Nestor followed her. Quinn ground to a halt.

"Do you mind if I see the kitchen? Always wanted to see what kind of industrial kitchen a vegan uses."

Alone, with a stranger, in her kitchen? "I don't think so…"

On the counter, her phone buzzed. Caller ID said West Brand.

Quinn ignored it. "I don't allow clients back there."

Nestor sighed. "I really would like to see your setup. These clients of mine, they're big in town and throw a lot of parties. Wife just turned vegan and I promised I'd check things out for them. Might mean more business for you."

How could she turn down business? Austin's voice sounded in her mind. *We need the money, Quinn.*

"This way."

Inside the kitchen he looked around. "Very impressive."

His gaze centered on the back door. Quinn walked over to make sure the door was open. Being locked inside with this, well, creep, gave her the willies. She withdrew her prized chef's knife, began slicing the carrots left on the cutting board.

The man paled a little. "Nice blade."

Quinn did not smile. "It comes in handy."

Nestor pointed to the walk-in cooler she'd had specially installed. "What's that?"

Still holding the knife, Quinn went to the door, opened it. He peered inside. "Wow, lots of stuff here. Enough to feed an army."

Having this man in her kitchen made her uneasy. "You'd better leave. You don't want the order to get cold."

She handed him the box filled with the enchiladas and burritos, covered to keep them warm.

He nodded and left, the bell tinkling as the door closed behind him.

Relief filled her. Quinn returned to the kitchen, placed the check on the table.

She pressed two fingers to her head. Another headache. Was her memory returning?

No, it must have been the smell of smoke from Nestor's clothing. So strange. A man who professed to like health food and smoked. Well, his clients liked healthy food.

Still, she couldn't ignore the gut feeling something was wrong about the man.

Maybe she should call West. Ask his advice.

You never wanted anything to do with him again.

Quinn returned to slicing carrots when a truck screeched to a halt at the curb. As she glanced up, West ran into the kitchen, Rex beside him.

Mouth tight, eyes glittering with focus. Something was dreadfully wrong.

"Thank God you're okay," he muttered. "Quinn, was your client here?"

"He just left. What's wrong?"

"Your client wasn't here for ordering food. He's the unsub who killed Tia." West gripped her arms. "Quinn, tell me, where did he spend his time? Was he in the kitchen?"

Mouth wobbling, she tried to form words.

"Quinn! Tell me!"

"Yes. He…he wanted to see my operation."

"Get back," West ordered tersely. "Rex, find."

"Find what?" she asked. Then it dawned on her. "Oh my God. We have to get out of here."

"No. I need to find that explosive device. No telling how powerful it is. Could take down this building and the one next to it." West glared at her. "I told you to get out!"

"This is my store. I'm not leaving you."

Nose down, tail up, Rex sniffed around the kitchen. She couldn't hang back while West and Rex placed themselves in danger. In the doorway, Quinn watched, clutching the chef's knife like a life preserver. Heart racing, she couldn't believe it.

A bomb in her kitchen?

The canine paced the kitchen, going back and forth, his nose to the floor. How could Rex discern anything with all the smells? Chili, tomatoes, onions. Cumin.

But she knew this was what West had trained him to do.

Pausing for a beat, Rex loped over to the steel table where Quinn had set down the last order. Tail beating the air, Rex sat.

He'd locked onto the scent of something.

"Good boy, Rex," West said, his voice pitched higher.

West crouched down and removed a box the size of a cell phone from under the steel table. A light blinked.

He raced outside, banging open the back door. "Rex, stay! You, too, Quinn!"

West slammed the heavy door shut.

The hell with that. Clutching the knife, she ran outside, closing the door as he raced to the empty field behind her building, throwing the object.

Puffs of gray smoke spun out and the ear-shattering bang jolted her off her feet, making her drop the knife. A piercing scream punctuated the blast. Screaming, screaming, it was her.

With a sickening thud, West fell downward. Clouds of smoke covered him. She couldn't see. Where was he?

Quinn started for him.

Someone darted toward her, lips pulled back in a fierce snarl, his eyes wild. Santo Nestor. Quinn started to run when he body-slammed her against the wall.

Quinn fumbled for the Taser on her belt. Panic blossomed, but she pushed it down. She thrust the Taser at Nestor, momentarily stunning him. But the shock was too weak. She'd forgotten to fully charge it.

From behind the door, Rex howled and scratched, desperate to get to West.

If she could let the dog out, he'd be a weapon. She jumped to her feet, the door within reach. Almost there…

Nestor grabbed her around the waist and threw her hard. Her head made contact with the hard pavement and she almost blacked out. She touched her brow and her fingertips came away red.

Red. Blood.

Tia, wearing red. Business suit. Shouting on the phone the day before the bomb went off and her world exploded. *You'll never have Pine Paradise, Noel! I'll die before I sell to you, bastard!*

That man, standing at her desk, the cruel smirk on his face the day the office blew up. Nestor. The wildness in his eyes, the smell of smoke…

Nestor removed a switchblade from his back pocket. "I should have slit your throat the first time I grabbed you on the street. This time, I'll do it slow, make you hurt. Your lover can't help you. He's dead."

A sob caught in her throat. Tears escaped from her eyes. She hated Nestor seeing her hurt. West couldn't be dead. He was too alive, too full of life.

Nestor kicked her in the belly. The rush of pain made her gasp, stole the breath from her lungs. Then he stomped on her back, forcing her to lie flat.

"You messed up my little show. Now you're gonna pay. But first, I'm having a little fun."

With the toe of his boot, he jabbed her ribs. Nestor tore her dress. With sickening dread, she knew what he planned to do.

Rape her, and then kill her.

Pain radiated into his ribs. A fierce ache pounded in his head. The explosion had tossed him sideways, knocking him flat. West struggled to his feet, groping for balance. Quinn was out there, alone with the perp. He had to get to her. His heart constricted. No time for panic, for the helpless feeling threatening to take over. *Use your training.* It wasn't Quinn out there, the woman he adored. Loved with all his soul. It was a vic and she needed help.

Enough dust cleared for him to see the building. Nestor had torn Quinn's dress as she lay on the ground. Now he unzipped his pants. West reached for his gun when a bout of dizziness seized him. Damn it, he couldn't risk hurting Quinn when he couldn't see straight.

But he had another weapon—his brain. West holstered his weapon.

"El Jefe," he sang out. "Want to try again? You screwed up, big-time."

Confusion on his face, Nestor scrambled to his feet. Sunshine glinted off the blade in his hand. "Where are you?"

Nestor turned, knife in hand.

Just as he'd hoped, Quinn made a run for it. But Nestor ran after her, grabbed her arm. Quinn, bless her, had retrieved the chef's knife she'd dropped. She slashed Nestor's face. A scream erupted from the man's throat as he clawed at the wound slicing his cheek open. He darted after Quinn, blood running down his jaw.

Screw that.

Out of the cloud of smoke and dust West raced forward, running full speed like a linebacker. West reached for his weapon, praying he could get in one good hit.

He fired.

Pink mist bloomed around Nestor's right thigh. Screaming, Nestor collapsed on the ground. West flipped the man over and slapped steel cuffs onto his wrists.

Red pooled from Nestor's thigh wound. West withdrew his phone. "Prisoner in custody. Send ambulance to Good Eats on Main."

West glanced at her. Quinn shook, gooseflesh on her arms, blood dripping from a scalp wound. Her pretty dress was ripped, exposing her bra and panties. "You okay?"

He shrugged out of his shirt, placed it around her shivering body.

Stricken, she nodded. West flinched, pulled his belt free and wrapped it around Nestor's thigh. A string of screams and curses followed. Quinn stared.

"You're bleeding and you're treating him!"

"I may have nicked an artery," West told her.

"Let him bleed."

"No can do, sweetheart. We need him for questioning." West tightened the belt around Nestor's leg and the man screamed again.

"Son of a bitch, that hurts, you bastard!" Nestor yelled.

"Shut up. Be grateful I don't squeeze it tighter for daring to hurt my woman." Grimacing, West sat back, gripped his shoulder. Blood stained the light gray shirt.

Sirens screeched in the distance. Unraveling the bandanna she wore in her hair, she pressed it against West's wound.

She could have lost him.

"Hey." West reached up, touched a tear trickling down

her cheek. "It's okay now, sweetheart. Bad guy is knocked out. He'll go to prison. No one will threaten you again."

"I'm not crying because of him." Quinn rubbed her cheek against his trembling hand. "I almost lost you, West."

"But you didn't. Takes more than a bomb and a knife to take me down." He considered as she applied more pressure. "Well, maybe an HK416. Assault rifle. That could do the trick."

How could he joke at something this serious? And then she saw the emotion clouding his gaze and knew that humor masked the fear he felt.

"You were scared," she said. "Not for yourself."

"I was *damn* scared. Haven't felt that kind of fear in many years. I thought…I wouldn't reach you in time. Your phone went to voice mail."

She opened the door and the dog rushed out. Rex whined, jumping up and down on West. He rubbed the dog's head.

"I'm okay, boy," he told Rex.

"I couldn't bear to talk with you again," she whispered, broken. "Because I missed you so much and I still haven't forgiven you for keeping secrets from me."

Her hands wouldn't quit trembling. Quinn felt as if someone had tossed her into a bucket and kept shaking it. West took one hand, kissed it.

"Am I forgiven now?" he asked.

The ghost of a smile touched her wobbly mouth. "Maybe. When you recover."

Six police officers stormed out of the back door, along with EMTs. One medic checked out West.

Finn Colton arrived next. Quinn's mouth wobbled. Finn, her cousin. Over there, Brayden. She knew them, knew these men now gathered around West, doing their jobs with quiet efficiency.

"Is he going to be okay?" she asked the medic.

"We'll take him in, keep him for observance."

"No way. I'm fine," West argued.

Finn held up a hand. "You're going to the hospital, Agent Brand."

"Don't argue with the chief," Quinn told him. She gripped his hand. "Please."

Another EMT began giving her first aid for the head wound. West scowled. "Only if you go with me, sweetheart."

"Deal. But this is nothing. I regained my memory." She looked at Finn. "I remember everything. About Tia, the explosion and Nestor."

"His real name is Aston Reston. He's a career criminal," West told her.

The medic pulled a blanket over Quinn's shoulders. "We'll bring you in as well to get checked out. Head wounds are tricky."

"Tell me about it," Quinn muttered.

An hour later, she sat by West's bed in the ER. Finn paced the room as West gave his report. The antiseptic smells bothered her, but not as much as the sight of an injured West, chest bare, the ugly white bandage on his shoulder.

"I still don't understand how my landlord is connected to this, other than this Santo/Aston person being a cousin. Why would Larson want to blow up his building?"

"Insurance would cover it."

West struggled to get up, but Finn pushed him down. "Easy, big guy. You're not going anywhere."

"I should have aimed for his damn heart," West scowled.

"Good thing you didn't," Finn told him. "Reston is in lockup. DA will apply pressure, get him to talk about who hired him to blow up Tia Linwicki."

"Reston did it, but I think the Larsons were connected," Quinn blurted out.

Both men looked at her. She blushed, touched her head. "Now that I got my memory back, I remember the conversation Tia had with Noel Larson on the phone the day before the explosion. She backed out on the deal to sell Pine Paradise. Larson wasn't going to own the deed to the property. She found out the Larsons were deeding the property to Aston Reston right after the sale. He planned to take it over, renovate the property with a loan from his cousins."

"A loan?" Finn raised his brows. "I'll bet the payback was letting the Larsons use it for illegal activity."

"Tia found out Reston would be on the deed, and she backed out. She told me with his record, she didn't want her family's property going to a convicted felon."

She'd been in a rush that day, anxious to get back to the store to fill a big catering order, and had tucked the conversation in the back of her mind. Until now.

It felt wonderful to recall everything now. Even the price she'd paid was worth it. Quinn knew she could finally get her life back.

Finn finished taking West and Quinn's formal statements and left. Alone with West, she held his hand.

His gaze met hers. "Quinn, there's still the matter of Demi. Did you give the jacket back to Demi recently?"

"No. I had loaned my compact to Tia last month. She never returned it. It was shortly before she met Larson at the abandoned hardware store. She told me Larson wanted to see it, maybe buy the property."

"That's how it ended up there. She probably dropped it." West gave her a level look. "Demi's jacket?"

"Honestly, I don't know. That's the biggest puzzle of all. Someone took it from my closet, but how? Only you and I had keys to my apartment."

"And security cameras would have picked up footage in the hallway." West shifted his weight on the bed. "Soon as I'm out of here, I'll look into it."

Chapter 21

It felt so wonderful to have her memory back and return to normal.

The day after police arrested Aston Reston for Tia's murder, Quinn felt as if she could finally move forward. West had returned to work, heading to the training center with Rex, but promised to meet her later. Humming, Quinn arranged baked goods in the glass case when the little silver bell tinkled over the door.

Quinn blinked in surprise. Gemma strolled inside. Her cousin Gemma Colton, from the right side of the tracks. Wealthy, spoiled and with a designer wardrobe any woman would envy.

Those things no longer mattered as much to Quinn.

With her chestnut hair and dark eyes, Gemma was a beauty. Today she wore a sleeveless turquoise blouse and designer jeans and turquoise heels. She looked around the store with interest.

"Hi, Gemma." Quinn wiped her hands on a dish towel. "Anything I can help you with?"

"I stopped by to see how you were doing. Everyone is talking about you and West."

So much for a secret relationship. Quinn didn't care. West was back on his feet, fully recovered, and Tia's murderer behind bars. She had her memory back. Life was good.

"Thanks. I'm doing well." Quinn motioned to the tables outside. "Would you like a kale smoothie on the house?"

Gemma's perfect nose wrinkled. "How about strawberry instead?"

Soon they were seated outside, the sun beaming down on them, a nearly cloudless sky overhead. Pedestrians strolling past nodded and smiled. Gemma must be right. Everyone kept talking and looking at her, but not in an accusing way.

More like respect. And curiosity.

"Your West is so brave. Putting himself in danger to save you." Gemma heaved a dramatic sigh. "You're lucky to have a man love you that way, Quinn."

Odd hearing that from Gemma, who always seemed to have everything in life. "He's a good man."

"It's amazing that you ended up like this. I mean, look at your father. He isn't an upstanding member of society. You have no lineage in town. So how did you get West to fall in love with you?"

Once, Gemma's words would have cut deep. Made her feel like that little girl who'd never been invited to the rich Colton parties. But those times were past. And the look on Gemma's face—pure desperation—tugged at Quinn's heart.

Maybe Gemma had no filter, but she wasn't cruel on purpose.

Gemma hadn't come here to check on her or make friends. Gemma needed some kind of assurance. "What's wrong?" Quinn asked gently.

Her cousin stared at her drink. "How can I get Devlin to fall in love with me the way West loves you?"

More surprises. "You've been dating awhile. It seems serious."

"Oh yes, he seems serious. About seeing me, and being with me. But I get the feeling he doesn't love me. Not like West feels about you." Gemma toyed with her straw. "Would Devlin risk himself to save my life the way West did with you?"

Sympathy filled her. "West is a trained agent, hon. Give it a chance with Devlin."

Gemma sighed. "You're so lucky, Quinn. I wish I could get Devlin to love me. Will it ever happen?"

Quinn sipped her kale drink. "Gemma, love isn't something you force. You let it happen, nurture it. You can't make yourself into someone different just to get the other person to love you. It's chemistry and conversation and a whole lot of forgiveness and compromise."

"Maybe." Her cousin looked thoughtful. "I can try harder."

It would happen or it would not. Gemma had to discover that on her own, just as Quinn had. Talk switched to the new recipes Quinn tested when West's pickup pulled up front.

Rex wasn't with him. Quinn's heart skipped a beat. Was everything okay?

Rising to her feet, Gemma gave her a hug. "Thanks." She glanced at West. "Thank you for saving her."

West nodded, but he seemed distracted. As Gemma walked away, West jingled his keys.

Something was up. "What's wrong? I thought you were

at the training center today. Is everything all right with Rex?"

"He's fine. I left him there to work with one of the other trainers while I checked something out. Come on. We need to have a little chat with your business partner. Where is he?"

They went into the store and into the kitchen, where Austin chopped vegetables at a cutting board.

"About time you stopped socializing and returned to work. I need help." Austin pointed to a pile of carrots. "Start prepping those and I'll make the sauce."

Another odd thing, much odder than Gemma paying her a visit. When had Austin grown so bossy?

West gently gripped her arm. "No, Quinn."

His gaze turned icy hard. "Austin, did you deliver a food order to a resort in the canyon near Pine Paradise?"

Quinn's heart skipped a beat as her business partner's face flushed. "Why? I've been trying to get us business, I've been—"

"You've been trying to get Quinn in trouble," West cut in.

"That's not true!" Austin's wild gaze whipped to Quinn. "Why would I do that?"

"Only one person could have taken Demi's jacket from Quinn's closet. One person who had access, besides myself and Quinn. We analyzed the wrapper found at cabin seven. Tests showed it contained traces of aspartame, the ingredient found in sugar-free gum." West's hardened gaze centered on Austin. "The key to cabin number seven has been missing awhile. Where did you put it, Austin? Before I bring you into the station for fingerprinting, anything you care to confess, Austin? Besides the fact you like to make origami and steal women's clothing?"

Quinn's heart skipped a beat. Dread filled her. Surely

West couldn't be accusing Austin. Mild Austin, who held Good Eats together while she recovered?

Her business partner paled. "I don't know what you're talking about."

"Oh, you do." West got into his face. "If you tell the truth now, it'll go easier on you. Do you really want to hurt Quinn any more?"

Austin glanced at Quinn with a plea in his eyes. Her heart did a triple flip. "West, what are you talking about? He didn't do anything."

"He paid your rent. I saw Larson, wanted to give him the back rent check you gave me, and the bastard told me Austin paid for it."

She could barely breathe. Helping her by taking over the business while she recovered was one thing. But paying the rent? Pride aside, it hinted to Noel Larson that Quinn had no money. It made her more vulnerable and she hated looking weak, especially to a slime like Larson.

"I told you I never wanted that, Austin. Why did you ignore my wishes?" she asked him. Her voice rose a notch, and she fought to keep it even. "I told you I had my savings."

Austin's mouth opened and closed. He backed up until he hit the stainless steel refrigerator, and then splayed his palms against it.

"The rent was overdue…"

"I had the money! All I needed to do was get the check to him. I was in the hospital."

West slowly walked toward Austin. "Spill it. Tell her, Austin. The truth. You were at cabin number seven. You took Demi's jacket and left it there."

Visceral pain sliced through her. She didn't want to believe it, but West wouldn't lie about this.

"Prove it." Austin pushed his glasses up his nose.

"You have the security cameras. Show me on tape where I sneaked into Quinn's apartment and took the jacket."

West grabbed Austin's arm, tugged him toward the closet where she stored papers and cans. Inside the closet, West pushed at the back wall.

Her mouth opened and closed in astonishment as a door swung open...to reveal a set of stairs marching upward.

West pointed to the hidden stairs. "I got to thinking about this place. Did a little research on the building and pulled the old blueprints. This set of stairs was originally intended to be used as the main access to the floor upstairs, which was a storage area. Then the owner had these stairs sealed off when the apartment became a separate residence. They lead straight to your bedroom closet."

Quinn fisted her hands. Now it made sense, the strange sounds she'd heard that one day when she napped...the cough and the feeling she'd been watched.

"You spied on me," she said.

"No! I only used the stairs to get Demi's jacket. I didn't realize you were there, Quinn." Austin reddened as he realized what he'd spilled.

"I thought the recording of the anonymous tipster sounded familiar. I just couldn't pinpoint how you did it. Tell her. Quinn deserves the truth," West snapped.

Her partner, her best friend, hung his head. "I found the stairs two months ago when I rummaged through the closet for last year's invoices to see if I could drum up more business from former corporate clients. You never go in there, you just shove the boxes inside, Quinn. I was going to tell you..."

"But you didn't," she said slowly.

"I didn't do it to hurt you." Austin finally looked at her. "Yeah, I planted the jacket and everything and called it in to the police. Hell, if Devin wanted to offer that much, why not take it? It would save the business. Six figures goes a long way in paying food bills."

Devlin Harrington's reward for the capture of Demi Colton. Money, it was always about money. She'd thought Austin was different, like West. Neither cared much about being rich.

Turned out she'd been wrong, just as she'd been so wrong about FBI agent West Brand. West Brand, who had been there for her through everything.

"You would frame my sister, my only sister, for money?" she asked Austin.

"Everyone knows she's guilty. You cared more about her than us, than our business! And she never gave a damn about you!" Now Austin shouted, her mild, cheerful partner who never raised his voice. How shrill he was, the anger leeching through his cutting words.

"She's family," Quinn whispered. "I care about her, and I cared about you, Austin."

"Oh right. You were letting everything go, Quinn. After you got all starry-eyed about him." Austin pointed to West. "I was the only one saving us. All of this, it's here because of me because I found new accounts that brought in money. The business should belong solely to me. You would have left me anyway, moving out with Big Shot FBI Man here, and I didn't have the cash to buy you out."

Quinn hugged herself, feeling herself come apart. Everything fell apart, burning slowly to ashes before her eyes. "Get out of my sight."

West beckoned to the patrol officer coming through the front door. She couldn't bear it. Quinn wanted to shut out the drone of the cop reading Austin his rights, her former best friend pleading that he hadn't meant to hurt anyone…

The officer led Austin away toward the patrol car. Quinn watched them leave, her chest hollow.

Brayden lingered, shuffling his feet. Finally he looked at them. "Reston's dead."

Her throat closed up. Reston was the link between finding evidence of the Larson brothers and Tia's death. Tia deserved justice.

"Killed himself with a homemade shank." Brayden rolled his shoulders. "The feds were about to get a confession out of him, since the DA offered him a sweetheart deal."

"Was it really suicide?" West asked.

"They're ruling it suicide." Sympathy filled Brayden's gaze as he looked at her. "I'm glad you're back, Quinn."

When everyone else left, West stayed at her side. "Are you okay, Quinn?" he asked quietly.

"Not really." Emotion clogged her throat. "What will happen to him?"

"He'll be questioned and charged with obstruction of justice. If he's a first-time offender, judge will go easy on him."

"He was my bestie," she whispered. "Why would he do such a thing? Austin loved Good Eats, he's always been there for me, and I never let him down. Why?"

A warm palm cupped her cheek. West lifted her face to regard his solemn expression. "Because people do things out of desperation, honey. Austin knew if your business closed shop, he'd be out of a job and the investment he put into the business."

"The business was floundering, but not that bad," she protested.

West stroked a thumb over her cold cheek. "Probably didn't matter to him. With the reward money, he could buy you out and control everything."

"Being in charge while I was recovering went to his head. He was the sales force behind Good Eats, and I was the cook. It worked out well. I never imagined he resented it." Quinn pressed two fingers to her temple. Could she trust anyone anymore?

Her only sister, on the run, suspected of killing men. Her best friend, framing her sister and wanting to snatch Good Eats from her. West was the only one at her side who stood by her. She'd told Gemma that love wasn't something you forced.

But love also meant being honest.

He kept touching her, gentling her with his reassuring touch. "Quinn, is it too late to repair what we had? I love you, and I want to spend the rest of my life with you."

She clasped his hand and pulled it away from her face. No more distractions. "I love you as well, but I have to know I can trust you. No more secrets."

"I'm sorry I had to investigate you, and put you under suspicion for hiding information about your sister. I had a job to do," he said.

"Then tell me what happened to your family. Everything, West."

This was going to be tough. Even now, as they walked upstairs to Quinn's apartment, he could feel his chest constrict. Memory was a funny thing. Sometimes it fled when you needed most to remember.

Other times, when you tried desperately to forget, it danced in your mind.

They went upstairs to her apartment. West sat on the sofa, legs splayed, hands braced on his knees. He stared at the opposite wall. Couldn't look at Quinn. Hell, he hadn't talked about this in years.

Maybe it was best to start at the beginning. He took a deep breath.

"My father was a cop, one of the best on the force in the

small town where I grew up in New York. Upstate, near Syracuse. His father was a cop, as well. Dad loved his job, but he came into contact with some real slime. He was on a case involving a suspect in a bombing. Alan Beam blew up a bank in a robbery, killed a security guard. Dad was the detective who made the case, arrested Alan. But the judge let Alan go free on remand—bail—because the state attorney didn't have enough evidence.

"I was dating Gina Fontanilli, the hottest girl in school. We were ready to take our relationship to the next level." He couldn't help a small smile at the memory—a good one. "My mother didn't want me going out, because she was worried about Beam being on the loose, and Dad ordered me to stay home. I sneaked out."

"Young love," Quinn said softly. "Any teenager would have done the same."

"I took Gina to the movies, and then to lovers' point… You can guess the rest." He shoved a hand through his hair. "Got a call on my cell phone, which I ignored because Gina… Well, I was preoccupied. And then I checked messages. My dad's partner told me to get my ass home ASAP. Something bad happened to my family."

"Oh, West," Quinn murmured.

He didn't answer her, couldn't, because if he stopped talking, he might never tell the story. "I came home to fire engines, flashing lights, and the house was on fire. Half of it was gone, just gone." West drew in a deep breath, struggling with the ache in his chest. "My parents and my two sisters were dead. I'm the only survivor."

She slid over to grip his hand. Her hand was soft, warm and reassuring. "The burns on your hand?"

"I ran to the house. The fire had spread to the front. Grabbed the doorknob to go inside, try to save them. Screaming, I remember I kept screaming. After I thought the hoarse throat was smoke inhalation. Cops told me I wouldn't stop screaming."

Moisture brightened her eyes as he glanced at her. "How did you survive the fire?"

West lifted his shoulders. "Firefighter pulled me out. Then they loaded me into an ambulance, treated me for the burn. But I didn't want plastic surgery. The scars fed my new purpose."

And then she looked at West, really looked at him. "Your father sounds like a wonderful man. I wish I would have known him."

"Dad gave me love and taught me duty, honor and to work hard. Every day I try to make my father proud. Every damn day I'm with Rex, training with him, on a case trying to find the bad guys, I try to emulate my father. He gave it his all, and that's what I try to do, as well."

Suddenly he realized the familiar, stabbing grief he'd always felt had turned into a distant ache. No longer did he feel the compulsion to dedicate all his life to the job. Life was more than work.

He had Quinn. Moved on.

"You're a good man, West Brand. Your father would be proud of you," Quinn said softly. "All this time, you've held that inside, not wanting to get close to anyone because you didn't want to lose them."

West nodded. Damn perceptive of Quinn. He thought about a quote he'd read once in high school, one that stuck with him at his family's funeral.

"Every man has his secret sorrows which the world knows not. And often times, we call a man cold when he is only sad." West recited the quote from Longfellow.

Once he'd thought himself that man. Viewed by other K-9 officers as distant and even cold, when all this time he held secrets in his heart—a past where a killer had destroyed his entire family.

No longer. He had reconciled his past and found a new beginning.

"West, would your father want you to be happy?"

He thought about his father, could almost see him giving the thumbs-up. *Go for it.*

"Yeah. Dad would want me to settle down, marry." The tightness in his chest eased a little. There would always be an empty spot in his heart and he'd always miss his family, but he was ready to live again. "Have a family and take risks. Life is about risks."

West got down on one knee, kissed her hand. "Quinn Colton, I ask you again, will you marry me?"

Eyes bright with tears, she nodded. "Yes."

"I can't promise I'll tell you everything, Quinn. It won't be easy."

"As long as there are no big secrets between us."

He rose and pulled her up against him. "We'll have to keep our engagement a secret. There's still a groom killer running loose."

"I don't mind secrets, as long as I'm in on it."

"I'll tell you another one. I'm leaving the Bureau." Gaze steady, he regarded her. "I talked to Finn about a permanent job here in Red Ridge."

Her breath hitched. "Oh, West. Really? I thought the FBI was your life."

"I like Red Ridge. Seems like a nice place to settle down." He grinned. "Quiet, kind of dull…"

Quinn laughed.

"The Bureau *was* my life." He caught her hand, kissed the knuckles. "But it's about damn time I paid attention to my heart—you."

She rubbed his hand against her cheek. "I want children."

"Two kids." He held up two fingers. "No more."

She laughed. "Since I'll be the one having the babies, I agree."

"Well, maybe three. Only if the first two are boys. I want a girl." He slid his arms around her waist and pulled her against him. "A little girl with freckles and curls, who looks like my darling Quinn."

With the Groom Killer still roaming free, West knew they still couldn't share news of their engagement. It didn't matter. Eventually he would stand at the altar, watching his woman walk toward him during their wedding. Worth the wait.

Agent West Brand kissed Quinn, the only woman he wanted to love for the rest of his life. The bad memories of his past had eased with what waited in store—Quinn Colton eventually becoming his wife.

He had gone from a tragic past he'd wanted desperately to forget.

Toward a bright future he would always want to remember.

* * * * *